WE DON'T MATTER

WE DON'T MATTER

Above the Rain Collective
2021

Above the Rain Collective
abovetheraincollective@gmail.com
North Georgia, USA

Contributing Editor:

J.A. Sexton

Publisher's note:

ISBN: 978-1-7377970-1-2

Cover graphics and interior formatting by J.A. Sexton
Original cover photograph by Austin Granger
Above the Rain logo artwork by Bee Freitag, text by Jack Freitag

There are people who pass through our journeys, on their way to another time. Their existence leaves a mark on our own, no matter how brief. To those who have come and gone, I knew you all for just a moment, but that moment has never left my walk.

See you on the other side.

Prologue

It wasn't there. Fuck. Aidan retraced his steps for the fifth time. He was sure this is where he'd hidden the camera. He'd run down the alley and tucked it behind the dumpster. He remembered tripping over a bag of trash after he'd thrown the camera bag into the street, then ducked behind the dumpster to hide it before he took off in the other direction. He was sure it was here, the bag of trash was just a few feet away. He put his back against the wall and held his breath as a police car drove slowly by. Once it disappeared, he let the breath out and realized how much the alley smelled like urine. Human urine. He took shallow breaths, to not let the odor absorb into his nasal passages and peered around. At the end of the alley was the fence he'd jumped over, being chased by the cop. There were three dumpsters in the alley. He'd stuck it behind the second one. To be sure, he checked behind the other two, but other than what appeared to be a very large rat staring back at him, he saw nothing.

He'd waited over an hour until everything had died down before circling back. In that time, it seemed unlikely anyone else would've found the camera. But it wasn't there. That he was sure of. Beyond the incriminating footage on the camera, his name and address were adhered to it with label maker strips. Cameras weren't cheap. He couldn't afford to lose it in more ways than one. Now, its disappearance was also putting him in danger.

The light on his phone illuminated the area with an incoming call. He quickly answered it to extinguish the light.

"Hello?"

"Where are you?" a soft male voice asked, obviously shaken.

"I went back for my camera."

"Jesus, Aidan. You need to get somewhere safe. They may be searching for you."

"I know, Zeke. But my address and phone number are on the camera. I need to find it."

"Shit. Do you think they found it already?"

"I doubt it. The fat cop chasing me didn't stop to look and gave up running after a few alleys. No one saw me put it there. I think throwing my camera bag helped divert them, so I had time to hide it," Aidan whispered, glancing around.

The alley was dark and he'd moved fast as soon as he'd been spotted. No one had seen him shove it behind the dumpster.

"What are you going to do?" Zeke's voice was tired. None of them had expected what happened that night.

"I don't know. I have to find it. It's proof and connects me to the scene. Let me just walk around a bit more to look, then I'll head home."

"Be safe, Aidan. Watch your back."

"Thanks, Zeke. I promise I'll be back soon."

They hung up and Aidan wandered out to the main street. It was almost four in the morning and it was now quiet. Just trash collectors and some homeless people milling around. Aidan kept to the shadows, watching. Mere hours before, the street had been filled with the chaos of people pushing and shoving to see what was happening. Now, it was silent. His eye caught a homeless guy sitting on the curb with long, scraggly, blond hair and a disheveled beard. The man was peering down at something in a bag as he smoked a cigarette. A light shined up on the guy's face and he stared up at Aidan, his eyes intense and focused. He waved his hand at Aidan, motioning him to come closer. Pointing at the bag, he gestured his head towards it and lifted the item slightly out of the bag.

Aidan's camera!

Aidan headed towards the man when the man's head suddenly jerked to the right. He shook his head vehemently, shoving the camera back into the folds of the bag. Aidan realized too late as to why when a police cruiser bore down on him. He glanced around for an escape, but he was trapped. The headlights of the car blinded him from finding a way out. Before he could move, he was thrown to the ground, his teeth clattering painfully. He groaned as it felt like his organs were being smashed together.

"Dont fucking move," an angry voice ordered him.

He was cuffed and dragged up by his elbows, coming face to face with the pinched, red face of the officer who'd thrown him down.

"Do you see it?" the officer asked another cop, who was searching around.

The other cop shook his head and shrugged. Aidan knew what they were searching for. His camera. He glanced at where the homeless man had been sitting. The spot was empty and the man was long gone. Aidan sighed in relief. He still didn't have his camera, but neither did they. They, the cops in question, shoved him into the back of the car, smacking his head against the frame of the car door. Aidan knew it wasn't an accident. The cops here for years had abused their power, and now he had proof. Well, had. Now, it was somewhere in the care of a homeless man, he hoped would know to keep it safe.

Chapter One

The alarm continued its grating repetition, despite being snoozed multiple times. Aidan groaned and sat up in bed. No matter how old he got, he never woke up on the first alarm. His mother used to yell at him when he was in high school because he missed the bus the majority of the time, and she was forced to drive him. Now, at the end of his final year of film school, not much had changed. He went to the bathroom and brushed his teeth, smoothing down his black hair with water. He splashed his face to try to wake up. Deep, purple circles lined his dark brown eyes.

Sleep never came easy for Aidan. He was usually up until two or three in the morning; working on projects, watching television, or dealing with the endless spiral of thought in his head until he was on the verge of hallucinating. Only then, could he fall asleep. He grabbed clothes off the floor and smelled them, not sure if they were clean or dirty. Washing them he could do, putting them away not so much. As a result, clean and dirty eventually ended up intermingled in a pile on the floor. They smelled fine, so he threw them on, heading to the kitchen to snag a juice and something to eat on his way to class.

His roommate, Mia, was in the kitchen cooking hashbrowns and eyed Aidan as he rooted through the fridge. Her long, wavy, chestnut hair was tied back with a piece of string to keep it out of the way. She leaned against the counter and sighed, nudging him with her foot.

"What are you going to do when you get a job?"

Aidan laughed and shook his head at her. "You sound like my mom. Hopefully, by then I'll get my shit together."

"Doubt it," Mia replied, flipping her hashbrowns. She threw bread in the toaster and pulled hot sauce out of the fridge.

They'd been roommates for a few years, so Mia knew him well. Mia had practically accosted him at the skate park his first year of film school, since then they'd been inseparable. They'd even briefly tried dating, but after their first kiss, Aidan just wasn't feeling it. It wasn't that Mia wasn't attractive, because she was. Aidan at times was mesmerized by her beauty. Her father was African-American and her mother was Hispanic. Her skin was a rich cocoa, her face marked with large, deep brown eyes and full lips, which sat perfectly below her button nose. She had curves in all the right places, and a laugh so infectious it almost made him itch. Everything about her was perfect, except he just didn't feel aroused by her. She was like a sculpture. Beautiful to look at, but in the end that was all.

If she'd been hurt by his lack of interest, she never let it show, and they'd moved on to one of the closest friendships he'd ever experienced. They were opposites in almost every way; her need for organization a contrast to his inherent chaos, but it made for a symbiotic relationship they both thrived off of.

"Hey, you coming to my performance tonight?" Mia asked, giving him a look that said it wasn't an option not to.

"Of course. TJ going to be there?" Aidan picked up his backpack and headed for the door.

"He'd better."

Aidan chuckled and ducked out the door, into the blinding sun. Not that he was complaining. It rained so much in Seattle, any sun was a welcome reprieve. He grabbed his skateboard by the door and booked through the streets to class. He was going to be late either way, but he reasoned a little late was better than a lot late. His professors didn't seem to see it that way but let it slide, considering he was one of their star students. His chaotic nature made everyday life a mess, but it brought a creativity and thinking that made him successful in school.

He'd forgotten to ask Mia what time her performance started. She was in the Cornish College of the Arts for Opera and was performing a solo at the student center that night. He'd just text TJ about it because if he asked Mia, she'd have his head for not remembering. TJ was a friend of his from back home in North Carolina, who came out the year after Aidan started school in Seattle. TJ went to a different college than Aidan and Mia, not being drawn to the arts and was focusing on a career in social work.

Once TJ came around and met Mia, he was always around. They began dating a few months later and were a pretty permanent couple at this point. TJ had his own place but they'd already discussed moving in together after she graduated. Aidan understood and had plans to head to Los Angeles then, anyhow.

He liked Seattle but was over the rain, also knowing he stood his best chances of doing film work in LA.

TJ texted back the time and Aidan stopped to set an alarm on his phone. If he didn't show, Mia would never let him live it down. He shot TJ a message to meet outside the side doors, so they could go in together to find seats. They'd known each other all their lives. They grew up in the same small beach town on the coast, learning to surf and skateboard together. Aidan's family moved out west after the death of his brother, Casey, when Aidan was fifteen. His parents felt it was time to leave. Although Aidan was sad to leave his friends, he'd immediately felt a connection with the west coast, he'd never felt in Crestview, North Carolina. He and TJ stayed in touch and when it was time to leave the nest, TJ began talking about moving out west. Once Aidan was in college, and TJ decided where he wanted his life to go, TJ applied and was accepted to school nearby.

Aidan slipped in the back door of the lecture hall, but not without notice of his teacher, who shook her head and kept talking to the class while giving him the eye. Classes flew by and Aidan stopped in to talk to his school counselor about graduation. They had finals in a couple of weeks and graduation right after. His parents were coming in for the graduation ceremony, and he'd already secured a couple of leads on jobs in the industry.

Things were moving fast, and he still felt it was somewhat unreal. Ultimately, he wanted to do documentaries, but at this point he just needed to get his foot in the door to build his resume. He and Mia had the apartment until the end of August, giving Aidan time to work things out, and TJ and Mia time to find a place closer to TJ's school. TJ had held off college for a year after high school, so would graduate the following spring.

After his meeting with the counselor, Aidan swung back by the apartment to shower and get dressed for the performance. Mia was gone and it was quiet. He considered lying down for a bit but thought better of it. If he didn't wake up in time, she'd never forgive him. He had a habit of unintentionally letting people down. Mia had a tough exterior, but she worried too much and wanted her crew around her. He showered, throwing on clean slacks and a polo shirt. The student center was too far to skateboard to, so he checked the bus schedule and saw he still had a little time to eat. A grumbling stomach during the performance wouldn't go over too well. He finished just in time to grab the bus and meet up with TJ.

TJ wasn't hard to spot, standing by the doors in a dark blue blazer, white button-down shirt, and tan slacks. Holding a dozen roses. His light brown hair was slicked back, and he shifted uncomfortably in what appeared to be brand new loafers. Aidan laughed as he walked up and TJ shrugged, grinning, his freckled face a cross between manhood and boyish charm.

"Shut up, Aidan. You know I gotta show out for my girl."

Aidan gave him a little shove and smiled. "I know it. She'd expect nothing less. You look sharp."

They'd come a long way from the shaggy beach bums they'd once been. Not that they didn't skateboard every chance they got. They took trips to surf now and then, but surfing in Washington state was completely different from surfing in North Carolina. Colder, rougher. It was fun, but took different equipment and was more exhausting. Plus, they weren't all that close to the ocean. Aidan missed the beach, just not the beach town where he was born. That small-minded southern town had put his family through hell after Casey died, with rumors and back-handed comments about his brother's death.

They made their way into the auditorium and found seats as close to the front as they could. Mia needed to see them, so she didn't feel alone up there. By the time she came on stage to perform, the auditorium was full and the lights had dimmed. She looked stunning in a long, burgundy, velvet gown and matching elbow-length gloves, her hair loose down to her waist. Around her neck, she wore a gemstone necklace and matching earrings that glittered in the spotlight. The skater girl they knew was transformed into a timeless beauty.

A stealthy glance in their direction, let them know she'd seen them. She stepped up to the front of the stage and the crowd hushed. She clasped her hands in front of her and glanced at the piano player, who began to play the delicate chords of Giacomelli's *Sposa Son Disprezza*ta. Mia's voice joined in, causing Aidan to hold his breath. Her voice carried across the rafters, into the audience. Aidan didn't know what the song was about but could hear the pain in the composition. He wasn't ashamed when tears came to his eyes. He glanced at TJ, who was letting tears run down his cheeks, both from the beauty of the music but also for his love of Mia. He met Aidan's eyes and simply nodded.

When Mia finished, the audience rose to their feet, clapping furiously. Aidan didn't know opera, but he did know what he'd just witnessed was astounding. Mia smiled shyly and bowed, her eyes meeting TJ's as he made his way forward to hand her the roses he brought. She knelt to take them, placing her hand on his cheek in appreciation. She stood back up and bowed again to the audience, still on their feet clapping. As she made her way off the stage, she glanced back at Aidan and TJ and smiled gratefully. Her boys. Her team.

After the performance, and a brief stop at the after-party for the performers, they made their way back to Aidan and Mia's apartment in TJ's car. Mia happily changed into shorts and a t-shirt, transforming back into the girl who liked punk music and eating with her hands. TJ grabbed drinks for them and sat down next to Mia on the couch, rubbing her legs. Aidan sat across from them in a chair. TJ peered at Mia and smiled, his blue eyes twinkling.

"You're so amazing. I mean, I always knew that, but what you did tonight was magical. I'm so proud of you."

Mia blushed and took his hand. "Shut up."

"Seriously, Mia. You're going to be a star," he insisted.

"I don't know about that, but I appreciate your faith in me." She grinned, snagging a handful of potato chips from the bag on the table. She glanced at Aidan.

"What about you? Did you like it?"

Aidan nodded. "It was sad but beautiful. What did the words mean?"

"It's about a woman whose husband is unfaithful, however, she still loves him and is broken-hearted."

"Wow. Yeah, I guess it is sad then," Aidan replied.

TJ squeezed her hand and leaned over, kissing her cheek. "Well, her husband was a fool."

Mia grinned. "Damn right he was."

It was getting late, so Mia and TJ retired to her room after a bit. Aidan dreaded attempting to go to sleep. He stayed up and watched television until his eyes could no longer stay open. It was after midnight when he climbed into bed. He closed his eyes, willing his mind to find the place it could disappear to. Instead, it started its spiral. Anxiety gripped his stomach, he couldn't put his finger on why. He reminded himself everything was going good. Everything was falling into place. He took slow, deep breaths and thought about the process of filmmaking. The idea, the execution, the editing. Focusing on concrete ideas and images always settled his brain. It was like counting sheep, but instead of sheep, he was going through the process of making a movie.

His mind wandered to what drew him to this path in the first place. His brother, Casey's, death. After Casey died from a drug-induced suicide, Aidan began to see the world differently. No longer just a kid living by the beach, hanging with his friends, trying to get his older brother's attention. Everything became film, a story through the lens. Layers under the surface, the untold stories. Every person a shell of memories, hopes, pains, images, connections.

He couldn't see a person without seeing their inner film playing out. His goal was to pull those out and make them visible. Every place he went, a reel of all who had been there before, the events which had, and would, transpire. Even when he wasn't behind the camera, he was. His brain was the camera, putting together the segments, adding the effects. The concrete became abstract, and the abstract concrete. An unending stream of images, needing to be connected into reality.

The only story he'd not been able to dig out; to analyze and develop, was his own. Inside him were too many fragments, pieces that couldn't be put together. Whether by inability or his brain's way of protecting him. He didn't know and wasn't willing to address it. When he felt it coming on, it came with a deep-seated rage, which in truth scared him. It was a door to a part of himself he couldn't handle.

He'd shifted his attention to what he could control. By focusing on the world and people around him, he didn't have to focus inward and on the pain which had been eating him up for years.

⏳

Chapter Two

The Lower Woodland skatepark was packed with exiting students, squeezing in a few last turns before the end of the school year. TJ and Mia headed to the larger bowl, and Aidan headed for a smaller emptier one. He dropped in on his skateboard, the sound of his wheels making a crisp swish on the concrete as he carved around the bowl. He practiced one-eighties and successfully nailed a handplant. Being out here made him feel connected to himself and helped release the pressure built up inside. Noticing his shoe was untied, he got to the top of the bowl and hopped out, squatting on the pavement to double knot his laces. The last thing he needed was to face-plant because his laces got caught in the wheels.

He noticed a tall, slim guy on the other side of the bowl, performing a Benihana; a trick where he ollied and brought his board forward with his front foot, while the back foot suspended in the air, as he grabbed the tail of the board before bringing it back under his feet. Aidan was impressed. The guy ended up back on the side Aidan was on and hopped out near him.

"Nice work, man," Aidan said honestly.

The guy smiled and nodded. He was blond, but like the kind of blond where his hair almost had no color to it. Between white and almost translucent. His bangs fell over his eyes, which were so pale, Aidan couldn't tell if they were gray or blue. Almost a shade between, not on the color scale. The guy appeared to be about mid-twenties and stood a few inches taller than Aidan. His skin was fair but golden from being in the sun, and he was muscular. Aidan stuck his hand out.

"Aidan. I haven't seen you here before."

The guy shook his hand, his own hand warm and strong. He glanced at Aidan and their eyes met for a second before he nodded, watching the other skaters.

"Zeke. I just moved here from Idaho with a construction job. Oregon before that. I think, maybe California prior. We move around a lot for jobs. I was searching for a skatepark, this one was recommended by one of the locals. I didn't know it would be so packed today. You from here?"

"Just for college," Aidan replied. "I'm graduating next week, then probably heading to California. LA. Pursuing filmmaking."

"Nice," Zeke responded candidly. He glanced at Aidan and held his eyes on him for a moment. "Glad to meet you, Aidan."

Aidan couldn't explain why, but Zeke's eyes on him made him feel exposed. He mumbled an agreement and grabbed his board, dropping back in the bowl. They skated for a couple of hours, chatting about techniques, skateparks, and Seattle. Mia and

TJ joined them a little while later and introductions were shared around.

By late afternoon, everyone was tired and started to wrap up. Aidan thought Zeke was interesting and wanted to get to know him better. He invited him back to their place to eat. It was more than a few blocks away, so they took a bus back and picked up Chinese takeout on the way from the bus stop to their apartment. Mia and Zeke chatted almost the whole way home about their interests and histories, allowing Aidan to get to know Zeke better without being nosy. Leave it to Mia to leave no stone unturned.

Zeke had moved around with construction jobs but was originally from Provo, Utah and began doing construction work as a teen to get out of there. He'd moved all over the midwest and west coast since. He read a lot, mostly non-fiction, and didn't watch television, except movies. He liked old country music; Hank Williams, Johnny Cash, Willie Nelson, and the sorts. He was twenty-four years old, the youngest of six children. When Mia asked about his family in more detail though, he clammed up and changed the subject. Mia also came from a large family, sharing about her siblings and parents which made Zeke relax.

TJ, being the ever-watchful boyfriend, made sure to hold Mia's hand at times, making it clear they were dating. Not that he appeared to have anything to worry about, as Zeke showed no interest in Mia outside of friendliness. Zeke did, however, make an effort to draw Aidan into the conversation and match his pace to Aidan's, so he didn't get stuck behind.

Once back at the apartment, they spread the food out on the table and grabbed plates, everyone taking a little of everything. TJ took sweet tea out of the fridge and paper cups from a cabinet. Mia ate with chopsticks, but everyone else went for forks. Zeke sat on the side of the table next to Aidan, again observing him quietly. Almost as if he was trying to read Aidan.

Aidan, in an effort to make conversation, blurted out the first thing that came to mind. "So, Zeke. You're from Provo, Utah? That's, like, ultra-religious country, right?"

Zeke turned red and immediately Aidan felt stupid for asking. Mia's eyes got big and she glared at Aidan as she kicked him under the table. Aidan winced, rubbing his shin. She was right, though. For all he knew Zeke was religious. He stared at his food, thinking how to apologize when Zeke cleared his throat.

"Indeed it is. It's why I left. They don't like people like me there," Zeke replied, his voice low.

"People like you?" TJ asked, before realizing what Zeke meant.

"Yeah, uh...the gay kind." Zeke's words hung in the air.

For Seattle, being gay wasn't all that unusual, but they hadn't meant to out him like that. After all, they'd just met Zeke. He was probably already feeling somewhat outnumbered and uncomfortable in their group. TJ's demeanor settled into relief and Mia smiled lightly, resting her eyes on Zeke's face.

"I'm sorry about them not being accepting of you, Zeke. That's unfair and must've been really hard for you growing up there. What about your family?" She placed her hand on his to show they universally accepted him.

Zeke shook his head. "When I say *they*, I include them. My family is pretty fanatical. I was raised in the church. Zeke is short of Ezekial if that helps give a better picture of how committed to the church my family is. All of us kids have names from the bible. There are certain things you can and can't be. You can't be gay."

"Hey, we didn't mean to put you on the spot. I mean, we just met and we aren't trying to, like, make you tell your life story," Aidan sputtered out.

He felt ashamed of them and embarrassed for Zeke, who'd probably never want to hang out with them again. The conversation had turned quickly, and it felt like there was no way out. Mia laughed nervously and TJ focused on his food. Zeke turned his pale eyes on Aidan.

"I'm not ashamed of my truth. It is who I am. I'm not making you uneasy, am I?" Zeke directed his words at Aidan.

Aidan did a quick gut check and shook his head. "No, man. I just didn't want you to think we were prying. I don't want to chase you away, is all. We should've been more respectful."

Zeke laughed, changing the whole scope of his face. Lines formed in his cheeks and his eyes seemed to light up. His laugh was deep but soft like his voice. He brushed the hair out of his eyes and leaned back, staring at them.

"Seriously? I just got here, have no friends, just told you I'm gay, and you're worried *I* will be chased off? I've lived in at least ten different towns and have never made a friend beyond having a drink after work. I work, read books, and skateboard. You're the first people who have ever invited me over. I'm not offended at all."

Aidan met his eyes and nodded. He hadn't considered how isolating Zeke's life probably was. Traveling around all of the time, not having a supportive family, being gay in an industry that was probably not that welcoming to homosexuality. He'd likely spent the last six, or so, years pretty much alone. Aidan felt bad for Zeke and was glad he'd invited him over. What was said, was said, they could move past it.

"Well, you're welcome to hang with us as long as we're around. Mia and TJ are staying at least another year, but I doubt I'll be here past the summer. Until then, it would be cool to have you around."

Mia got up and clicked the radio on. They all had eclectic music tastes but agreed on the alternative rock station. They cleared the table and moved to the living room, spreading out to get comfortable. Aidan plopped down on the couch and Zeke sat next to him. Mia sat down on a bean bag chair on the floor, and TJ lay down next to her, his head in her lap. The rest of the evening, the conversation revolved around music, world events, future plans, and movies. Zeke immediately fit in with the group, it was almost as if he'd been there all along. Aidan was bummed when it got late, and he could see everyone else was getting tired. His night was probably just beginning. TJ headed out since he had an early class, and Mia turned in shortly after.

Zeke and Aidan talked for another hour about different places they'd been. Aidan shared a little about growing up in North Carolina and his family moving to Washington, but not why. It was a door he wasn't ready to open up with anyone new. The conversation faded out, and they sat quietly listening to music for a bit. Finally, Zeke got up, yawned, and stretched his arms up, his hands almost brushing the ceiling. While they were only a few inches different in height, Aidan was stocky and Zeke was long and lanky.

Zeke checked his phone, shaking his head. "Man, I didn't realize how late it was. I have to be at the site at six in the morning. I'd better head out. I really appreciate the company and dinner, though."

"Anytime, seriously. We all have day classes but are pretty much around at night unless we hit the town. Let me get your number and give you mine; I'll let you know what we're up to." Aidan pulled out his phone and typed Zeke's name in.

They exchanged numbers and Zeke walked to the door, almost reluctantly. He grabbed his board, slinging his bag over his shoulder. He extended his hand and smiled, lines crinkling in the corner of his eyes.

"Thanks, Aidan. I'm glad we ran into each other today."

"Yeah, me too, Zeke. Let's plan to skate at some point this week." He shook Zeke's hand, holding it for a second before letting it drop.

Zeke gave him a two-finger wave from the corner of his eyebrow and headed out the door. Aidan stood frozen by the door, trying to figure out what just happened. His brain was spinning, attempting to put the fragments together. He was glad they met Zeke as a friend, but at the moment they shook hands before Zeke headed out, Aidan felt something different. Something deep inside of himself he hadn't felt before.

The world just shifted and exposed part of him, Aidan didn't know was there. When he shook Zeke's hand at that moment, he felt an energy bubble up from inside him, making him want more. More of what, he didn't know. But it created a connection between them he didn't quite understand. Almost a desire.

A spark.

Chapter Three

Aidan didn't meet up to skate with Zeke that next week. Graduation came on in a flurry, and his parents came to town the day before graduation, shuttling him around for new shoes, a haircut, and all the trappings they felt were necessary for a proper graduation. They stayed in a hotel nearby and only stopped by the apartment briefly to pick him up for dinner. The apartment was too small for entertaining, and even though his parents knew he and Mia were just roommates, they still weren't totally comfortable with him living with a girl.

They were polite to Mia, but standoffish, which she wasn't accustomed to. Her family was big and welcoming, hugging everyone and forcing people to stay for dinner. It was what drew Aidan to Mia in the first place. She'd chased him down at the skatepark that first day, and introduced herself without batting an eye. Aidan appreciated her openness and would miss it terribly, once they all went their separate ways.

His parents had become more protective after Casey died, his mother constantly checking in on him. He understood and made every effort to assure her he was okay. It wore him down some days, though. He loved his parents and appreciated everything they'd done for him, but it was smothering at times. His mother's worry was a bag of rocks he was forced to carry through life. He missed Casey, too, but he wasn't Casey. Casey was always on the edge of life, even as a kid. He'd been chasing after something which wasn't within his grasp. He was seven years older than Aidan, the product of their mother's first marriage. That ended when Casey was a baby, and she raised him alone until she met Aidan's father. They married and Aidan came along shortly after. He adored Casey, however, Casey was so much older, Aidan just couldn't keep up. He felt like he spent his life staring at the back of Casey, disappearing out of view.

Aidan struggled with anger after Casey's death, fighting at school and almost getting suspended. His parents took it as a sign to pack up and leave the only place he'd ever known. His father started a job in Tacoma, Washington, and Aidan found the change in environment allowed him to focus his attention outside of himself. He buckled down at school, getting a decent scholarship to college for film. He never gave himself a moment to truly think. Except at night, and even then he found ways to put his brain outside of itself. He knew it wasn't necessarily healthy, but it was the only way he could cope.

Now, he was graduating and wouldn't have never-ending projects to keep him busy. He needed to start work as soon as possible because he'd learned downtime meant anxiety. He'd been offered a partially paid internship with a film company in Los Angeles and a couple of other part-time gigs, but it wouldn't be enough to cover the bills. He was trying to figure out if he could take them all and work out the schedules.

He was at the table, charting out scenarios in a notebook he kept handy when the knock came. He got up and greeted his parents at the door. He was taller than both of them by some twist of fate and peered down at them. His father was of Russian Jewish descent and quite a bit older than his mother. Her family immigrated to the United States after World War II from Italy and were also Jewish. They weren't strictly practicing but did observe standard Jewish holidays. Casey's father hadn't been Jewish, his last name Duncan, so they also observed non-Jewish holidays when Casey was alive. As kids, they felt luckier than other kids because of this. They got double holidays.

Aidan was a cross between his parents with dark hair and eyes like his mother. He had black eyebrows set above his eyes in a way that made him appear meaner than he was. His mother was small and very Italian looking, with kind, tired eyes. She was a fretter, always waiting for the other shoe to drop. His father now had silver hair and lines around his eyes, showing he'd spent a lifetime of considering. He was an accountant, so he was always considering. How things fit, how to make everything balance, how to get blood from a stone. Aidan looked like his mother and acted like his father. Always analyzing.

He bent down to kiss his mother's cheek. "Hey, Mom. I'm almost ready, just have to get my bag. You want anything?"

She shook her head and smiled. "No. But I think we need to get there. Our reservation is for six."

It was five-thirty, the restaurant was literally two blocks away. Aidan chuckled to himself. Neither of his parents had ever been late to anything. He grabbed his bag from the bedroom and took a deep breath. Dinner was going to be a series of questions about his plans for the future. Although his parents didn't love the idea of film, they were supportive as long as he had a plan. He played his responses over in his head, ones that would put their minds at ease. He ran a comb through his hair and met them back by the door.

They walked to the restaurant in silence, and his father held the door open for them when they arrived. The restaurant was packed and loud, with people standing in line to get their names on the list. His parents had been smart enough to make a reservation. They were sat towards the back in a quieter corner. Aidan chose a seat with his back to the wall, facing into the restaurant. He felt better if he could see what was going on. He spied Mia across the restaurant with her family, all who were talking at once and laughing. TJ was with them and had obviously been welcomed in. Mia sat next to him with her hand firmly clasped in his. For a moment, Aidan felt a twinge of jealousy. Not about her, but that they'd found something so right. They were both his friends, but somehow he was still on the outside, looking in. At least in that regard.

He peered at the menu and shifted uncomfortably in his seat. He wasn't hungry, but if he said that, his mother would worry. He ordered soup and a salad. His parents ordered and the waitress gathered the menus as she departed, leaving them in an awkward silence. His father reached down into a bag he'd been carrying, then handed a package to Aidan. It had a card from both of them, congratulating him on graduating. Aidan unwrapped the present and sat in disbelief at what was inside. Even if his parents weren't thrilled with his career choice, they'd certainly done their research.

Aidan laid the paper aside and stared, grinning at the gift. It was a high-end, professional video camera and camera bag. He'd been wanting one for a while but they ran a couple of thousand dollars. At least. He was speechless and glanced up at his parents. His mother was smiling and his father met his eyes.

"That's a good one right?" His father asked, picking up the manual which came with the camera.

"Yeah, Dad. This is amazing. Thank you both so much!" Aidan didn't want to make a scene, but tears were pricking at his eyes. He rubbed his nose and bit them back. "I love you both. Thank you."

Their food arrived, so Aidan very carefully packed the camera into the bag, making sure it was all secure. He couldn't wait to try it out. He ate without even thinking about the food, his brain making a checklist of all of the places he wanted to film. Once they were done with dinner, they walked back to Aidan's apartment. His parents were tired and his graduation ceremony was the following morning. He hugged them, letting himself into the empty, quiet apartment. As soon as he could, he pulled the camera out and spread out the manual and pieces to get familiar with them. He just had to get through graduation and would have a few weeks of freedom to film.

He walked through the different aspects of the camera, filming in the apartment to get a good feel for the camera. He could hold it in one hand if needed, and the clarity was amazing. He made a mock documentary of the apartment, then watched it to see what kind of tricks he could use. It was movie quality and he felt a sense of giddiness, even with the goofy bit he'd filmed. He packed it up, heading to bed. Mia was still not home and would probably stay with TJ or her family at the hotel. Aidan clicked on the television for background noise and stretched out in bed to read the manual. Surprisingly, he dozed off before midnight.

The next morning, he woke up and focused on getting ready, even though he wanted to play around with the camera. He thought about taking it with him but decided against it, knowing his attention would be pulled elsewhere. He showered and dressed, stopping at the mirror to make sure he was *parent* presentable. With the new haircut, new shoes, suit, and tie, he almost appeared like an actual adult. He knew TJ would give him shit about how he was dressed, just like he did to TJ at Mia's performance.

He made it in time for the practice run-through and saw Mia a few rows ahead. Her last name was Gordon, his Osher, and they were sat alphabetically. She saw him and waved. This was it. They'd been together almost from the beginning, now they'd graduate and go their separate ways. Aidan pushed the thought down. He'd come to the school alone and met Mia shortly after. TJ joined them in Seattle the next year, but other than the two of them, Aidan didn't really have any other friends. No one he'd miss when he left. He'd miss TJ and Mia. A day didn't go by, they didn't see each other.

The graduation went off without a hitch, a few graduates trying to make their mark by taking their time on stage to garner a little attention with campy jokes and loud bravado. Aidan accepted his diploma and smiled at his parents, who looked on proudly. His mother was crying, sniffling into a tissue, and his father was just nodding over and over, a small smile playing at the corner of his mouth. Aidan was glad to make them proud. To bring them some joy, in what had been a hard life. He thought of Casey and wished he was there to see it. He could picture Casey cheering him on in the audience, giving him a big thumbs up. It was just Aidan, now.

After the ceremony, his parents headed out to make it home before dark. Aidan met up with TJ and Mia, who were saying goodbye to her family. They all hugged Aidan, too, congratulating him. Aidan, Mia, and TJ had agreed to have a small party back at their place to celebrate. A few school friends were invited, but not too many since the apartment was small. Aidan didn't have anyone, in particular, he'd invited, so when they got back, he cracked a beer and sat out on the steps. He wasn't a big drinker, but today seemed like a good time to have one. A few more people showed up than he was expecting, and he decided to lock his room, so he didn't have strangers in there. Especially with his new camera.

As he was heading in, he paused and thought about Zeke. The party had been planned prior to meeting him, so he hadn't been invited. Aidan honestly didn't want to spend the evening with a bunch of people he didn't know. He texted Zeke and asked if he wanted to come over to the party. He headed in to make sure his camera was locked in his room, then checked his phone. Zeke hadn't replied. It *was* short notice, though. Shrugging it off, he went back out to the party.

Mia and TJ were doing shots in the kitchen with a crowd, so Aidan stayed away, snagging a few beers instead, and went back outside. More people were going into the party as he grabbed a seat on a bench at the front of the building and sipped on his beer. It was still light out; he imagined the party would go on well after dark. He felt his phone buzz and peered down at it. There was a message from Zeke.

"Hey, sorry, just saw your message. Offer still stand?"

Aidan quickly typed back. "Yeah, come on by."

"Do I need to bring anything?"

"Nope, just yourself."

"On my way."

Aidan waited out front, not wanting to get absorbed into the chaos of the party. Their apartment held about six comfortably, and there had to be at least twenty people in there already. He stretched his legs out, drinking his beer. After a bit, he saw Zeke come skateboarding around the corner and waved him over. Zeke maneuvered around people on the sidewalk, rolling up to the bench where Aidan was sitting. Aidan squinted up at him and handed him a beer.

"Glad you could make it, man. We're better off out here. It's a madhouse in there."

Zeke took the beer and sat down beside Aidan, wiping sweat from his brow. He took a long swallow of beer and stared at Aidan, his light eyes resting on Aidan's face. Normally, Aidan would feel uncomfortable with this kind of attention, but for some reason with Zeke it didn't seem intrusive. He met Zeke's eyes and nodded. Zeke sat back, letting out a long, slow breath. They sat in silence, sipping on their beers before Zeke spoke softly.

"Thanks for inviting me over, Aidan. I was hoping to hear from you."

Chapter Four

Aidan's camera went everywhere with him. There was nothing too mundane to film; within a week he had hours of footage. Mostly he played around with it, tried out effects and erased it. It was gaining familiarity with the camera, making it an extension of himself he was working on. Eventually, it needed to almost not exist other than as another eye of his own. He was touched by his parent's thoughtfulness, this was their way of saying they supported his career choice. He still hadn't made a formal decision on what offer he was going to accept. It pretty much came down to where he'd be able to grow the most, be encouraged to have a voice. He knew he was required to put in the time on other people's projects, but he also didn't want to feel like he was just doing grunt work.

Although Mia graduated, she decided to start pursuing her Master's for music studies. TJ had a year left on his Bachelor's for social work but was also planning to continue school after that. They talked about eventually moving back to California where Mia grew up, bringing their skills to disadvantaged neighborhoods. It wasn't official, but they'd started to mention the word marriage in conversations, speaking about it in a practical sense. Neither was pushing the issue, but as far as Aidan could tell, they'd made up their minds it was where their relationship was heading. School was first, that much was clear.

Zeke and Aidan met up a few times a week to skate and their friendship grew stronger. Both knew in time, work would call them to different places, but they tried to focus on their time together while they had it. Zeke was an enigma, open about certain things almost to a fault, but like a steel trap on others. Aidan began to learn what to talk about and what to avoid. Zeke had a quirky sense of humor and deadpan sarcasm. Aidan sometimes missed the intention, not sure if he'd offended Zeke. Then a smile would start to crack at the edges of Zeke's mouth, and he'd lose his straight face.

A couple of weeks after graduation, Aidan packed his camera and skateboard to meet Zeke at the skatepark. He wanted to film some action shots, so he could work on editing a skateboard trick video. As he snagged a juice out of the fridge, he saw a performance invite with a big red circle around the time. Beside it, a note from Mia that simply read, "Be there!"

Aidan laughed and snapped a picture of it with his phone, so he wouldn't forget. Mia was performing at the civic center and being her first non-school public performance, he was obligated to attend. He'd need to head home by the afternoon to shower and get dressed. He set an alarm on his phone.

By the time he made it to the skatepark, Zeke was already in the bowl on his board and practicing handplants as he came up on each side. Aidan sat down and began filming before Zeke noticed him. Zeke was a masterpiece, every muscle in his body contributing to his motion. Some skaters were more loose and sloppy, but everything Zeke did was intricate and thought out. Even if another skater wiped out in front of him, it was as if he expected it, quickly adjusting around them, not losing a beat. Aidan had skated his whole life and wasn't half as good as Zeke.

On a round, bringing Zeke to the side Aidan was on, he spied Aidan and popped out, grinning like it was nothing. He pulled off his helmet, brushing his sweaty hair back off his face as he sat down next to Aidan. Aidan handed him a bottle of water. Zeke poured about a quarter through his head and shook his head, sending little droplets everywhere. He was wearing a tank top and rubbed the droplets that fell on his arms into his skin. He guzzled the rest, peering at Aidan.

"How long have you been here?"

"Not long. Long enough, though, to get some good footage of you." Aidan opened the viewing screen on the camera to show Zeke.

Zeke nodded and laughed. "See now, if I'd known you were filming, I would've fallen flat on my face."

"I sincerely doubt that," Aidan responded. Zeke never fell flat on his face.

Zeke eyed him for a moment, reading how he meant it and glanced away. Aidan watched him quietly, fidgeting with his camera. Zeke's face was angular. Long nose, high cheekbones, strong but pointed jawline. With his light hair and eyes, he appeared like an elven warrior. Zeke glanced over, catching Aidan staring at him and raised his eyebrows. Aidan shrugged as his cheeks flamed.

"I was just thinking you look like what Orlando Bloom's character in the Lord of the Rings movies should've looked like," he hastily explained.

"I've never seen them. We weren't allowed to watch anything like that growing up. Devil's handiwork and all." Zeke laughed, a trace of bitterness at the edges.

"Oh. So, he was like an elf king or something like that. But you look more like an elf than he did. Girls loved him though," Aidan responded.

"Lot of good that would do me," Zeke replied, chuckling. "Guys love it, too?"

"Guys wanted to *be* him."

"Okay, I can take that. So, it's a good thing, you're saying?" Zeke met his eyes, the intensity between them made Aidan waver.

"Yeah. I mean, you look like an elven king. Not of this world." Aidan felt his hands get sweaty and rubbed them on his cargo shorts.

Zeke watched the other skaters and thought about this. He turned his head back to Aidan, his eyes serious. "Don't be offended, Aidan. But do you actually *like* girls?"

Aidan felt his face get hot. He wasn't sure why, but anger rose in him and he stared hard at Zeke. "Jesus, Zeke! What kind of question is that?"

Zeke looked down at his hands. "Sorry, man, it's just a question. You never talk about girls, you aren't dating anyone. Just forget I asked. I didn't mean to piss you off."

Aidan stood up, snatching his camera. He walked to the edge of the bowl and began filming. He pushed the anger down, realizing less than anger, it felt more like shame. What the hell was wrong with Zeke? Just because he was gay, everyone else was, too? Aidan could feel the sweat on his palms causing him to lose his grip on the camera and caught it right before it slipped out of his grasp into the bowl. He was too shaken to film, so he went back and put his camera in the bag. Zeke was still sitting and didn't make eye contact. Aidan sat back down, sighing heavily.

"Sorry for the over-reaction on my part. You just caught me off guard. So, when I was fifteen, my brother took a bunch of ketamine, then jumped off the pier in our hometown and drowned. Since then, I've been trying to not be inside myself. Mia and I tried dating when we first met, but it just wasn't there. I love her, her personality, but I wasn't feeling it. It's about me. I don't even truly know who I am. If I think too long on it, I find myself slipping into a dark spiral, so I just stay busy. All of the time. Like until I'm so exhausted I pass out."

Zeke listened and nodded. He pulled his legs up, putting his elbows on them as Aidan spoke. When Aidan was done, Zeke cleared his throat and peered at him.

"I'm sorry about your brother. I didn't mean to allude to anything. I was speaking my thoughts out loud and shouldn't have said that. Was he your only sibling?"

"Casey? Yeah. I loved him so damn much. He was seven years older than me, and to me, he was a god. He was a sensitive person, you know. He felt things deeper than everyone else. He was always so philosophical. I guess, in the end, it was too much for him." Aidan rarely talked about Casey with anyone, but talking to Zeke about him seemed natural.

"Man, that really sucks. I'm sorry. If you ever need to talk, anytime, I'm here. I know what it's like to feel abandoned." Zeke's voice was so sincere, Aidan glanced over at him. Zeke met his eyes and nodded. "I mean it."

Aidan chewed his lip thoughtfully. "Watch your offer, this shit keeps me up most nights."

"Anytime. Day or night."

They took a pause in their conversation to skate, and for Aidan to get some film footage. A little while later, Aidan heard his phone going off and checked to see why. His alarm was sounding with the name *Mia* blinking on it. Mia's performance! He quickly gathered his things, waving to Zeke, who was coming back over.

"Hey, I gotta go. Mia's performing at the civic center, I better go home to change." He threw his bag over his shoulder and took a swig of water. He needed to hurry.

"Nice! Opera, right?" Zeke asked as he unclasped his helmet and clipped it to his bag.

"Yeah, she's amazing!" Aidan started to head off, then stopped to turn around. "Hey, would you want to go? I'm sure she'd love the support."

Zeke's eyes lit up. "Hell yeah, I'd love to go. Text me the time and address, I'll run home to change."

Aidan sent him the snapshot of the performance invite, making Zeke laugh over Mia's note. They each headed off in their own direction. On the way home, Aidan thought about Zeke's question about girls and considered it more deeply. He'd gone to prom and other school events, but typically the girl asked him or it was a friend. He'd never done more than kiss a girl and while it felt nice, it didn't drive him to want more. He'd always chalked it up to his own head and losing Casey. But what if it was more? He found girls pretty at times but like with Mia, it was like looking at a beautiful piece of art. He didn't need it to go further. Maybe he had just not met the right girl. Maybe someone was out there, he'd kiss and feel desire. He shoved the thoughts down, focusing on making it home and to the event on time.

No one was home when he got there, he'd noticed Mia was spending more time at TJ's. They'd talked about possibly moving in there when her lease was up, but it wasn't pet-friendly and they both wanted to get a dog. Aidan set his bag down and jumped in the shower. He thought about the footage he'd gotten of Zeke skating, how fluidly Zeke moved on the board like it was part of his own body. He thought about how Zeke's muscles adjusted with every motion. As this thought crossed his mind, Aidan found himself slightly aroused, realizing he was getting hard. Shame flushed through his body, and he scrubbed his skin hard to redirect his thoughts. It was just the warm water and exertion from the day, he convinced himself. He hurried through the rest of the shower and toweled off. He glanced at himself in the mirror as he dried his hair, his cheeks were flushed with red spots. What the hell was going on with him?

He checked his phone, he was running late. He quickly threw on shorts and a polo, trying to look nice but also stay cool. He combed his hair and thought about bringing his camera. Filming wasn't allowed inside the venue, so he decided against it. It would be just another thing to carry and since he was taking the bus, he didn't want to risk losing it. He slipped it under his bed, giving himself one last look in the mirror. The thing was, girls had always liked him. His thick black hair, dark eyes, olive skin, and black eyebrows drew them to him. They told him he was dashing, quite often he found love notes shoved in his locker. The opportunity had been there. The feeling had not.

He climbed on the bus and found a seat near the back. As the bus made its way through town, he watched all of the people on the street, thinking about their lives. Their histories. Their joy and suffering. He wasn't alone in loss, he knew that. He felt alone, but maybe more so from the walls he'd built around himself. Mia and TJ were family to him, even so, he'd not let them all the way in. He felt something for Zeke. An immediate connection, a friendship that came easy. The bus pulled up to the civic center and Aidan stood up to step off. As he exited into the evening air, a thought occurred to him, he knew he'd have to address. He walked slowly towards the civic center, mulling it over in his mind.

Maybe Casey's death, and how he felt, were not solely connected. He was fifteen when Casey died, but what if Casey hadn't died? Would he still have felt this way? Was it deeper inside of him and those events weren't correlated, but merely two paths joining at the same time? Maybe he was running away from himself because he saw something forming within him, he wasn't comfortable or familiar with. At that time, and since, he'd focused on Casey's death because it allowed him to not focus on himself, on a truth he wasn't ready to face.

A truth Zeke was now bringing to the forefront.

Chapter Five

The person at the center of Aidan's mind was standing outside the civic center, leaning against the wall. His white hair was brushed off his face, and he was wearing light linen pants with a white button-down shirt. Aidan felt underdressed seeing Zeke but shrugged it off with the summer heat. Zeke saw him coming and stood straight up, raising his hand. Aidan came towards him, feeling more nervous than he should. They were friends. That hadn't changed, no matter what turmoil was going on inside of Aidan's head. Zeke couldn't read his mind, they were just two friends hanging out. To see opera. That made Aidan chuckle and relax. That's what guy friends did, right?

"Hey, Zeke. You been here long?"

"Not too long. I wasn't sure exactly where it was, so caught an early bus to scope out the area. It's nice down here."

Zeke smelled clean, like bar soap. Aidan moved towards the door, not trusting himself too close to Zeke after the shower incident. Nothing like that had ever happened before, he was sure it was coincidental to his thought pattern. Zeke followed and they found TJ down by the front. He'd saved a couple of seats and they slid in, trying to get comfortable. Aidan was in the middle and leaned in to ask TJ if they'd found a place to live yet.

"Nah," TJ replied. "Everything is so expensive that allows dogs. We may just have to stay at my place until one of us is actually working."

"Or you could sneak a dog in?" Aidan teased.

"Mia wants a damn Great Dane puppy. There is no hiding that."

They laughed and the lights flickered, reminding people to find their seats. Aidan looked at the program and was surprised to see Mia was the star of the show. It was a full opera and she was performing a large number of songs. He rested back in his seat to get comfortable, glancing at Zeke, who was peering around the auditorium. Zeke leaned back, catching Aidan's eye and smiled, raising an eyebrow. Aidan handed him the program, pointing out Mia's name. Zeke grinned and nodded, impressed.

The lights dimmed and people quickly found their seats. The curtain rose and Mia was standing alone, the piano player off to the side. A full orchestra was in the pit and they began to play. Mia's voice rose above the instruments, rising to a crescendo as she held a high note. TJ had his hands pressed to his knees, obviously nervous for her. But she was perfect. Aidan found he was holding his breath and let it out.

Zeke whispered, "wow."

As the song came to an end, the three guys relaxed, releasing the tension they'd been holding in their bodies. Mia had this. This was her territory. The rest of the night was equally amazing, and Aidan found himself moved by the music. Zeke was mesmerized, his mouth hanging open at times.

At one point, Zeke shifted in his seat and his knee rested against Aidan's. He didn't notice, but Aidan did. Aidan couldn't deny the heat from Zeke made him feel something. He eased his leg away to not make it apparent. Zeke's eyes were focused on the stage. Aidan was confused and frustrated. He'd been able to control every thought, every feeling since Casey died. It was the one skill he'd developed, after being devastated by losing the one person who meant the most in the world to him. Now, the thought of Zeke, or him touching Aidan's leg, made Aidan flustered. Which made him angry at himself. He moved so he was leaning more towards TJ, and made himself pay attention to the performance. By the end of the evening, only Mia was the only thing on everyone's mind. TJ brought her flowers, like before, however this time he had to wait in line behind admirers. Mia was friendly and polite with the people, but her eyes changed when she saw TJ. He was her rock.

It took much longer for Mia to get out to join them. By the time she made it out, most of the crowd had dispersed. TJ wrapped his arms around her as she rested her head against his chest, relieved to be just herself again. The group walked over to a nearby diner to grab food. As they sat, Aidan grew concerned when Mia and TJ sat on one side of the booth, leaving the other side for him and Zeke. They'd be close to each other, and he needed to keep his shit together. Aidan slid in, pressing himself against the side of the booth. Zeke slipped in next to him, but slightly out so he could let his legs stretch outside of the benches. This gave them a little breathing room.

"Man, that was impressive," Zeke told Mia. "Does your voice get tired?"

"Oh yeah. By the end of the performance, my throat is tight," Mia explained.

"I've never really heard opera like that. Being raised in the church, a lot of singers come through, but nothing like what you just did. It's hard to believe such a powerful sound comes out of your tiny self." Zeke laughed, shaking his head.

"When I was little, it was all I wanted to do. I sang in church, too. My family isn't bible-thumping religious, but we went every Sunday. Once they realized I could sing, I was always up at the front, belting away. I knew I wanted to keep doing it."

Their food arrived and they dug in, falling silent until everything was pretty much gone. They chatted for a bit before heading out. TJ and Mia headed back to his place, as Aidan checked the time for the bus schedule. He wasn't quite ready to be home alone, but was out of money and couldn't kill time either. Zeke peered at his phone, sighing.

"Hey, I'm off tomorrow. You want to hang out for a bit?" he asked as they headed towards the bus stop.

Aidan didn't have anywhere to be either, so that sounded better than going home to fight off the spiral. "Yeah, I have some beer back at my place. We can watch a movie or something."

Zeke nodded. He watched Aidan for a second like he wanted to say something, then looked away. Their bus pulled up and they got on, standing because it was crowded. The bus jerked away from the stop, causing Aidan to fall back into Zeke.

Zeke caught him and laughed. "Hold on. It's going to be a bumpy ride."

For some reason, Aidan didn't think he meant about the bus and blushed. They got off a block from Aidan's apartment and walked slowly towards it. The night air was surprisingly cool with a light breeze blowing. When they got to the door, Aidan paused as he fished his key out of his bag.

"It's nice out. You want to sit outside?"

Zeke tipped his head. "That sounds good."

They grabbed a couple of beers and sat on the steps. Conversation between them was always easy, and Zeke talked about different places he skateboarded. No one else on the construction crew skated, so he'd find places once he settled into a new area and go alone. Sometimes the construction sites worked well, but he was also drawn to abandoned buildings. Aidan wanted to film at abandoned places, so they agreed to go scavenging the next day. After a couple of beers, they moved inside and put on a movie neither was watching. Zeke got up to use the bathroom and Aidan watched him leave the room.

When Zeke came back, he sat down next to Aidan, his leg touching Aidan's. It felt purposeful. Aidan acted like he didn't notice but also didn't move.

"Can I ask you something?" Aidan asked.

Zeke nodded but didn't speak.

"How did you know you were gay? If you aren't comfortable, you can ignore the question." Aidan felt like he'd swallowed pepper.

Zeke considered the question and then spoke, "I guess I kind of always knew. When I was little, we had this pastor who was super Las Vegas. Shiny suits, slicked-back hair, a master on the microphone. I was enamored by him and would just sit and stare. My parents thought it was early seeds of their son having the calling, but really I was so drawn to him. Then as I got older, I found myself feeling that way about other boys, then other men. I don't think I was ever confused or questioned it. It just was who I was. I mean, girls just didn't do anything for me."

"When did your family figure it out?"

"I told my mother when I was eighteen, thinking because she was my mother she'd understand. Even though they openly spoke about their hatred of 'the gays'. She listened but didn't say much, other than it was the devil trying to confuse me. Later, my father came in and beat the hell out of me. I was more emotionally hurt than physically, and he almost killed me. They were my parents, you know? They brought me into the world. They were strict but were still my parents. But not after this. To them, I was no longer their child. They told me it was conversion therapy or get out. Their love had a switch they could turn off. If it ever was love."

Aidan felt such a deep pain for Zeke, he choked back tears. He stared down at his hands and shook his head. "Conversion therapy? Like where they convince you that you aren't gay?"

Zeke snickered bitterly. "Convince? More like shame, beat, torture you until you say you aren't gay. So, I left. I snuck out that night to the nearest construction site and got a job with them the next day. When the guys would leave for the day, I'd sleep at the site. By the time we moved on, I had enough money saved to always have a place in each town. I never spoke to my parents again. That was six years ago."

"Fuck, man, I'm sorry. I can't imagine."

"Aidan, we all carry our scars, we're the walking wounded, right? You lost your brother, I lost my family. We both carry a lot of pain. It's why I like you. You seem to get it." Zeke's voice was gentle but strong.

Aidan met Zeke's eyes and nodded. Zeke was the first person he didn't feel like he had to make his suffering okay for. With Zeke, he didn't have to pretend everything was fine, so they could move on with their day. Losing Casey had broken him. Losing his family had broken Zeke. But they came out stronger in some ways, too. Not too many people would understand, but they could understand each other. Aidan sighed and leaned back against the couch with his eyes closed. He wasn't tired but his brain was. He felt Zeke get up to go to the kitchen. He came back with a couple of beers and sat back down. Aidan opened his eyes and smiled.

"Thanks. I mean, for the beer, but also for listening and telling me about yourself. I always feel like people shift when I start to talk about my life, about Casey. Like, they go from a friend to putting a pity bubble around me. I appreciate you not doing that and trusting me with your past." Aidan took a sip of his beer.

"Likewise. People go from being a friend to acting like I have a disease when I tell them I like dudes." Zeke laughed and gave Aidan a little shove.

Aidan thought about what Zeke had said about always knowing he was gay. He never questioned it. It was like knowing he had light hair. It was what it was. Aidan wasn't that in tune with himself. He wasn't sure about almost anything, except being a filmmaker. That was concrete, he could semi-control it. Personally, it was easier to not think about how he felt, or wanted, on anything else.

Zeke leaned back against the couch, his leg resting against Aidan's. Heat rose from his leg but rather than pushing away,

Aidan let himself feel it. It felt nice. Natural. They sat watching, but not absorbing, the movie for a bit when Zeke glanced over.

"Is it cool if I just sleep here? I don't want to go all the way home. I can crash on the couch if that's alright."

"Yeah, for sure. I have an extra blanket and pillow I can give you." Aidan got up, grabbing those from his room. He brought them to Zeke, who was yawning. "There's an extra toothbrush in the cabinet. Mia likes to stock up."

Zeke rubbed his head and stood up to go to the bathroom. "Thanks, Aidan. Tomorrow we can go explore, find some shit to get into."

Aidan chuckled and headed to his room. Once he heard Zeke go out of the bathroom, he went to brush his teeth. Zeke was already crashed out on the couch by the time he was done, and Aidan paused to look at him. Zeke's legs were over the arm of the couch and he was sleeping with his hand on his chest, his face turned to the side. Aidan shook his head, went to his room, and climbed into his bed, amazed at how quickly Zeke fell asleep. He was tired but his brain wasn't done yet. He thought about Zeke lying on the couch, and what it would be like to lie next to him. Shame started to rise in him, but he forced it away. He needed to consider what he was thinking. He had to allow himself to feel something. He let his mind go back to imagining Zeke lying next to him. Putting his arm around him. It didn't seem wrong. It was comforting to think about. He pictured Zeke lying face to face with him, their eyes locked.

The thought made Aidan smile to himself, and his brain finally let him sleep.

Chapter Six

The next day, they headed out early to check out abandoned sites. TJ let them borrow his car since he and Mia were hanging out around town. Zeke had already explored most of the sites in his free time and led Aidan to the best ones. They went to an old hospital, grain silo, brewery, and found a way into the Seattle Underground. They skateboarded where they could, and Aidan got hours of footage. Most of the places were creepy, but Aidan found a familiarity in exploring and thinking about the people who'd been there before. He could almost picture the places in full action, the sounds and smells. They'd packed food and sat on a wall at the Georgetown Steam Plant to eat by late afternoon. Everything echoed around them, yet felt claustrophobic at the same time.

"I don't know why, but I find this oddly comforting," Aidan said between bites.

Zeke laughed, understanding. "Yeah, I get it. I always find abandoned places to feel more home than home, you know?"

Aidan did. It was as if at the moment they were there, it was all theirs. He liked the idea of living in an abandoned place but as he'd seen, the rats had pretty much claimed those spaces. They were fearless, too. More than once, Zeke and Aidan backtracked because of a rat refusing to move. Zeke put his stuff back in his backpack and started doing tricks on his board. Aidan pulled out his camera and filmed, appreciating how seeing Zeke through the camera eye was different than in person. In person, he was aware of all of their surroundings, through the camera's limited eye it seemed as if Zeke was all alone in endless darkness.

Zeke glanced over grinning, as his board slipped out from under him and he hit the ground. "Stop distracting me."

Aidan peered over the camera. "Stop distracting *me.*"

It came out way more intimate than he intended. Zeke got up and stared at him, raising an eyebrow. He brushed off his shorts and shook his head.

"You know, Aidan, you gotta watch how you say things, so they don't get misconstrued."

Aidan laughed nervously at Zeke's words. Maybe he *had* meant it the way he'd said it. He chewed his lip and met Zeke's eyes. He didn't want to play with Zeke's emotions, but he also wanted to know if what he was feeling was real. There was no easy way about it. He nodded, focusing back on the screen. Zeke came and sat back down next to him, finishing off his water.

"We should probably head back towards home," Zeke said, his voice deep and tinged with frustration.

Aidan turned the camera off, packing it carefully in the bag. He could feel Zeke's presence next to him and felt like Zeke was waiting to say something. He glanced at Zeke, who was watching him, his pale eyes unblinking. Aidan put the bag down and waited for Zeke to speak. Instead, Zeke leaned in and kissed him lightly on the lips. Aidan was stunned but didn't pull away, feeling a strong desire awaken inside of him. Zeke didn't do anything else and sat back.

"So, I ask you again, Aidan. Do you even *like* girls?"

Aidan stared at him and thought about it. It all became apparent. He shook his head and muttered, "No, I suppose not."

Zeke smiled knowingly and nodded. "I didn't think so. You ready to go?"

Aidan stood up but felt disconnected from his body and sat back down. He leaned over, placing his head in his hands. Zeke put his arm over his shoulders and they sat quietly. Aidan didn't know what to do with this revelation, and Zeke didn't press. Finally, Aidan took a deep breath and stood up again. Zeke slung his bag over his shoulder, grabbing his board. Aidan rode his board out, letting the pull of the motion distract him for a bit. He was in turmoil but also felt lighter, clearer.

Zeke drove them home and the conversation was stilted about random nothingness. Aidan tried to not make eye contact; by the time they made it to the apartment, the tension was weighing them both down. Zeke switched off the car, turning to face Aidan.

"Look, I did that because I could see this in you. You're my friend and you torture yourself with who you think you need to be. I admit, I wanted to for a while but don't want to lose you as a friend. If you minded, let me know. I'll never do it again, and we can just be friends. But you have to know I'm attracted to you."

Zeke ran his hand through his hair, pushing it out of his eyes. It fell back over as soon as he moved his hand.

He watched Aidan, waiting for a response. When Aidan just sat there quietly, Zeke nodded and opened his door. Aidan wasn't trying to be hurtful, he was at a loss for words. They walked in silence to the apartment, but when they got to the door Aidan reached out, placing his hand on Zeke's arm.

"I didn't mind. I don't know what's going on with me, but I feel something for you, Zeke. I'm just not familiar with what this all is. Give me time, okay? For now, your friendship means everything to me."

Zeke let out his breath and smiled. "That's better than nothing."

Mia and TJ were cooking when they got in, and the conversation quickly picked up between them. Aidan showed them the highlights of the footage he took of the abandoned places, and they all agreed to go again the following week. Zeke and Aidan fell back into their normal selves, but every once in a while their eyes would meet and one of them would end up blushing. This was new territory for both of them. Mia sensed the change, eyeing Aidan.

"What's with you? You're acting all weird," she teased.

He shrugged, knowing she'd get it out of him before long. She squinted her eyes at him and glanced at Zeke. Aidan followed her gaze and flushed, putting his head down. She grabbed his arm to lead him out of the room.

"Aidan, you better tell me. I know what I'm thinking, so you'd better set me straight."

Aidan met her eyes and simply nodded. She knew. Her mouth dropped open and she hugged him.

"It's about time you figured it out. I was wondering how long it would take," she said knowingly.

"You knew? How?"

"Aidan, when we kissed, I suspected. Trust me, every guy that has kissed me, except you, pushed it further immediately. You were nice and polite, but that was all. That night we met Zeke, I saw you watching him and wondered how long it would take for you to realize you were attracted to him. I'm glad he came along to speed up the process," Mia explained.

Aidan shook his head and felt a weight lift off of him. Maybe all these feelings he was struggling with, trying to push down, were him just denying his true self. It was too much to take in all at once, he needed time alone to figure things out.

"Thanks, Mia. I'm still not sure what the hell is happening, but it helps to hear that from you."

She took his hand and they went back in. TJ and Zeke were deep in a discussion about the future of renewable energy, so Aidan snagged a soda and headed to the living room. He sat down on the couch and put his head back, closing his eyes. Being gay wasn't something he'd considered, however, now was something he couldn't dismiss. He opened his eyes and watched Zeke in the kitchen. He was leaning against the counter, laughing. In his skate shoes, long cargo shorts, and tank top, he didn't fit the cliché of a gay man. Then again, neither did Aidan. Maybe that was part of the problem. His whole life, being gay was portrayed in a certain way in the media, and he'd never related to that idea.

Zeke glanced over and caught his eye. Neither blushed. He bowed out of the conversation with Mia and TJ and came over, sitting next to Aidan.

"You alright?"

Aidan bobbed his head. "Yeah, just trying to make sense of this. Of myself."

"Okay. If you want to talk..." Zeke trailed off, staring at his hands.

"Zeke, thanks. Today wasn't the first time I was aware but was the first time I accepted it. I...I *am* attracted to you. I just don't know what to do with that."

Zeke's ears turned red, but he didn't look up. Aidan put his hand on Zeke's back, leaving it there. Nothing about it felt wrong. Zeke eyed him and smiled. They didn't need to say anything else. Mia saw them from the kitchen and winked. The rest of the evening went like it always did, everyone talking over each other and cutting up. Zeke had to work the next day, so he stood up to leave by dark.

"Alright, I gotta catch the bus home. As always, it's been fun," he said as he picked up his bag, meeting Aidan's eyes.

"Hey, I can walk you to the bus. I want some fresh air, anyway," Aidan blurted out, making TJ raise his eyebrows.

"Sure," Zeke said as if it meant nothing.

They walked out as the last bits of sun disappeared into the night. They made their way to the bus stop. It was empty and they stood quietly waiting for the bus.

"I was going to say you could just crash over but..." Aidan didn't know what the follow up to that was.

"But we need to figure some things out," Zeke finished.

Aidan chuckled. That was an understatement. "Zeke, can I...um...fuck, I don't know what I'm trying to say. Can I do something?"

Zeke stared at him confused, nodding slowly. Aidan stepped in close to him, sliding his arm around Zeke's waist. He leaned in and kissed Zeke, more firmly than Zeke had kissed him before. Zeke relaxed and responded, his tongue lightly touching Aidan's. Aidan pulled back and stared at Zeke. There was no doubt, now. What he felt then, versus any time he'd kissed a girl, was completely different. With girls, it had been warm and soft but enough. With Zeke, he wanted more. He stepped back, tipping his head. Zeke reached out, touching his hand.

"You okay?"

Aidan grinned. "Yeah, more than okay. It all makes more sense."

Zeke reciprocated the grin as his bus came down the street. "Hey, see you soon?"

"For sure. Thanks, Zeke."

Zeke climbed on the bus and gave him a quick wave. Aidan watched the bus pull away until it was no longer visible and strolled home. He stopped outside the door, smiling to himself. He could still taste Zeke on his lips and felt butterflies in his stomach. No matter what, at least now he knew. He couldn't think about what all it meant, or how he'd deal with it moving forward. He just knew he had answers to who he was, and that was enough for now.

Today had been a good day.

Chapter Seven

Whether out of shyness or fear of messing things up, Aidan and Zeke didn't see each other for a week. They talked every day through calls or text, but neither could bridge the gap to see each other. Finally fed up, Mia demanded they all go out together. They planned a day to explore the town, including abandoned buildings, and she made sure no one backed out. Aidan told TJ about his feelings for Zeke, but TJ didn't seem too surprised. He was quiet and thought about it, then shrugged.

"You like who you like, right? If you like Zeke, then that's how you feel." TJ had always been the logical one growing up. He was never wild or messed around with drugs. He surfed and got straight A's in school. He never seemed to have anything to prove to anyone.

Aidan figured that's why their friendship had lasted so long. TJ was a brother to him in more ways than one. TJ was the only one who stood by him when Casey committed suicide, and the town turned on his family. Well, TJ and Casey's best friend, Smith. Smith had gone to prison over selling drugs, and he and Aidan didn't talk for a couple of years because of it. He'd been the one who'd sold the ketamine to Casey. Over time, Aidan had come to realize that Smith was trapped just like Casey. Smith eventually left the town with his girlfriend Sam, and Aidan had made contact again. Smith now went by Smitty and was sober, running his own restaurant in the Outer Banks of North Carolina. Aidan missed them terribly and wished he could see Smitty again. TJ knew Smitty and Sam, too, it was their small connection to the world they grew up in.

The day Mia planned, and forced on everyone, came and TJ agreed to drive since he was the only one with a car. The three of them headed over to pick up Zeke. Aidan kept wiping his palms on his shorts, trying to breathe slowly. He hadn't seen Zeke since they kissed at the bus stop. Zeke came bounding out of his place towards the car. Mia was sitting in the front with TJ, so Zeke climbed in the back with Aidan.

"Thanks for picking me up! Where to first?" Zeke asked, giving Aidan's hand a quick squeeze.

"I was thinking we could head out to the abandoned hospital? Start creepy, right?" Mia answered.

"Yeah, cool. I can show you some eerie places there for sure," Zeke replied and leaned back, his shoulder touching Aidan's.

Aidan glanced at Zeke, who met his eyes. Zeke gave a short wink and grinned.

"Missed you," he mouthed.

Aidan nodded, feeling his cheeks get hot. TJ's car was small, so they were crammed in next to each other. TJ drove like he was on a racetrack, tossing them side to side. They couldn't help but touch, which helped Aidan get over his bashfulness. By the time they got to the old hospital, they were joking around like the friends they were. TJ popped the trunk, so Aidan could grab his camera, and they headed into the hospital. It was dreary in the middle of the day and weird sounds seemed to be everywhere. Just rats and the building settling likely, but it still made everyone jumpy.

Mia chattered away, not afraid to go anywhere. More than once they looked around and she was gone, just to pop out of a completely different area. Aidan filmed as they went, careful not to step on rotting floorboards. They were hoping to catch something on film they'd never seen or couldn't explain, but for now, he just needed to watch his footing. They made it to a higher level of the hospital and found a spot where a large window had been pushed out. Aidan stepped forward, the fresh air a welcome relief from the stale corridors. It was overcast and seemed like it might rain, which was kicking up a strong breeze. As it blew through the darkened halls, it made a low wail, causing the hair to stand up on Aidan's arms.

Zeke came up beside him and they stared out the window. The breeze blew their hair off their faces, cooling them down. Mia and TJ wandered down the hall to a room she'd wanted to peek into. The creepier it was, the more Mia was drawn to it. This left Zeke and Aidan alone. Aidan peered at Zeke, reaching out to touch his hand. Zeke glanced over and held Aidan's hand in his. It was warm and firm. Aidan was waiting for things to not feel right, for one of them to pull away, but it didn't happen. They stood holding hands, watching out the window until they heard Mia and TJ coming back down the hall.

"Hey, you ready to move on?" Mia asked. "It's supposed to start raining, so we better do anything outside first."

They headed back down to the car. Mia caught Aidan's eye, delicately smiling. She'd seen them holding hands, and wanted Aidan to know she was happy for him. The rest of the morning, they went from abandoned building to abandoned building, Zeke being their consummate guide. For having been only in Seattle for a few months, he knew his way around better than any of them.

They ate the lunch they'd packed, trying to decide where to go next when the rain hit. Really, more like a monsoon. They were at the old brewery and ran in to find a place to stay dry. Aidan set his camera down, covering it with a rain jacket he'd brought. The camera was more important to him than his own skin. Once he was sure it would be dry, he went to look out at the rain. Mia and TJ had disappeared into the brewery, and he wasn't sure where Zeke had gone. He stepped out into the rain, turning his face up with his eyes closed, letting it fall on his cheeks. He still really missed the ocean and diving deep underwater, so he could feel nothing but the weight of the water on his body. This reminded him of that as he let out the breath in his body, allowing the rainwater to consume him.

He opened his eyes and shook his hair, now soaked from the rain. He rubbed the water off his cheeks and peered around. Zeke was standing under the ledge watching him, with the most understanding expression on his face. Aidan flushed, embarrassed he'd been caught so vulnerable, but Zeke shook his head. He walked over and placed his hand on either side of Aidan's face, kissing him deeply. Like the rain, Zeke's kiss washed over Aidan, making him feel fragile and safe at the same time. He put his arms around Zeke as they stood in the rain, kissing and holding onto each other.

When the rain let up, they slipped back under the ledge and attempted to dry off. The insecurity of the car ride was gone, they felt nothing but enjoying each other's company. Aidan checked on his camera which was still completely dry. Mia and TJ came back, looking flushed themselves, and the four of them loaded back in the car to head home. Everyone was drenched, so they decided to at least regroup before heading back out. Back at the house, Aidan dug out dry clothes for Zeke and changed in the bedroom, while Zeke changed in the bathroom. Although Zeke was taller, everything Aidan wore, for the most part, was just t-shirts and long shorts. Zeke had a thinner waist but cinched the shorts with a belt. Aidan admired him when he came out, liking to see his clothes on Zeke's body.

Mia and TJ rested for a bit in her room. The rain and travels had worn them all out. Aidan was tired but didn't want to leave Zeke by himself. He glanced at Zeke and cleared his throat.

"Hey, I'm tired. I don't suppose you want to come lie with me?"

Zeke laughed, cocking his head. "Sure. I'm pretty beat, too. Don't try anything though, buddy."

Aidan blushed, knowing Zeke was kidding but also knowing he wasn't. They went to Aidan's bed, which like the rest of his room, had piles of nondescript clothing and items everywhere. He shoved everything off, so Zeke would have a place to lie, apologizing for the mess.

"You know I'm a neat freak, right?" Zeke teased.

"Well, then you're going to lose your mind here," Aidan replied.

Zeke chuckled and rested on his back, on the side Aidan cleared. Suddenly, Aidan felt self-conscious and sat on the edge of the bed. Zeke sighed, placing his hand on Aidan's back.

"Just like camping. We're just sleeping in the same tent."

Aidan nodded, then grinned. "*You* are the one talking about pitching tents, dude."

Zeke laughed out loud and put his hand on his chest. "Fair enough. Bad analogy."

Aidan lay down on his back next to Zeke, kicking his shoes off. They didn't say anything for a bit and when Aidan turned to say something, he saw Zeke was already asleep. He seriously could fall asleep anywhere. He watched Zeke's chest rise and fall in sleep and reached out to touch his jawline. The touch stirred Zeke, who took Aidan's hand and put his fingers to his lips for a moment before he let go.

Aidan closed his eyes and let sleep overtake him, finding comfort in the warm body next to him. It had been since he was a little boy and would climb in Casey's bed when he was scared or lonely. Casey had always let him, putting his arm over him, assuring Aidan it was alright. It was the only time Casey stopped moving long enough for Aidan to catch up with him. Not a day went by that he didn't miss Casey, or internally rage at him for leaving him behind. He was his everything. He dozed off listening to Zeke breathe, picturing Casey's smiling face in his mind.

When he woke later, it was dark and he was alone. He could hear Zeke and Mia talking in the kitchen. He stumbled out, feeling almost drunk. He never slept that deep and was having a hard time coming out of it. When he came into the kitchen, Mia took one look at him and giggled. He checked his reflection in the windowpane and could see why. His hair was sticking up all over, and he was completely disheveled. Zeke eyed him, biting his lip.

"Come on, sleepy. Let's get you put together." He took Aidan by the arm, leading him to the bathroom. He wet his hands and smoothed Aidan's hair. "Wanted to let you sleep. You were pretty out."

"Yeah, I don't usually sleep. Like almost ever," Aidan admitted. "I guess having you around helped."

Zeke nodded, then leaned against the sink. "Aidan, you were talking in your sleep. Super anxious, stressed talking. Have you ever spoken to anyone about Casey?"

Aidan shook his head. It was something he felt he'd never be able to contain again if he opened it. He rubbed his nose and bit back tears. "I can't."

Zeke stood up, putting his arms around Aidan. "If you don't, this could kill you. Like Casey."

"I don't do drugs."

"There are a lot of ways to kill yourself, Aidan. You're still doing it, just slower." Zeke's voice was adamant.

Aidan knew he was right. If he didn't deal with losing Casey, he was going to lose himself. A crack shot down the wall he'd built around himself. He sat down on the bathroom floor, releasing the pent up pain and tears he'd been holding in for years. Zeke sat down with him and rubbed his back. Aidan felt like he did the day they told him Casey was dead. Scared, alone, and breakable. He'd deflected it with anger and numbness for so long, but it was time to face losing Casey. He cried until he felt dry and paper-thin. He looked up at Zeke, expecting to see judgement or discomfort. Instead, he saw kind eyes, watching him.

"Aidan, you have to stop believing you're alone."

"I am, Zeke. I always have been."

"I'm here, right? As far as I can tell, I'm sitting in front of you and not a figment of your imagination."

Aidan laughed softly. He blew his nose and sat back. "Yeah, but for how long?"

"Jesus, Aidan. As long as you want me to be. Not everyone leaves," Zeke said with conviction.

Aidan knew Zeke meant it, but still, he couldn't trust it. It was easier to put up a wall between them than to go through all of that again. Zeke watched his face change and sighed, resting his elbows on his knees. He leaned forward.

"Fuck. Casey really did a number on you. You were just a kid. So was he. He wasn't running away from you, he was running away from himself. He didn't know what he was doing to you. You have to forgive him, and set yourself free."

Aidan nodded. He knew Zeke was right. He peered up to meet Zeke's eyes and didn't waver. He grasped Zeke's hand in his own. His voice sounded far away when he spoke.

"I'm trying."

Chapter Eight

Zeke stayed the night, and they sat in Aidan's room, talking everything out. Mia had heard them in the bathroom and was concerned when they came out. She could tell Aidan had been crying. Her protective nature stepped in, staring from him to Zeke. Aidan met her eyes to let her know he was alright. She watched Zeke and nodded. She could see Zeke was comforting him and took a step back, allowing Zeke to be the person Aidan leaned on. Aidan smiled weakly at her, she was still his best friend.

They grabbed food and drinks and disappeared into Aidan's room, turning on the television for background noise. Zeke sat cross-legged on the bed. Aidan sat across from him, holding his knees to his chest with his arms. The change in location had paused their openness and Zeke took a deep breath.

"Okay, let me start. You know a little about what happened to me, but let me tell you everything." He reached out and took Aidan's hand in his, as much to steady himself as to be there for Aidan.

"Like I said, I think as long as I knew I was a sexual being, I knew I was gay. My first crushes were on guys. By the time I was twelve, other boys were passing notes to girls in school, and I was thinking about the boys, instead. I never told anyone, because being raised in the church, it was made very clear that liking people of the same gender was a sin. I'd hoped I'd grow out of it and pretended to like girls, so my parents weren't suspicious. But in our church, there is an expectation of marrying into the congregation. My parents had already picked a girl they wanted me to marry. It was presented as my choice, but ultimately to have their, and the church's, acceptance, I had to go along with it. So, not arranged but pressured. Or maybe arranged, I guess."

Aidan's eyes were wide with disbelief. In this day and age, he couldn't imagine being told who you should marry, even if you were straight. He tried to picture a younger Zeke being presented with those choices, and it made his stomach turn.

"The girl? She was fine with it?"

Zeke shrugged. "I never asked. It wasn't up to us, honestly. She was nice and we were in the same youth group together, but I didn't know or even really talk to her. They couldn't force us, but they could shun us...which was almost worse."

"What was her name?" Aidan didn't know why he was asking or why it was making him feel jealous.

"Rebecca."

"So, if you had not come out and refused, right now you would be married to some girl named Rebecca? With a bunch of kids?"

Zeke chuckled, squeezing Aidan's hand. "Yeah, I guess. A slew of kids, too, because they also don't believe in birth control, and most people get married at eighteen."

Aidan shook his head and sighed. "I'm glad you aren't."

"Me too. Anyway, around that time, I decided to talk to my mother before it went any further. I told her I didn't want to marry Rebecca, and she thought it was just because it was Rebecca specifically. She told me I'd eventually fall in love with her. When I told her I wouldn't fall in love with any girl, she stared at me blankly. I told her I was gay, but she refused to listen, saying the devil had gotten into me and I needed to repent. This went on for a while, eventually, she refused to talk to me. When my father got home, I could hear them in the kitchen talking about me and the devil. My father came in and beat me until I passed out. When I came to, I was alone in my and my brother's room. My older sister came in, telling me they wanted to see me. I was dizzy and could hardly stand up, my left eye swollen shut and clotted with blood. I made my way to the kitchen table where they were at. They wouldn't let me sit. They called me all kinds of slurs and told me if I didn't go to conversion therapy, they'd put me out on the street."

Zeke took a deep, shaky breath, wiping away a tear that had slipped down his cheek. "These were my parents, you know? The people you depend on and feel like should be there for you. Either way, they were disgusted by me and told me they didn't love me or consider me part of their family. I was devastated. Conversion therapy would just keep a roof over my head and allow me to still marry Rebecca. Otherwise, I was nothing to them. A disgrace. So, after agreeing to conversion therapy, that night I packed what I could and slipped out. I wandered for a while and slept at a nearby construction site. Well, sort of slept. I knew I had a concussion and tried to stay awake for periods of time. The next day, I went to the construction site office to ask for a job. The foreman took one look at me and brought me on. I couldn't see out of that eye for months, even after the swelling went down. That job ended, and the crew was about to move on. I was offered to stay on with them. I've done it ever since."

Aidan sat in silence, afraid to speak. He was horrified at what he'd heard. The value of Zeke's life was only what it brought to the church. Zeke was staring off, still stuck in the memories. Aidan squeezed his hand to bring him back. Zeke looked back at Aidan and his eyes shifted into focus on him. He smiled bashfully.

"Anyway, that's my story."

Aidan moved closer, sliding his arms around Zeke. Zeke had spent years learning how to encapsulate his pain, so other than letting his head rest against Aidan's shoulder, he didn't show other emotion. Aidan sat back and leaned against the headboard.

"My turn, huh? I've told you a lot about my family and what happened with Casey, so I'll tell you the one thing I haven't told anyone. For a long time, maybe still, I've blamed myself for Casey's death. I don't know why. I was a kid, but somehow I thought if I'd just listened more, things would've been different. Had I read the signs, I could've helped him. I was so intent on me meaning something to him, I didn't see he didn't mean anything to himself. We always said Casey was on a cloud, off in his own world. But it wasn't until recently, I came to grips with the reality that the world wasn't free and beautiful. It was dark and torturing him. He started using ketamine to escape that world, eventually using it to escape this one. Casey always talked about how things should be better, how people should care more. He tried spirituality, like new-age type stuff, I guess, but he still felt trapped. I was so angry at him for leaving me. He was everything to me. I looked up to him, I turned to him, I relied on him. I felt abandoned when he killed himself. Like he'd done it to me. I lashed out, got fucked up, and tried to destroy everything good in my life. I blamed myself. Over time, that wore me down, and I decided I'd bury the pain in staying busy and not let myself feel or think. I guess that's how all of this escaped me for so long. I wasn't feeling anything. Now, I look back and see how much pain Casey was in. Now, I feel like a selfish little shit for only thinking about myself."

Zeke leaned next to Aidan, resting his hand on Aidan's leg. "You had the right to be a selfish little shit. You were hurting, too, and in all reality *were* abandoned by the one person you cared the most about in the world. Casey didn't mean it, but it happened. Maybe forgiving yourself will be the next step. Think about fifteen-year-old Aidan, let him know it's okay to be an angry kid, facing a huge unknown."

Aidan hadn't considered that. He was always seeing himself with the knowledge he had at the time, creating a cycle of shame for not being better. But he couldn't have known all of this back then. All he knew was losing Casey. He didn't know if he would've been able to come to this without Zeke. Every time he talked about Casey, he'd done so with an unending wall of shame he couldn't ascend. Zeke had helped him over that wall, and let Aidan of the past be free of expectations he knew nothing about. Aidan glanced at Zeke.

"I truly appreciate you, Zeke. I've been locked on this fucking merry-go-round for years. Within the short time of knowing you, you've helped me not only accept who I am but helped me face all of this crap I've been carrying."

"Aidan, I can say that literally from the first time I laid eyes on you, I could see that weight. I saw you at the skate park that first day before we spoke, and you were in the bowl. Your face was set in such determination, but it wasn't determination to land the trick. It was determination to not feel anything. I wanted to reach out to you but didn't know you or how open you were. The wall you were behind was apparent. When you spoke to me, I was genuinely surprised as I took you as someone who didn't usually speak to anyone."

That was a fair assessment. Aidan had switched out anger for numbness, and the world was simply a screen of stories being played out in front of his eyes. Until he met Zeke and was absorbed in; to feel pain, love, and hope. Aidan leaned in, pressing his lips to Zeke's. Zeke ran his fingers through Aidan's hair and drew him closer. They kissed each other for a minute, then Aidan pulled back.

"When I was little, Casey used to let me climb in his bed and would hold me when I was scared. My mother was affectionate, but it was Casey who made me feel safe. He'd always tell me things were going to be okay. I believed him on such a deep soul level, that when he died, I truly didn't know what to believe anymore. I didn't feel safe. I was always standing on the edge of the cliff with one foot dangling over. Everything, and everyone, seemed so fragile, so out of reach. It wasn't until you held me, I realized I was the one who was so fragile, so out of reach. Somehow, you found me at the edge of the cliff and pulled me back, Zeke. I don't know how, but you make me feel safe again."

"No matter what, we have each other," Zeke replied, his voice so low it was just above a whisper. "I've never felt about anyone the way I feel about you, Aidan. It's not just attraction, though it's also that. It's knowing I'd stand in front of a bullet meant for you, to protect you. Now that I've found you, I don't want to let go."

Aidan stared at Zeke, so many emotions squeezing at his chest. "Zeke, have you...well...have you been with anyone you loved before?"

Zeke thought about it, measuring his words. "I've been with other people, yes. Nothing serious or long term. I sort of tried different people out, you know? Like, to figure out what I wanted. But it was always like trying a new meal to be polite. I didn't know what I was supposed to feel. Until now. The first night I came over here, I immediately knew I wanted to know you more...deeper. I was so drawn to you, I couldn't get you out of my mind. I'd never felt like that. What about you? Have you ever loved anyone?"

Aidan met Zeke's eyes and shook his head. "Not like this. Not like I love you."

Zeke's eyes widened and he stared at Aidan, taking in what he'd heard. Aidan nodded and held Zeke's hand.

"I love you, Zeke."

The change in Zeke's face was a beautiful thing. He smiled in a way he'd never smiled before, and the lines around his eyes softened into a vulnerable sadness. All his years of being rejected and searching had come to an end. He kissed Aidan's fingers lightly.

"I love you, Aidan."

They gathered each other close and lay intertwined with the magic of what they'd revealed. Not since he'd been a small child, tucked in his brother's arm, had Aidan ever felt so sure he truly belonged.

Chapter Nine

Mia announced she was moving in with TJ since they couldn't find a new place, and he needed to renew his lease by the end of the summer. But she'd pay her rent for the remaining lease on the apartment with Aidan. Aidan was sad to see her go but understood they were ready to get their life together going. He suggested Zeke move in as he was staying in a month to month studio apartment, which was run down and not in the best part of town. Aidan hadn't considered the implication of the suggestion, thinking of it as a logical solution and not them moving in together as a couple. Zeke was surprised by the suggestion, however, and being his usually open self, questioned it.

"You do realize if I move in, it wouldn't be as a roommate, right? Like, we've passed that point. I could take Mia's room but we're still a couple. That comes with all kinds of other issues to consider."

Aidan thought about it, then mentally kicked himself for being so single-minded. Of course, if Zeke moved in, it would put their relationship on fast forward. They'd admitted their love and committed to each other as a couple, but moving in was a much larger leap in a new relationship. He'd only been thinking about it in a practical sense for Zeke.

"Well, when you put it that way, I guess I hadn't thought about all the aspects. I was thinking more in the friendship sense, not so much where that would put us in our relationship," Aidan replied quietly, feeling stupid for not thinking it through.

Zeke had been standing between the kitchen and living room and came to sit beside Aidan on the couch. "This is really important to me. I don't want to do anything to fuck it up, you know?"

Aidan nodded. This was new to both of them, as neither had been in a serious relationship before. They hadn't even been intimate beyond kissing and holding each other, so moving in was probably out of order. He smiled and rubbed his head, laughing.

"Sorry for jumping the gun. My practical side gets in the way of sensibility sometimes."

Zeke chuckled, sliding his arm around Aidan. "One of the things I love about you. You want to head to the skatepark soon?"

"For sure, I need to work some energy out, anyway," Aidan responded sheepishly.

They loaded up to catch the bus to the park before it got crowded and hot. Seattle summers, despite being so far north, were hot and humid; most people tried to get activities in before the afternoon. When they got there, it was still pretty empty. They skated until mothers with children on scooters showed up, making it dangerous and not fun. They decided to walk home, so they could explore a bit and strapped their boards to their bags. The walk was a long one, but they took their time enjoying each other's company, finding unique shops they wouldn't have seen otherwise. They stopped in a small metaphysical shop, which reminded Aidan of Casey as soon as they stepped in the door. The aroma of incense smelled like Casey's bedroom. For a moment, Aidan thought about stepping right back out, however, as part of facing his past, he knew he needed to soak it in to address the feelings it brought up.

Zeke headed over to a wall with bins of crystals and stones, while Aidan went over to the incense, determined to find the one that reminded him the most of Casey to buy. A lady, who appeared like she was in her mid to late forties, was reading behind the counter and smiled kindly at them without speaking. She was pretty with very little makeup, slightly graying, shoulder-length hair and lines on her face, showing a lifetime of laughter and compassion. She didn't intrude on their browsing and went back to her book.

Aidan searched through the incense, landing on two that together smelled exactly like he remembered Casey did. He gathered a handful of each and wandered over to Zeke, who was holding different crystals in his hand. Zeke glanced over at him and the incense. He guided Aidan's hand, holding the incense to his face and breathed in.

"Nice. Very warm and earthy," he said.

"Casey. It's how he smelled," Aidan replied.

Zeke watched him, reading what it meant to Aidan to cross that line. He nodded, furrowing his brow and squeezed Aidan's hand lightly. He placed a crystal bar in Aidan's other hand and closed his fingers over it. Aidan could feel a vibration through his hand and his eyes widened. Zeke smiled knowingly.

"That's selenite. Good for clearing negative energy. I carry a small piece in my pocket most times. I'd like to buy that for you if you're cool with it?" Zeke pulled out a small battered piece of selenite from his pocket, blowing lint off of it before showing it to Aidan.

Aidan opened his hand and peered at the slightly translucent white crystal bar in his hand. The color reminded him of Zeke's hair, and the fine lines which ran the length of the crystal felt thick and thin at the same time. He smiled at Zeke.

"Yeah, I'd like that. Thanks."

Sometimes he wondered if Casey hadn't sent Zeke his way. They had similarities, except Zeke was sure of who he was and wasn't trying to fit in. He accepted he was different and had been forging his own path since he was a child. His confidence was unnerving at times. Casey had felt out of place his whole life and didn't know what to do about it. It trapped him in a spiral, eventually dragging him under. Zeke was the big *fuck you* in the face of society. But they both held a deeply compassionate side, allowing them to see beyond what others couldn't.

Zeke took the crystal and a few other stones to the register. Aidan found a wire holder which would fit Zeke's piece of Selenite and a cord, so he could wear it around his neck, instead of it beating around in his pocket. He took it with the incense to check out. Zeke was done, perusing some books by the register while Aidan paid. The lady watched both of them, and as she handed Aidan his change, she bobbed her head at them.

"You make a nice couple. Opposites, but balanced. Light and dark," she said bluntly.

Aidan blushed, wondering how she knew.

Zeke grinned. "Thanks," he replied without batting an eye.

She reached out and touched Aidan's hand briefly. "You carry a lot of heaviness. He can help you lighten the load. You feel things differently than other people. It can be a curse or a blessing, depending on how you hold it."

It all felt too surreal to Aidan. He muttered thanks as he bolted out the door. He stood out on the sidewalk, feeling like the world was spinning. His chest was tight and he felt panic rising in him. Zeke came out and drew Aidan close to him, guiding him to the side of the building.

"You okay?"

Aidan shook his head.

Zeke put his arm around him and didn't say anything else. Aidan felt like he was shaking on the inside and took slow deep breaths. It had been too much all at once. He was trying to deal with unpacking the containers inside of himself, but not all at the same time and not unexpectedly. After a few minutes, his head settled and he glanced up at Zeke.

"Sorry, man. I thought I could handle it. The walls started to close in on me," Aidan explained.

Zeke nodded. "Believe it or not, I do understand. I didn't come to this place all at once. I stumbled around lost for a long time. Give yourself a chance to process this. There's no rush, and I'm here for you each step of the way."

That's one thing Aidan had, Zeke hadn't. Zeke was forced to figure it out all on his own. Aidan took Zeke's hand and held it in his own, feeling the vibration travel between them. He breathed easier and pulled the wire wrap on the cord out of the bag, showing it to Zeke.

"Let me see the crystal from your pocket," he said.

Zeke reached into his pocket and took out the already dusty again selenite. Aidan let go of Zeke's hand, taking the crystal. He brushed it off, blew on it, and put it in the wire holder. He slipped the cord over Zeke's neck, kissing him softly on the lips.

"Now, it will be safe."

Zeke put his hand over the selenite necklace and stared at Aidan. His eyes glistened with emotion. "Damn, Aidan. You're so fucking thoughtful. No one has ever been that way to me."

Aidan shrugged, the tips of his ears getting hot. "You're worth it."

They continued their walk home, holding hands. A few blocks from the apartment, Aidan heard a rev of an engine, followed by a sharp, crushing pain in his shoulder. He didn't know what happened as he bent forward with the force of the pain. He peered up to see a dark green, pickup truck driving away, as he distinctly heard them scream, "die, faggots!" at Zeke and him. Aidan snatched the bottle they'd hit him with off the ground, pitching it as hard as he could at the truck. The back window shattered loudly with the impact of the bottle. The truck hit its brakes and slammed into reverse, coming back at them.

Zeke grabbed his arm, yelling, "Oh, shit!"

They booked it down an alley. They could hear the guys chasing them, and made as many twists and turns as they could to get them off their tracks. They could tell they were putting distance between them, as the slurs the guys were screaming at them were getting fainter. They turned down an alley and saw an extended ladder for a fire escape. They scrambled up it and Zeke yanked the ladder up as soon as they got to the landing. They ran up the side of the building on the series of landings and steps. They reached the roof and climbed over, leaning against the wall so they couldn't be seen. The guys were moving through the alley, but they could tell by the frustration in their voices, they'd no idea where Zeke and Aidan went. Zeke clasped Aidan's hand, chuckling as he tried to catch his breath.

"You fucking destroyed their window," he said with admiration.

Aidan had. The old rage he'd felt in his teens, had torn out of him in a second, making the bottle into a bullet that ripped into their truck. He laughed, feeling all of the tension drain out of him. He had to admit, it had felt good. They hid there for a while until it had fallen quiet and Zeke peered over, seeing no sign of the guys below. They stood up and looked over the buildings as the sun started to set. It was beautiful, bringing an odd contrast to running for their lives earlier.

"You think we'll run into them again?" Aidan asked as they made their way down the fire escape.

"Nah, their plates were out of state. But let's go through the alleys home to be safe."

They wound through the alleys until they came to the back of the apartment, letting themselves in the back gate. Once inside, Aidan realized he smelled from sweating and was filthy from lying on the roof. His shoulder throbbed and was starting to stiffen up. Zeke went to the kitchen to guzzle water, so Aidan went to take a shower. He stripped down and climbed in, allowing the hot water to loosen his shoulder and wash the dirt away. He heard the door open and after a moment Zeke stepped in the shower with him. He'd not seen Zeke naked and it caught his breath. He was beautiful; muscular and lean. Zeke, for one of the first times, seemed bashful and watched Aidan to make sure it was alright for him to be in there.

Aidan reached out and drew Zeke close to him, the water cascading over both of them. They washed each other's bodies, taking time to admire what had previously only been behind clothes. Zeke looked at Aidan's shoulder where the bottle had struck him, touching it gingerly. Aidan winced. It was going to leave a large bruise and a welt had formed. Once they were done washing their bodies, they moved to lie in the bed, facing each other. The water from the shower beaded on Zeke's skin. Aidan reached out to run his fingers along Zeke's thigh, the water evaporating with his touch.

Zeke stopped Aidan's hand, his desire for him apparent. Aidan moved his hand between Zeke's legs and slid in close to him, hearing Zeke moan softly. Zeke put his hand down on Aidan and lightly drew his fingers up and down the hardness, as Aidan's mind and body opened to a pleasure he'd never known. Neither could hold back any longer and brought each other to the peaks of ecstasy in every way possible, with a yearning demanding them to each other.

After they were spent, Aidan wrapped his arms around Zeke and held him as close as he could, the sweat from their bodies intermingling. Zeke mumbled something Aidan couldn't hear.

"What, Zeke?"

"I was saying I changed my mind. I want to move in."

"You do? Are you sure? I don't want to put any pressure on us."

"After that, there's no pressure. I want to feel you next to me when I sleep."

Aidan kissed Zeke's neck, and Zeke turned his face to him. Aidan bit his lip, smiling.

"Me too."

All the sleepless nights, all the dark thoughts and panic he'd carried for so long by himself might not go away, but at least he wouldn't have to face them alone anymore.

Now, he had a light to his darkness.

Chapter Ten

Within a week, Mia was packed and Zeke had moved in. Zeke reorganized Aidan's chaos and made their bedroom a sanctuary, instead of a large laundry basket. The bathroom was cleaned out of unnecessary supplies and organized. Aidan almost didn't recognize his spaces. Mia had always kept the living areas clean, but anywhere Aidan went was a trail of disarray and confusion. Zeke was minimalist and clean. Even more so than Mia. Aidan promised to make a better effort at keeping the area crap free. Since Mia's bedroom was empty, they left her bed but set up a film editing station for Aidan to work at.

Aidan knew he needed to make decisions on what he was doing now that he'd graduated, but the newness of living with Zeke took his mind away from committing. Zeke still worked construction and Aidan was rapidly running out of money. His parents had agreed to help pay while he was in school, however, gave him a month after graduation to figure something out on his own. That month was just about up, and he still had two months on the lease to pay. He needed to find work in the short term, and make a long term decision on where he was going. He was pouring over his bank statement when Zeke came in from work, snagging a drink out of the fridge.

"What's that?" Zeke asked, sensing Aidan's frustration.

"Bank statement. My original plan had been to leave pretty much after graduation to go to California for work, but I put it off and now I'm broke. Trying to figure out how to make ends meet until the lease is up."

Zeke nodded and sat down. "I mean, I can help with the bills. I do need to buy a car, though, because the site is way too far from here to take a bus every day. But I have money saved. What's the total?"

Aidan slid the budget sheet he'd drafted up over to Zeke. Living in Seattle wasn't cheap and now that his parents weren't helping, there was no way he could swing the rent. Even with Zeke. Zeke peered at the sheet and sat back in his chair, running his hand through his hair.

"Wow, it really is steep here. I suppose because you're right downtown. I can definitely help, but this is bigger than me. I could probably get you on the crew for the rest of the summer. They're always looking for extra help."

"You could? I've never done construction before."

Zeke took Aidan's hand and flipped it over, palm up. He ran his thumb across the smooth skin. "I know. I've got gloves you can start with until your hands toughen up."

Zeke picked up his phone and called the foreman, who was more than happy to have another set of hands at the site. Aidan could start the following week. Aidan was relieved but embarrassed he was in the situation in the first place.

"Thanks, Zeke."

Zeke smiled and touched Aidan's shoulder. "What? Not have the chance to have you around more? I look forward to it. You've got to have work boots there, though, don't want to drop anything on your foot or put anything through it. What size do you wear?"

"Ten, if it's the same size as my sneakers."

"Ah, mine will be too big then. We can go find you some. I need to go look for a used car tomorrow, anyway. We can do that first and find the boots after. Also, don't wear nice clothes, like wear stuff you don't care if it gets ripped or stained...because it will. Anything you wear will become work clothes."

Aidan was nervous about working construction. He'd never built anything, or worked anywhere, for that matter. He went to college straight out of high school, and since his scholarships covered his tuition and books, his parents agreed to cover his housing and expenses. He was thrifty and only got what he needed, but he still never needed to fend for himself. He thought he would've gone right into a film job, and still could, but wanted to finish out his time in Seattle.

The next day, they got up early and went to used car lot after used car lot. Zeke didn't want a car payment but also didn't want a total piece of junk car. By lunchtime, they were pretty discouraged and started scouring the newspaper. They circled any listings they could get to and began making calls. Most of the cars were junk, but they finally came across an older Jeep Cherokee within Zeke's price range that ran well. The interior was rough, the seats torn, and the headliner coming down in certain places, but the mileage was decent and the engine purred. Zeke talked the guy down a couple of hundred dollars and paid cash. They drove the Jeep out, heading for a supply store where they could get boots.

Zeke was an expert, transforming into an experienced construction worker quickly finding boots with steel toes that fit Aidan perfectly. Aidan had never worn anything but skate shoes and felt strange in the boots. Zeke checked the fit and gave his approval. Once they were home, they went through Aidan's clothes, sorting out ones that would work for the site. Zeke handed him a spare pair of work gloves and a tool belt. The hardhat would be provided at the site. Aidan was set to start work in a couple of days, but he was still afraid he'd make a fool of himself. He wanted to prove to Zeke he could do this since Zeke had gone out on a limb to get Aidan the job.

The following Monday, they got up early and drove to the construction site. The sun was just coming up and Aidan yawned, wondering why they had to be there so early. By mid-morning, hauling lumber in the summer sun, he understood why. He was wearing shorts and a t-shirt, but the hardhat was hot, the boots were hot, the gloves were hot. He was sweating out of every pore on his body. At lunch, he pulled off everything he could and poured water over his head. No wonder Zeke was nothing but muscle, Aidan had used muscles he didn't even know existed.

The other guys were polite but not overly friendly. Zeke worked hard and was part of the crew, but he held himself away from the general chatter. It was pretty filthy and coarse, so Aidan was fine to stay back. The other guys were traveling construction workers, spending most of their time with each other. Some had wives or girlfriends in different places, but since they were around each other all of the time, there was no filter. The assistant foreman was a woman, so they changed their tune when she came around, but the rest of the time their conversation was not fit for most ears.

Zeke had introduced Aidan as his friend, knowing exposing their relationship would cause them too much grief and possibly cost them their jobs. Aidan was fine to not be noticed, he just wanted to do the work and go home. What he couldn't get over, was how hard Zeke could work. He never stopped. When Aidan would carry three boards of lumber, Zeke could carry six. In the time Aidan could go up and down a flight of stairs, Zeke would pass him multiple times. It wasn't that Aidan wasn't strong, it was that Zeke was almost inhuman. This alone kept the other guys respectful, and at a distance.

Aidan stopped for a bottle of water, watching Zeke from afar. Zeke moved with such precision and focus, Aidan almost felt ashamed of himself. He was stunning to watch, and Aidan caught the assistant foreman staring at Zeke intently, with a look of desire on her face. Aidan realized Zeke was on a lot of people's radars. As if he sensed Aidan's thoughts, Zeke turned towards him and grinned as he picked up an armful of pipes, throwing them over his shoulder. He gave a quick wink and disappeared into a building. Aidan smiled to himself. Zeke chose him.

By the end of the day, Aidan's legs were shaking from exertion, all he wanted was to go home to fall into bed. They walked to the Jeep and climbed in. Zeke glanced at Aidan.

"Rough day? The first couple of weeks are the worst, but you'll build up strength. My first weeks, I didn't think I'd make it. Plus, I didn't have gloves or boots, so I was blistered and bleeding everywhere."

Aidan felt better hearing that and was grateful for the boots and gloves Zeke had given him. Despite those, he had cuts all over and could feel blisters on his hands inside the gloves. He slowly slid off the gloves, pressing the liquid sacks on the fleshy parts of his palms. They were tender, tomorrow they'd be worse. Zeke peered at his hands, shaking his head.

"Best thing is to drain them, put some witch hazel on them to dry them up, and cover them for tomorrow. It's still going to hurt, but you don't want them to burst inside of your gloves. Then it will be painful and slippery, which will rip them open more."

Aidan winced at the image. The idea of doing this all over again was too much to think about, so he pushed it aside. Zeke made dinner when they got home, and Aidan stood under the shower for far too long. Zeke came to check on him as the water started to get cold. Aidan stepped out, clean but sore all over. Zeke checked the blisters and drained them with a needle. He soaked Aidan's hands in witch hazel, leaving them uncovered to let them air dry.

After dinner and a couple of beers, Zeke led Aidan to the bed and gave him a massage, digging his fingers into Aidan's muscles to loosen the knots. Aidan groaned in pain.

"How do you do this every day?" He sat up and stretched his arms.

"I'm used to it now. I suffered a lot at first, but pride and survival helped me push through."

Aidan recuperated in the bed, enjoying how the mattress supported his body. Zeke brought him some aspirin and climbed into bed next to him. They watched television until Aidan felt the weight of sleep dragging him under. He glanced over at Zeke, who was already asleep, and leaned his head against Zeke's shoulder until he dozed off.

The next day, he woke up in the most physical pain he could ever remember. Zeke was ready with aspirin and pushed him towards the shower. By the time the hot water had run out, the aspirin had started to kick in and Aidan knew he could push through. He moved slowly, treating his hands with care. Zeke helped cover the starting to dry up blisters, and helped Aidan tie his boots. Aidan stood up ready for another day as Zeke gathered him in a huge hug.

"So fucking proud of you," he whispered in Aidan's ear.

Aidan grinned, shaking his head. "I have a whole new appreciation for you, Zeke."

Zeke smiled and shrugged. "Just survival right?"

They made it to the site with the rising sun, and Aidan took a deep breath. Today was going to hurt, but this was where he proved himself. He did his best to keep up with Zeke and though he couldn't, he kept up enough to earn the respect of the rest of the crew. The end of the day came with another painful ride home, another hot shower, bleeding hands, and Zeke's kindness to get him through.

Mostly, it came with Aidan proving to himself that he was strong enough to make it on his own. Day after day, he pushed on and pushed harder. By the end of the first week, he didn't hurt as much and the blisters were beginning to callous. Within a couple of weeks, he felt a strength in his body and fluidity of movement he'd never felt before. He could see the changes in the mirror, the lean angles which come from using every muscle. He'd always been fit, but this was different. This was his body running on all cylinders. At the skatepark, he found his body made more sense. He could manipulate his movement, so the board was an extension of himself.

Zeke noticed the changes, too, and stopped him on the way out of the park one night, slipping his arm around Aidan's waist. "Aidan, you have always been beautiful, but now I don't think I can keep my hands off of you."

Aidan laughed and pulled Zeke closer. "Then don't."

Chapter Eleven

Mia was astounded at the changes in the apartment when she and TJ came over for dinner a few weeks later. Not only had Zeke taken control of Aidan's chaos, he'd also added a semblance of style as well. Neither she nor Aidan had done anything in the way of decorating, beyond posters on the wall and a bookshelf made out of four cinder blocks with boards. Zeke found some discarded furniture in the alley and painted it bright colors, along with the bookshelf boards, then added cultural sculptures he'd collected on his travels. He didn't have furniture of his own, being so transient, but he brought a flair of unique pieces to the apartment, making it seem more like a home and less like a flophouse. He added lamps and replaced the bean bag chair with more actual seating, allowing all of them a place to sit.

"Damn, this looks nice," TJ said as he and Mia came in. "You know there is a huge box outside the door, right?"

Aidan didn't and went out to see what it was. The box was fairly flat but taller than him. He'd no idea what it was and peered at the return address. It was from Sam and Smitty, his brother's friends from North Carolina. He dragged it into the living room, then grabbed a knife out of the kitchen to open it. Once it was open, he saw a card and pulled it out. He opened it and grinned.

Aidan!
> *We're so proud of you and all you've accomplished. Congratulations on your graduation. Now go change the world. But come see us first. We miss you!*

> *Love,*
> *Sam and Smitty*

He closed the card and kneeled to unwrap what was inside the box. TJ came over and they both gasped when Aidan slid the paper away, revealing a long wooden surfboard with intricate colored wood inlay. Sam had learned to make surfboards a few years back, having since become one of the most sought after surfboard artists in the country. TJ had actually taught Sam to surf while Smitty was in prison, and she'd started a fund in Casey's name to offer surf lessons, mentorship, and college scholarships to kids in the town after. TJ had been one of the original mentors in the program for the kids and received a scholarship to college through the fund as well. This led him to a desire to pursue social work.

Aidan teared up, running his hands down the board in awe. Sam had stood by him after Casey died and never let the connection fade. She and Casey had become friends just months before he died, but they'd connected. She'd been changed by his death. Casey and Smitty had been friends for years and losing Casey had almost killed him. They were now family to Aidan, he was grateful they never let him go. TJ helped him get the board out of the box and leaned it against the wall. It was art, but Aidan was committed to using it as well. Sam would want him to.

Zeke ran his fingers over the inlay and whistled. "This is the most amazing thing I've seen. You still surf?"

Aidan laughed...something Zeke didn't know about him. "I used to. I haven't been in almost a year, but we used to surf all the time back home. TJ is good. He has taught lessons. I'm like Casey, totally chaotic."

"Why doesn't that surprise me?" Zeke laughed, placing his hand on Aidan's back.

"For real," Mia concurred and took out her phone. "Let me get a picture of you three with the board."

They moved around the board as she snapped some pictures. Aidan grabbed her hand to pull her in, and they squeezed together to get all four of them in the shot with the board.

"Send those to me, so I can send them to Sam and Smith," Aidan said.

"Okay, but let me get one of just you with the board, too."

Mia took a few more pictures, making Zeke get in one with Aidan and sent them to Aidan's phone.

"Hey send me a couple of those, too?" Zeke requested.

Aidan changed his screen to the four of them together and felt pangs of sadness, knowing in just a month or so they wouldn't be together anymore. His eyes caught TJ staring at the board, and knew he wanted to address a distance he'd sensed growing between them since Zeke had been around. He and TJ had been friends their whole lives, and he didn't want that to fade away. He snagged a couple of beers, tapping TJ on the shoulder.

"Can we talk?"

TJ nodded and they went out to the steps to be alone. TJ was quiet, so Aidan bridged the gap.

"Are we cool? I feel like we're not as in sync."

TJ glanced at him, then down at the ground. "Yeah, man, I'm sorry. Life is changing fast, I'm struggling with all of it."

"Is it because, you know...because I came out?" Aidan fumbled over the words.

"I won't lie, I was surprised, but no. We love who we love, and it doesn't change who you are. I mean, Zeke being around, definitely changes the dynamic, but even if you were dating a girl it would be the same. Maybe. I guess because you also have a lot in common, too, I feel sort of pushed out. I'm sure you felt that way when Mia and I started dating."

Aidan had, but because Mia was female, he and TJ still had things in common being guys, which kept them on the same level. He could see how Zeke filled both roles, a partner and a guy friend. He hadn't thought about how that might shut TJ out.

"TJ, you're my oldest friend. There isn't a time in my life you weren't there, and you came all the way out here because of me. I'm sorry if I shut you out in any way. I feel bad that you moved out here, and I'm planning on leaving soon."

"No, don't. I'd never have met Mia and she's the love of my life. I can't imagine not being with her. And knowing us, we'll circle back around at some point. Besides, you were my lifeline out of that town. We're brothers. Just make time for me sometimes, okay?"

Aidan felt genuinely bad. He was so wrapped up in his relationship with Zeke, he hadn't been the best friend to TJ. "I'm sorry. I promise I will. Now that I have the board, you want to drive out to the coast?"

"Fuck yeah."

They finished their beers and got up to head in. Aidan had become more comfortable with intimacy since meeting Zeke and reached out to hug TJ at the door.

"We're family, don't forget that."

TJ grinned, the same grin he'd had since they were kids, and it warmed Aidan's heart.

"You know, Aidan, Zeke's been good for you. You're more here, now. Like, not behind a wall. I'm happy for you, please know that."

Aidan knew. They headed back in and Mia glanced between them, reading they were good. She smiled in relief. These were her boys, she wanted them to be there for each other. Zeke started talking with TJ about surfing, expressing an interest in learning. Mia joined in and before long, they'd made plans for a trip the following weekend to drive out to the coast. Aidan silently thanked Sam for making it happen and sent her a picture of the four of them with the board. She quickly sent back a smiley face. Aidan loved her, and Smitty, as much as his own family.

The following weekend, they drove out to the coast in two cars. Aidan had his old board for Zeke to use, and his new board for him to use. TJ brought a couple of boards he owned as well. Neither Mia nor Zeke had ever surfed, and Aidan learned on the drive Zeke had never even been to the ocean. Aidan was raised by the ocean and couldn't imagine having never seen it. He grasped Zeke's hand and squeezed it, glad he was the one to show it to him.

When they pulled up to face the ocean, Zeke sat staring, speechless. Aidan touched him on the shoulder.

"Come on, let's go to the shoreline."

Zeke nodded and unbuckled slowly. He opened the door, taking a deep breath of the salty air. Aidan came around his side and took Zeke's hand as they walked to the water's edge. There's no way to explain what it's like to watch someone see the ocean for the first time. Seeing it in pictures and movies does *not* do the expanse of water justice. Zeke peered from end to end, trying to take it all in. Tears slipped down his cheeks in amazement. He slipped off his shoes and moved towards the water, letting go of Aidan's hand. Aidan snapped a picture as Zeke stepped into the waves. Zeke raised his arms towards the sky, tipping his head back, the sun glinting off his light hair. Aidan gazed in awe, being sure to capture the moment in pictures.

Zeke dropped his arms at his side, standing motionless. Aidan came up behind Zeke and wound his arms around him, resting his hands on Zeke's chest.

"Wow," Zeke whispered. He turned and held Aidan as tight as he could. "You left this?"

"I left Crestview, but I've never left the ocean," Aidan explained.

"Casey," Zeke said, his voice gentle, understanding as Aidan nodded.

They walked back to the car and unhooked the surfboards. TJ went over how to use the leashes and basic safety with Zeke and Mia. They followed him to the water and he started teaching them the basics. As it always was for Aidan, he felt Casey strongly at the ocean, so he wandered down the beach to be alone with his memories and feelings. Once he felt properly isolated, he paddled out into the water. He caught wave after wave, letting the tears fall. Only here, could he truly mourn the brother he'd never see again. He sat on his board for a moment and bawled, allowing the abandoned kid he'd been, grasp the finality of his brother's death. After the tears had run dry, he paddled back into shore and made his way down the beach to his friends. He realized an hour had passed, and he was grateful for his time alone with Casey's memory.

TJ had them out trying to get up on waves, so Aidan sat on the sand and watched. Zeke seemed to take to it naturally, of course, and was up and moving along the waves almost effortlessly. Aidan appreciated that amazing man was his, snagging his video camera to capture the moment. He propped the camera, holding it with his elbows resting on his knees and began filming. TJ was close to Mia, helping her learn how to brace her knees to stay up on her board. She fell off and climbed back on, sitting on her board to catch her breath. TJ paddled over to her and they leaned in to kiss.

Seeing it through the camera's eye, Aidan felt like he was spying on their intimacy but knew this was all part of capturing true human nature. He could see TJ take Mia's hands and say something to her. She nodded, wrapping her arms around TJ's neck. When she let go, he could see TJ wipe a tear away from his cheek, then one from hers. He reached into a sealed pocket on his shorts and drew out something. Aidan zoomed in and could see it was a ring. TJ slipped the ring on Mia's finger and they kissed for a long time. TJ had officially proposed. Aidan was shocked, grateful somehow he'd caught the moment on film.

He shifted the focus to Zeke surfing and found himself turned on, watching Zeke maneuvering the waves. As he was fighting the desire, Zeke turned his eyes towards him and a shot of lightning energy went through him. Zeke gave an impish smile, disappearing behind the barrel of the wave. Aidan filmed for about fifteen more minutes, then put the camera away and pulled a sandwich out of his bag. The other three were making their way back to shore. They all sat and ate, exhausted from the time spent surfing.

Aidan turned to Zeke. "You caught on fast."

"Yeah, it's kind of like the theory of skateboarding. The board is an extension of yourself. But different because the waves are powerful! It knocked me on my ass plenty of times." Zeke laughed, his eyes glittering.

After lunch, TJ and Mia told them they were going to stay in the nearby town overnight.

"Oh, congratulations by the way," Aidan told them.

Mia blushed and stared at him. "How did you know?"

"I caught it all on film," Aidan admitted, patting his camera bag. "I mean, I'd no idea TJ was about to propose. I was just filming you all surfing, then he did it. I hope you don't mind?"

"Mind? Are you kidding? Thank you! I was so caught off guard at the moment, I couldn't even take it all in," Mia exclaimed. "Now, I have something to show my family. I love you, Aidan."

Aidan smiled, his cheeks warm. TJ gave him a thumbs-up, and Zeke congratulated the both of them, peering at Mia's ring. It was a simple band with a black opal, catching rainbows in the sunlight. Mia kissed TJ on the cheek and beamed. They'd openly talked about marriage, but TJ still made it something special for them. She got up, taking TJ's hand and they loaded up to leave. Aidan watched them head towards TJ's car, becoming aware his family was continuing to grow and solidify. He turned back to Zeke.

"You want to surf some more?"

"You know it. Besides, we haven't surfed together yet. I want to do this with you."

They paddled out, but before they got ready to ride the waves Zeke leaned in, kissing Aidan hard on the mouth, his tongue teasing Aidan's. This sent waves of undeniable longing through Aidan. Aidan stared at Zeke and shook his head, feeling himself get hard. Zeke shrugged, aware of what he was doing to Aidan. He mouthed the word, "later" and got up to ride a wave. Aidan took a deep breath, then jumped up to ride alongside the one person who had found a deep desire within him.

Chapter Twelve

The summer heat brought tensions in the city, and certain precincts of the police department were cracking down on loitering. This was a term they broadly used to move people on from areas they didn't want them in, particularly the homeless, poor, and in tourist-driven areas. Residents pushed back and small protests broke out throughout the city. The problem wasn't unique to Seattle; the national news told of similar incidents across the country.

Aidan and Zeke were leery of going out after dark but also didn't want to stay silent on an ever-increasing police state they were witnessing. Mia and TJ lived in an area near a homeless encampment, at the heart of the issues in Seattle. They were growing concerned for their own safety, as well as the residents. Some nights, when tensions were higher, they'd stay with Aidan and Zeke, but the frustration of feeling they couldn't be home was taking its toll.

None of them could claim to be a fan of the police, however, they'd stayed away, remaining neutral up to this point. This was becoming harder to do. The police in their area were increasingly using heavy-handed tactics and not being held accountable. Mia had seen this type of policing in California where she grew up, but Seattle had not been known for brutal behavior overall. Times were changing, and everyone was on edge. Zeke and Aidan tried to make an effort to spend time at TJ and Mia's place, so their friends didn't always feel chased away from their home.

TJ had come to school on a scholarship but his mother had not been well off enough to help with living expenses, so he'd rented a cheaper apartment near the border of a large homeless encampment in the city. The police often made their presence known, and tried to move the encampment out as higher-end housing and tourist attractions moved in. There were public encampments in Seattle, however, this one wasn't official, allowing the police to believe they could harass the residents.

Aidan and his friends often walked the encampment, handing out water and food vouchers, talking to the residents. Aidan would ask permission to film, finding most of the homeless residents were open to speaking about their situations. He didn't know what he'd do with the footage but had them sign waivers for use before filming them. Contrary to how they were portrayed by the media, most were either living out there by choice, not feeling like they fit in modern society, or were struggling with untreated mental or physical disabilities. Some were just down on their luck, having lost jobs and homes. Drug use and alcoholism did exist but were often the result of homelessness, not the other way around.

While it was disheartening, Aidan and Zeke began to feel connected to many of the residents. They came a few times a week, getting to know many of them by first names or nicknames. TJ and Mia knew most of them, as it had become part of their neighborhood and daily routine. Mia was fluent in both English and Spanish, so she volunteered with a local assistance group as a translator when needed. The group worked with the homeless to find more stable housing, jobs, and health services. TJ worked part-time with the group as part of his social work service hours for school. This helped subsidize his housing. He and Mia also worked a couple of nights a week at a group home for recovering addicts to cover their bills.

It was a night in late July when the tensions in the city hit an all-time high. The police were under scrutiny by a watchdog agency for breaking policies and were being questioned over humanitarian concerns. Zeke and Aidan had spent the day with Mia, TJ, and the assistance group, checking on all of the encampment residents. Temperatures were skyrocketing in the city, creating the danger of people overheating, suffering heat strokes, or dying. The group pulled coolers around full of iced water bottles and tried to find places for the residents to shelter during the heatwave. Most residents didn't want to leave, because it meant either taking their belongings or possibly losing them. Regardless, the encampment was home, they didn't want to be displaced. The police had been circling all day, being careful to not be seen breaking any policies, but using intimidation on the residents with their presence. Everything was at a breaking point, with no relief in sight.

Aidan and Zeke went back to TJ and Mia's to eat dinner with them before heading home. TJ and Mia had headed back a bit early to throw food on the grill and were ready with cold drinks when Aidan and Zeke arrived. Zeke sat down, taking a big gulp of iced tea. The mood was somber.

"It isn't good. The police are circling like they're about to pounce on their prey," Zeke muttered, discouraged.

"At least they're being watched closer now," Mia offered.

"That is just making them more pissed off. They won't keep it under wraps for long." Zeke glanced out the window and shook his head. "I've got a bad feeling."

They all did. The residents of the homeless encampment were feeling trapped, and the heat was making them testy and restless. The police didn't like having their hands tied and were on the verge of snapping. It would take just one incident to set off the powder keg. One justification and the police would spring with their claws out. The local groups could only hold things off for so long before they lost control, and everyone knew it. The city officials were turning a blind eye on both sides, only addressing issues after the fact, instead of preventing them.

The group ate dinner mostly in silence. No one felt like mindless chit-chat, and the real conversations were breaking them down mentally. Even though other parts of the country were dealing with similar frustrations, they felt Seattle wasn't on the national radar and was on the cusp of a complete meltdown. Aidan and Zeke knew they needed to head home for work in the morning but stayed as long as they could, in case the crack which was forming burst wide open. Finally, after midnight they resigned themselves to leaving and took one last stroll through the encampment. On their way out, they saw a police car creeping along the edge, the driver looking hard for something to make an issue about.

Unfortunately, it didn't take long for them to spy their prey and move their car towards it. On the sidewalk outside of the encampment, one of the residents was acting irrationally, walking back and forth, talking to himself, and smacking himself in the head. The police pulled up and got out, questioning the guy, who was not responding to them. They ordered him to stop but he kept moving back and forth, hitting himself. Aidan and Zeke watched tensed as Aidan slipped his camera out of his bag, stepping back into the shadows to film. Zeke was ready to intercede if he had to, but by doing so would put his own safety on the line.

The shorter police officer who'd been driving had his hand on his gun and was yelling at the homeless man. The man became more agitated as their voices raised. Aidan clicked the camera on and started filming as Zeke moved in closer to see if he could help. The other police put his hand up to Zeke, telling him to stay back. By this point, a small crowd was forming and some of the other residents tried to talk to the police about the man, but they weren't listening. He was special, they were saying, different. The police kept ordering the man to stop, then taking his opportunity, the shorter police stepped forward and put the man in a chokehold, causing the man to start screaming.

Another police car pulled up, and two more officers stepped out into the scene. People were yelling for them to stop, that the man was mentally disabled. Zeke tried to push through the crowd. Aidan went to set his camera down when Zeke glared at him, motioning for him to keep filming. Mia and TJ had come out after they heard the ruckus and were trying to reason with the police.

The officer now had the man down on the ground and the man was flailing, not understanding what was happening to him.

TJ calmly told the police he was a social worker and worked with the assistance group, but they screamed at him to stand back. The man on the ground was frantic, like an animal in a trap. Mia was crying by now, and the crowd had grown substantially.

A small, black-haired, honey-skinned, pregnant woman pushed through the crowd and was beseeching the police to listen to her, but couldn't get them to understand in her broken English. They shoved her away impatiently. Mia realized the woman was speaking Spanish and began to speed translate what the woman was saying to the police.

"This is her brother. His name is Enrique. He is autistic. He doesn't understand what is going on. He wouldn't harm anyone. They're at the camp because she lost her job and the shelters won't let them stay together. He needs her to communicate for him. Her husband is ill, she was tending to him when her brother wandered away from their camp. She asks you to please stop and let him up, so she can calm him down. He self-harms, but he is gentle. Please stop!" Mia was getting distraught, trying to get them to listen.

One of the officers seemed unsure and was staring from Mia to the cop pinning the man on the ground, but he didn't intercede. The man had stopped moving, and his sister couldn't wait any longer. She grabbed the arm of the police officer holding her brother down and cried, begging him to stop. The police officer reacted and hit her in the face with his retractable nightstick. Blood gushed from her face, and the crowd absorbed her quickly to get her to safety.

In striking the woman, the police officer had let go of his grip on the man. The man stumbled to his feet, out of breath and confused, calling for his sister. He glanced wildly around, attempting to move away when the police officer ordered him to stop. The man, still not understanding, headed towards the crowd. The police officer raised his gun and shot him. He crumpled to the ground in a heap.

The crowd cried out but stepped back, fearing for their own lives. As if a call to action went out, the rest of the police surged towards the gathered people with their batons drawn. The crowd tried to retreat but couldn't move fast enough. One of the officers started coating the crowd with pepper spray, causing cries of outrage and pain. Panic set in and people began to run, tripping over each other in their attempts to get away. The police officers seemed to enjoy watching the crowd falling and covering their eyes.

Aidan had lost sight of Zeke and began to freak out. Ambulances arrived at the scene and the police immediately banded together to get their facts aligned. Aidan shifted the camera to get a better angle, which must have caught the light, making one of the police officers glance over in his direction. As soon as he saw Aidan with the camera, the police officer began to move towards him. Aidan ran down the closest alley and tripped over a bag of trash. He hit his knee on the concrete, painfully ripping his skin open.

In the hopes to throw the police officer off his tracks, Aidan chucked his camera bag into the street. This bought him a few seconds and he closed the camera, shoving it behind a dumpster. He took a mental picture of where he put it, so he could come back for it. The officer paused at the bag in the street but realizing it was empty, came down the alley after Aidan.

Aidan jumped the fence at the end and ran, taking as many turns as he could to try and lose the police officer. After a bit, he realized he was now alone and climbed up onto a roof to catch his breath. He watched from the roof to see what was happening on the streets below. From the far side of the roof, he could make out the area where he'd come from. More police had arrived, and the ambulance was taking the man that was shot away. Aidan didn't know if he'd survived, as he was lying motionless the last time Aidan saw him.

The police were confidently talking like they'd diffused a dangerous suspect. Even though the homeless residents were trying to explain what happened, no one was listening. Aidan saw TJ speaking to the police but knew they didn't care what he had to say. To them, he was part of the problem, enabling the encampment to exist. They wanted to evict them through any means necessary, but the volunteers were making that impossible.

After what seemed like forever, almost everyone had dispersed and Aidan climbed down to circle back and get his camera. He'd caught everything on film, which would show what occurred. His phone showed multiple missed calls, however, he'd turned it off on the roof, so it wouldn't give him away. Zeke was freaking out asking where he was, but Aidan couldn't respond.

His legs were shaking as he crept back through the alleyways. The blood from his knee had pooled down into his shoe, and his foot was stuck in it like glue. He was terrified; he just wanted to get his camera and get to the safety of his home. The police were still patrolling the area, so he needed to be careful to duck into the shadows whenever they passed. Zeke messaged he'd headed home to see if Aidan was there, and to please let him know if he was safe.

Aidan quickly texted, "Scared but okay." He closed the screen to extinguish the light.

He made it back to the alley and discovered the camera was gone. Panic rose in him, realizing his name and address were on it. If they saw the footage and his information, they'd be able to track him and his friends down, connecting them to the scene. More importantly, he needed to find the camera and prove what they'd done. It was clear they were covering their tracks. They were going to blame this on the man and the encampment. He'd seen it in the past, their protocol was to quickly surround each other to back up a narrative, making the officer seem like he was defending himself or others. City officials were right on their heels, supporting the department, using the narrative to carry out their desired policies.

His phone went off again and he answered it as fast as he could, covering the light with his hand. "Hello?"

"Where are you?" Zeke asked, his voice filled with fear.

Chapter Thirteen

Aidan's head throbbed as he sat in the back of the police car, from them smacking it against the roof when they shoved him in. He leaned his head against the cold glass, trying to stop the dizziness. His insides felt scrambled and his back ached. His mind played over what just happened, seeing the homeless man on the curb with his camera. Attempting to get to him, but getting thrown to the ground by the police. He could taste blood in his mouth, and his knee which had clotted over was torn back open, bleeding down his leg. The fear had been replaced by rage, and the officers in the front were talking about him like he was a piece of garbage.

"So, what are you, Middle Eastern or something?" one of the officers asked with an air of disdain.

Aidan didn't answer him. His skin was tan, his hair black, and his eyes dark brown, but the assumption only proved their profiling. The officer glared back at Aidan, opening his wallet. He stared at Aidan's school ID. The name of the school clearly surprised him, and he raised an eyebrow.

"Cornish School of the Arts? What are you? A rich kid, slumming?"

Aidan peered out the window staying silent, picturing bashing the officer's head in.

"You're only making this harder on yourself. Aidan...uh, Osher. What kind of name is Osher, anyway?"

Aidan bit the inside of his lip, tasting fresh blood pool up. *Jewish, you stupid fuck,* he thought to himself. He knew staying silent was his best bet and needed to ask for a lawyer once they got to the police station. They didn't have anything on him. They were trying to get him to talk to slip up and say something they could use. They'd read him his rights; he fully intended to use them.

At the station, they yanked him out of the back, painfully banging his elbow against the door. Once inside, Aidan squinted at the bright lights as they uncuffed him to book him for loitering and take his fingerprints. They took him back to an interrogation room and left him alone for a bit. An officer came in after a bit, sitting down across from him.

"Do you know why you were arrested?"

Aidan stared at him without speaking.

"Looks here like you were loitering and filming the police."

"I have no idea what you're talking about. I was just walking through the area and obviously don't have a camera," Aidan said quietly. He knew filming the police was legal, but the less they tied him to anything, the better. Loitering was only a ticket and a fine, so they'd no reason to hold him.

The officer shifted uncomfortably and stared at the report. He wasn't one of the ones who'd arrested Aidan, and it was becoming clear Aidan shouldn't be there. Aidan was also bleeding and a black eye was forming, which wouldn't help their standing with the watchdog group.

"Uh...okay... what were you doing there?"

"Where?"

"It says you were walking along the street after three in the morning?"

"Since when am I not allowed to walk along the street? There's no curfew." Aidan knew he had the upper hand. He hadn't broken any laws, and the only thing they could say was that he was somewhere he wasn't supposed to be. But there was no law against it.

"Well, your residence is listed across town. Why were you over here at this time?"

"That's none of your business. People go places. I was taking a stroll. Unless you can say what you're arresting me for, you are required to let me leave. If you *are* arresting me, I request to call my lawyer. I also want it on record the officer threw me on the ground, smacked my head against the car, and used racial profiling on me."

The officer fell quiet, reading through the report again. He got up and left the room. Aidan was exhausted and in pain but couldn't show a break in his armor. He sat staring at the wall. They'd taken his phone and any personal belongings when they booked him. He knew Zeke was probably panicked he still hadn't come home. Hopefully, he didn't text anything about the camera or what happened. Zeke was smart and knew Aidan was in danger, so had kept his messages generic before and probably still would.

After about thirty minutes, the door opened and Aidan was told he was free to go. He was handed a plastic bag with his belongings and escorted to the door. He made it a distance from the station before pulling out his phone. Zeke had messaged but only asked if he was okay again. Aidan scrolled through his messages, nothing had given any of them away. Even his pictures just looked like college friends hanging out. He sighed and made it to the bus stop as the bus he needed pulled up. He climbed on and sat in the first seat. He caught his reflection in the glass, he appeared like he'd been in a street fight. His lip was busted and his eye was bruised. Blood ran down his leg and a knot had formed on the side of his head. The bus driver didn't seem to notice or care. By the time he made it to his street, he could see the faint light of day forming in the sky and it started to lightly rain. He felt like he was being watched, but saw he was alone on the street.

Aidan climbed the stairs to the apartment, removing his keys from his pocket. Knowing he was safely home, he began to shake so badly, he couldn't get the key to slide into the lock. He shook his head and tried again when the door flew open. Zeke grabbed him, bringing him into his arms.

"What the fuck, Aidan? Where the hell have you been?" Zeke asked, holding him tightly.

Zeke felt so warm and safe, Aidan couldn't speak. Zeke drew back and stared at Aidan, taking in all of his injuries. He met his eyes and tried to read what happened. Aidan took a weak breath.

"The cops found me and took me to jail," he finally answered.

"Aidan," Zeke said, his voice gentle. He gathered him close as Aidan let the rage and fear slip away.

Aidan leaned his head against Zeke's shoulder and sighed. "They didn't have anything on me. I didn't have my camera and wasn't doing anything. They questioned me, but let me go when I told them they'd either have to charge me, and let me speak to a lawyer, or release me. They were fishing. I told them I was reporting their abuse of me as well. They threw me on the ground, smacked my head against the roof of the car, and yanked me around. I hurt everywhere."

Zeke rubbed his back, listening. He didn't move and held Aidan against him. Once Aidan steadied himself, he drew back, staring at Zeke. Zeke just nodded, but Aidan could see he was fighting back tears. He'd been worried and knowing what they did to Aidan, hurt him to the core. Aidan touched Zeke's cheek and dropped his hand.

"I need to shower. Can you take some pictures of my injuries, first, before I clean them up?"

Zeke nodded, picking up his phone. Aidan stood still as Zeke took pictures of his face, head, and knee. The knee was torn pretty bad and could require stitches. Zeke placed his fingers on Aidan's face, wincing.

"I'm going to call out of work for us. It's supposed to rain pretty hard, anyway, so they may close down the site for the day. Go hop in the shower. I think I can butterfly your knee closed when you're done. I'm going to run down to the pharmacy and get a couple of things. You alright if I leave?"

Aidan bobbed his head and walked to the bathroom. He turned on the shower, sitting on the edge of the tub for a moment. He was still really dizzy and disoriented as a wave of nausea came over him. He lifted the toilet seat, vomiting violently into it. Once he was sure he was done, he took off his clothes and stepped in the shower, the hot water sending searing pain through him. The water turned red at his feet and his knee started bleeding again. He rinsed his body slowly, willing to keep himself from passing out from the pain, then cut the shower off. He dried off, using the towel to keep the blood from pouring down his leg again. Zeke still wasn't back, so he crept into bed, lying naked on his back. He left the towel on his knee to staunch the bleeding as the room spun around him. He heard Zeke come in and set his keys down. Zeke came to the room and saw Aidan lying on the bed.

"Bucket," Aidan whispered urgently as he felt nausea overtake him again.

Zeke ran to the kitchen and snatched the bucket from under the sink, making it back just in time to get it to the side of the bed as Aidan leaned over and vomited. He vomited until he was dry heaving and leaned back on the bed again. His head was pounding and the room continued to shift and move. He groaned as shakes overtook him. Zeke pulled the blanket over Aidan, leaving his knee exposed as he took bandages out of the bag from the pharmacy. The skin on the knee was laid open, leaving a gap. He drew it together, securing it with butterfly bandages. Once he lined the skin up with the bandages, he rinsed it with witch hazel and put a gauze pad over the top.

Aidan kept his eyes closed to keep the room from spinning and took shallow breaths to quell the nausea. Zeke asked him to open his eyes to check his pupils.

"You have a concussion," he confirmed, brushing Aidan's hair from his eyes.

Zeke climbed into bed and put his arms over Aidan. This helped Aidan feel like the room had stopped moving. He rested his head against Zeke's chest. He dozed off into a nightmarish, fitful sleep. Zeke stayed with him, waking him up on a regular basis to make sure he would. Aidan was only awake enough to use the bathroom or eat the crackers and broth Zeke insisted on. He vomited for a few hours, but by the afternoon it had let up, and he was able to keep light food down.

When he slept, he dreamed he was being chased and running. At times he was being stabbed or shot and heard explosions that would jolt him awake. At one point, with one of these explosions, he jerked awake and sat up. The room was dark and it was pouring outside. He groaned, placing his hands on his head. He'd been taking aspirin every few hours, but it wasn't helping. He needed to pee and swung his legs over the edge of the bed, feeling like he was on a rocking boat. He stood up and snagged a pair of shorts off the floor, sliding them on. His knee felt like it weighed a ton when he moved, so he held onto the wall as he made his way to the bathroom.

Zeke was nowhere to be seen and panic rose up in Aidan. He didn't want to be alone. He went to the bathroom and as he came back out, the door opened. Zeke came into the apartment, carrying bags of food. He saw Aidan wavering at the bathroom door and rushed over to support him, guiding him back to the bed.

"Where were you?" Aidan asked, his fear sounding like an accusation.

"Sorry, you were sleeping and I ran to get us some food. You have to eat more than broth and crackers. I got us some sandwiches and got you pediatric electrolytes."

Aidan stared at Zeke. "Like the stuff for babies?"

"Yeah, it's electrolytes. You need to replace what you've lost and it has less crap in it than sports drinks."

Aidan nodded and sat on the edge of the bed. He took the bottle, taking tiny sips. It tasted terrible, like sweet saltwater.

"Have you seen any cops around?" he asked after swallowing the nasty mixture.

Zeke shook his head. "Not any more than usual. But they do seem to be driving by slower. Could be in my head, though."

"Probably not. Have you heard anything about the guy they shot?"

"I talked to Mia early, she called to check on you." Zeke sighed and measured his words. "Aidan, he didn't make it. He died on the way to the hospital."

The dam broke in Aidan and he started to cry. Zeke slid on the bed over to him, winding his arms and legs around Aidan. The guy had done nothing wrong. He was dealing with his own demons and they killed him. They'd say he was a bad person, that he was a threat and they had no choice. Aidan thought about the homeless guy and his camera.

"I need to find my camera. A homeless guy had it. He was motioning to me when the police came and arrested me. He disappeared. Fuck! I don't know how to find him and can't just be walking around down there. They already have me on their radar."

"What did he look like?"

"I don't know. Pretty skinny, white guy with long, dirty, blond hair and a thin, rough beard. He was wearing, like, maybe a green or blue button-down shirt with the sleeves rolled up and dark jeans or cargo pants. I really can't remember, it all happened so fast."

"Huh," Zeke muttered and slipped out of the bed. He put his hand under Aidan's elbow and helped him stand, guiding him to the window. "Like him? This guy has been hanging around this afternoon."

Aidan peered out the window. Leaning against a tree was the homeless guy who'd shown him his camera. He must have seen the address on the side and come over to find Aidan. He was smoking a cigarette, acting nonchalant. When Aidan looked down, the guy glanced up to the window and nudged the bag at his feet. He went back to smoking, staring down the street.

Chapter Fourteen

Zeke slipped on a rain jacket and flipped the hood over his head, drawing the strings tight to hide more of his face. He grabbed the trash and went out to dispose of it. The rain was starting to pick up, so he skirted the side of the building to the cans. He threw the trash away and banged the lid down, getting the attention of the guy under the tree. Zeke motioned his head towards the back alley. The guy looked over, watching Zeke as he slipped around the back of the building and through the gate. Zeke left the gate open and went back into the building through the backyard. He bolted up the steps, waiting outside the door until he saw the guy come through the back gate and follow him up the stairs. He opened the door to the apartment and waved the guy in when he came around the corner.

"Hey, I'm Zeke. Aidan's friend. He owns the camera."

The guy eyed him carefully, glancing around the apartment. Aidan had slipped on a shirt over his shorts and was painfully making his way down the hall towards them. Zeke ran to help him and assisted him in getting to the couch to sit down. The guy watched them but didn't move from the door. Aidan peered up at him, meeting his eyes.

"Thanks for finding me." His voice was hoarse and weak.

"I'm sorry they got you. Looks like they roughed you up. I'm sorry I dipped, but I couldn't stop them and knew you didn't want them to have your camera."

Aidan nodded and shifted, attempting to ease the pain in his back. It had locked up and any movement was excruciating. "No worries, man. I appreciate you keeping it safe. I'm Aidan by the way."

"Chris," the guy said, moving closer as he pulled the camera out of the bag. He handed it to Aidan.

Aidan tried to reach out for it but a blinding pain shot through him and he sucked in his breath, closing his eyes. Zeke took the camera and sat down next to him, motioning for Chris to sit down near them. Chris was hesitant but took the chair across from them, leaning forward like he was ready to run at any moment. Aidan rested back against the couch, beads of sweat popping up on his brow and took shallow breaths until the pain passed. He opened his eyes and placed his hands on his camera gratefully.

"How did you know it was there?" he asked Chris.

"I was down there when it all broke out. I didn't see you filming until the police did, then saw you haul ass down the alley. From my vantage point, I could see down there and saw you duck behind the second dumpster and come out. You kept running with the cop after you. I waited a bit, but you didn't come back. I knew the garbage trucks picked up around four and your camera would get crushed when the dumpsters were set back down, so I made my way down there and found it. I live at the encampment; the cops didn't pay me much mind while I wandered around, waiting to see if you'd come back."

Aidan flicked the camera on and scrolled through the footage, sighing heavily as he watched what happened on fast forward. He closed the screen and shook his head, feeling hot shame wash over him. He should've tried to stop them. Nausea came over him and in a flash, Zeke was there with the bucket as he vomited up the sandwich he'd just eaten. Zeke sat next to him, rubbing his back and handed him a washcloth to wipe his mouth. Once Aidan was done, Zeke took the bucket to the bathroom and dumped it in the toilet, then rinsed the bucket. Aidan looked up at Chris.

"You saw what they did?"

Chris nodded. "Yeah. I know Enrique and his sister, Anna, from the encampment. They came about a month ago. She was supporting all of them. Her husband has some sort of illness, so she lost her job having to care for him and Enrique. She tried to get them in a shelter, but they would've been separated and can't be. Enrique is basically mute. He only says some words and Anna communicates for him. She was getting help for him with the assistance group, but it takes a while."

Aidan didn't know what to say. Zeke was standing at the door of the bathroom, listening.

"Damn," he said, running his hand through his hair. "I heard he didn't make it."

Chris shook his head. "They came and talked to the volunteer group, then took Anna and her husband to a hotel after they told her. She's devastated. Enrique was her only family, other than her husband. That fucking cop broke her nose, too. People have been coming around, asking questions about what happened. Not sure who they are, but I'm guessing it's a mixture of media, police groups, and the watchdog group. I think you have the only actual footage though."

Aidan considered the weight of all this. He needed to get the footage to someone to expose what happened. But who? He thought back through his classes, how amateur footage was used and credited. He worried for his safety in putting it out there himself but wanted to make sure he kept the rights, so it couldn't be abused. He needed to act quickly to make sure justice was served for Enrique. His head wasn't in the right state to figure it all out at the moment.

"You hungry?" Zeke asked Chris, who nodded gratefully. Zeke took a sandwich out of the bag, handed it to Chris, and motioned to the kitchen. "There are drinks in the fridge, too. It's all up for grabs."

Chris got up, went to the kitchen for a soda, and came back. He cracked the soda and took a long drink. He stared at Aidan, cocking his head. "They do all of that to you?"

Aidan bobbed his head and sighed. "More or less. I tore my knee open running from the cop. They threw me pretty hard against the ground, which tore it open more. Busted my lip, fucked up my back, and gave me the black eye. Something doesn't feel right inside either. Then they hit my head hard against the top of the door frame while putting me in the back. Felt like I was going to pass out."

"Yeah, they like to do that," Chris replied, understanding.

"Goddamn pieces of shit," Zeke said, his voice tight with anger. He'd seen what they'd done to Aidan, but hearing it put into words made him want to beat the hell out of them.

"And I'm a white, well, Jewish guy in brand name clothes. But apparently, they thought I was Middle Eastern or something."

Zeke jerked his head towards Aidan and stared at him. "What? Because you have olive skin with black hair? That's an awfully broad assumption. I mean, you look more Italian or Greek than anything."

"Yeah, but he isn't just white, you know? They see the world as white and not white. You can't assume they're smart," Chris spit out. "We live in a racist and classist society. Trust me, had they known you were gay, too, that would've been another strike against you."

Aidan and Zeke glanced at each other and back at Chris. How had he known?

Chris laughed. "Other than the fact I can see how much you care about each other right now, I saw you holding hands before all hell broke loose down there," he explained. "I'm an observer, always watching people. I guess that comes from my time overseas in the military. Never can let your guard down there."

"You were in the military?" Aidan asked, a little surprised. The guy in front of them was dirty and disheveled.

"Eight years. Multiple Middle East tours. Joined right out of high school. I came from a small very conservative town in Oregon, thought I was defending my country, you know? Fucked my head up pretty good."

"How did you end up here?" Zeke asked.

"Long story short, I saw a lot of shit people's brains aren't meant to see; it altered everything in me. I got out and tried to 'assimilate', but I just can't. I moved to Seattle, thinking it being such a big city, I'd find where I belonged, but I kept losing jobs and finally ended up at the encampment. I don't fit in there either, but no one tries to make me. I'll be honest, my brain is fucked up. I don't sleep well, I get woken up by noises that aren't there. I see people's faces when I close my eyes and hear people talking to me when no one is around. I've tried different meds from the VA but it doesn't help. The lady from the agency that comes around says it's PTSD. I don't know. I just refer to it as the haunting."

The haunting. Aidan felt he understood that more now than ever. He'd always felt haunted, but now it was chasing him. He watched Chris and thought about how one thing could be the difference between being part of society, or being considered an outcast.

"Hey, you're welcome to stay in our extra room. Shower, whatever. I need to go lie back down. The room is starting to spin again. I can't tell you enough how much it means that you saved my camera and got it back to me."

Chris bobbed his head and watched as Zeke helped Aidan stand up. They made it down the hall into the room with Aidan slightly hunched from back pain. He sat on the edge of the bed to try and steady himself. Zeke brought him aspirin and put the bucket next to the bed. Aidan lay down, groaning. Zeke kneeled down beside the bed and slid his arm over Aidan.

"I love you," he whispered.

Aidan nodded with his eyes closed and placed his hand over Zeke's. Flashes of light went off in his head, making him feel like he was falling. He grasped the side of the bed until it stopped.

Zeke held him until Aidan dozed off and wiped the sweat off his brow with a cloth. Aidan had felt feverish but refused to go to the hospital. Zeke turned the lights out, making sure there was water and aspirin beside the bed. He slipped out to let Aidan rest.

Screaming woke Aidan a few hours later in a panic, and he gasped, trying to catch his breath. The apartment was quiet except for the murmur of Zeke and Chris talking in the other room. He could still hear screaming but realized it was in his head, not around him. He sat up and swallowed, pushing back the bile rising in his throat. He tried to speak but no words came out. His chest was tight, not allowing him to breathe. He finally was able to take small breaths, wishing he could somehow lure Zeke to the room with his mind. He tried to call out, but his voice crackled in a faint whisper.

The room was closing in on him; dragging him into a dark tunnel, further and further away from the door and Zeke. A large buzzing filled his ears, while images of Enrique fighting for his life, and the police throwing Aidan to the ground, played over and over in his mind. He dug his nails into his leg to keep from the tunnel from taking him out of his body. He took every effort and breath in him to yell as loud as he could to Zeke, which was still a weak sound but louder than it had been.

Zeke dashed into the room, and one look at Aidan's face told him Aidan was deep in a panic attack. He climbed into the bed and faced Aidan, sliding his arms and legs around Aidan to let him know he was there with him.

"Aidan, listen to my voice. I'm here with you. You're okay. Feel me holding you, feel my arms and my legs, feel my hand stroking your back. You're safe in our home. You aren't going anywhere. You aren't dying. This is panic trying to convince you otherwise. Let my voice be your guide back."

Zeke kept repeating this over and over until Aidan could latch onto his voice. Aidan gradually began to feel Zeke wrapped around him, and he focused on Zeke's hand moving rhythmically up and down his spine. Zeke's voice was a beacon out of the tunnel. Aidan followed it until he could catch his breath. His body was drenched in sweat and he let his weight fall against Zeke. They stayed intertwined for a time as Aidan's breath returned to normal. He sat back and gazed at Zeke.

"Thank you."

Zeke nodded, wiping the sweat off Aidan's face with his hands. He leaned in and kissed him. "I'm sorry you're going through this."

"At least I have you," Aidan replied honestly. If he didn't, he thought he might lose his mind.

"PTSD," Chris said from the door.

Aidan glanced at him and furrowed his brow. "What do you mean?"

"You have Post Traumatic Stress Disorder. It's not just a war thing, that just put it out there into the mainstream. People get it for a lot of reasons that are trauma-based."

Aidan thought about that and it terrified him. "What do I do about it?"

Chris shrugged, sighing. "Fuck if I know."

Chapter Fifteen

Zeke stayed next to Aidan the rest of the night, and Chris took him up on his offer, crashing out in Mia's old bed. Aidan woke often, but every time Zeke put his arm around him to remind Aidan he was safe and not alone. By morning, they'd gotten some rest but were groggy. Aidan climbed out of bed and made his way to the kitchen, while Zeke used the bathroom. He was moving a little better but still felt like he'd been beaten with a baseball bat. Chris was in the kitchen and had made coffee. He handed Aidan a cup, motioning for him to sit down.

"Baby steps, dude. You take milk, sugar?"

"Milk," Aidan replied gratefully. The trek to the kitchen had taken it out of him, but he didn't want to be in the bed anymore.

Chris handed him the milk and sat down across from him. "You get any sleep?"

Aidan nodded. "A little. These nightmares though."

"I know them well," Chris commiserated. "You hungry or anything?"

"No, just coffee."

Zeke came in and kissed Aidan on the top of his head, then poured a cup of coffee. "Hey, Chris, shower's free if you want. I think I got some clothes that would fit you if you want to throw your stuff in the washer."

The way Zeke said things never came across as condescending, but rather like a friend sharing what they have. Chris nodded and smiled, his face lined with gratitude.

"I'll take you up on that. Don't suppose you have a razor and scissors I could use? All this hair has been hot."

"For sure," Aidan replied. "Under the sink, there's, like, everything. My old roommate, Mia, was a stasher. There are toothbrushes, toothpaste, soap, razors, just about anything you could think of. Use what you need."

"Speaking of Mia. She and TJ are heading over in a bit to talk about what happened. She's pretty shaken up. They may head to California for a bit," Zeke explained. "Hey, Chris, let me get you those clothes."

Zeke and Chris went back to the room to sort through clothes. Aidan thought about Mia, how she was trying so hard to stop the police from hurting Enrique. She'd been crying but they'd shoved past her, treating her like she didn't exist. He wanted to see her, so he was glad they were coming over. Aidan went to use the bathroom before Chris showered and was shocked when he peed out blood. He stared at it, attempting to figure out what it meant. He heard a knock at the door and closed his shorts to open it.

Zeke was standing there. "Aidan, you okay?"

Aidan shook his head, pointing at the toilet to the blood. Zeke peered in and bit his lip. His face was worried, but he tried not to let on.

"You peeing blood?"

Aidan nodded. Chris came to the door and saw what they were looking at.

"They must have bruised your kidneys when they threw you down. Probably why your back is hurting so much. Quit taking aspirin, it's thinning your blood."

"How do you know so much?" Aidan asked.

"You learn a lot in the military. Especially on deployment. Just rest and it should start to heal. If it doesn't, or you start seeing clots, you have to go to the emergency room."

Aidan made it to the couch and put his feet up at Zeke's insistence. His kidneys needed to heal. Chris hopped in the shower and Zeke brought Aidan some juice, sitting with him. He was scared but didn't want Aidan to see it. Aidan knew him well enough to know.

"Zeke, I'm okay. I just have to heal."

Zeke met his eyes, his pale eyes locked on Aidan, unblinking. He didn't say anything but took Aidan's hand in his own. Chris came out a little while later, dressed in a pair of Zeke's cargo shorts and a t-shirt. He'd trimmed his beard short and asked Zeke if he could help him cut his hair. Zeke laughed, taking the scissors.

"Alright, but you asked for it," he teased.

"Trust me, anything is better than this."

They dragged out a kitchen chair and Zeke got to work. He lopped off most of the length right off the bat, then tried to shape Chris's hair. He used Aidan's hair as a reference since he couldn't see his own, doing a decent job. Chris's hair was still a little shaggy but above his neckline and off of his face. It looked like a surfer cut, making him appear much younger. Chris went to the bathroom to check it out and finish shaving. A soft knock came at the door and Zeke peered through the eyehole. He opened the door to let Mia and TJ in. Mia had clearly been crying. After one glimpse of Aidan, she rushed over and put her arms around him.

"Jesus, Aidan! What did they do to you?" Her voice was horrified.

Aidan put his hand on her arm, liking the way her wavy hair tickled his nose. She sat back and peered at him, touching the black eye and busted lip.

"I'm okay. They're assholes."

"Have you gone to a doctor?" TJ asked, obviously worried.

Aidan shook his head, glancing at Zeke. "I can't. They know who I am. Our friend we just met, Chris, rescued my camera from behind the dumpster. I have footage of the whole incident. They know I do, but don't know I do, if that makes sense."

TJ bobbed his head. They knew. Aidan needed to fly under the wire for now.

"I mean, are you going to be alright?" Mia asked.

"I think so. I'm pissing blood, but Chris says if that lets up and doesn't get worse I should be good. Concussion, too. Not at my best, I admit," Aidan said, in an effort to make light of the situation.

"Fuck, Aidan," Mia whispered.

Zeke came over and sat next to Aidan with new bandages for his knee. He pulled off the gauze and the blood-soaked butterfly closures. The wound was holding together but was going to leave an ugly scar. He cleaned the wound and dried it, adding new butterfly bandages but leaving the gauze off for airflow.

TJ leaned in, peering at the wound. "Gnarly."

"Yeah, thanks to Zeke, not as bad as it was. I don't know what I would've done without him."

Zeke blushed, meeting his eyes. They smiled at each other as a moment passed between them. Mia watched them, sighing as she placed her hand on Zeke's arm in gratitude.

"Thanks, Zeke, for taking care of our boy."

Zeke grinned at her, winking. Chris came out of the bathroom and both Aidan and Zeke's mouths fell open. He was clean-shaven and with the haircut and Zeke's clothes, he appeared at least fifteen years younger than they thought he was.

"Wait, how old are you?" Aidan asked incredulously.

"Thirty-one," Chris replied and gave a bashful smile.

He was less than ten years older than them. Cleaned up and without all of the hair, he revealed a boyish face with dark blond hair and delicate features. His eyes were a vibrant green and he looked even younger than he was. Embarrassed by them staring, he blushed, glancing away.

"Damn, Chris. You're quite a looker," Zeke teased.

Aidan felt a pang of jealousy, although he knew he had nothing to worry about. Zeke was right though. Chris was handsome and had just a touch of awkwardness which made him endearing. He held a sadness in his eyes that showed his age and what he'd seen, but other than that, he could pass as one of Aidan's classmates. Chris waved them off and laughed.

"Introductions?" Mia asked, confused.

"Oh, yeah, this is our friend Chris. He found my camera and kept it safe when I was arrested. He brought it here and stayed last night. Zeke gave him a haircut. He used to have long hair and a beard that covered a lot of his face," Aidan explained.

"Nice to meet you, Chris, I'm Mia," Mia said, extending her hand.

Chris took it and no one missed that he found Mia attractive, as he met her eyes then looked down, his ears turning red.

"This is my fiancé, TJ," she continued, to not send any mixed messages.

Chris shook TJ's hand and smiled. TJ was more secure in his relationship with Mia, now, and ignored Chris's embarrassment.

"Nice to meet you, man. Good save on the camera."

Chris nodded and headed to the kitchen. Aidan started to try and get up when Mia and Zeke jumped up at the same time, asking him what he needed.

"Well, since you asked, I've got to take a piss, so unless you can do that for me, you have to let me get up."

TJ laughed at this and winked at Aidan. Growing up, Aidan had always been the sarcastic one, so it was good to see he felt well enough to do that. Zeke helped Aidan up and stood out of his way to let him pass. Aidan went to the bathroom and while he was still peeing blood, it seemed lighter, more watery. Or maybe he was just trying to convince himself of that fact. He glanced in the mirror and almost didn't recognize his reflection. The black-eye bruising had spread down his cheek, now a deep shade of purple. His lip was split, swollen, and bruised, giving him a bee-stung look. The lack of sleep had given him a gaunt appearance, and his skin had a greenish cast.

Zeke was waiting outside the door when Aidan came out and gave him a questioning look.

"Still peeing blood but it seems lighter, I think. I saw myself in the mirror. I guess if you love me like this, then you truly love me," Aidan joked.

Zeke tenderly brushed his bruised cheek. "I truly love you."

"Zeke." Aidan didn't know what else to say. Zeke was everything, but how could he put that into words?

Zeke cocked his head and grinned. "I know."

They made it back to the living room and sat down. Aidan pulled out his camera, handing it to TJ and Mia.

"It's hard to watch, but I have to figure out how to get this out there."

Mia took the camera and pressed play where Aidan had it cued to. TJ moved in and watched as Chris came around to see as well. Aidan couldn't see but could hear everything happening on the recording. He sat tensed, shaking as it played through. When the gunshot rang out, he saw TJ had tears running down his cheeks. They'd all been there, but there was something about seeing it on video which made them feel even more helpless. Rawer. Mia put the camera down, shaking her head with her eyes wide. No one said anything. Finally, TJ cleared his throat and met Aidan's eyes.

"So, what do we do now?"

"I don't know," Aidan answered. "I can send it to the media, but want to make sure I protect all of us in the process. I need to do it soon before they completely tarnish Enrique's name, and people move on from holding the police accountable. Like in the next twenty-four hours."

"They're already putting out there Enrique was acting dangerous and went towards the crowd, making it sound like he was going to hurt people. Not that he was trying to get to his sister. They said the cop thought he had a weapon, and someone in the crowd must have picked it up. Anna has tried to speak out, but people are beginning to side with the police."

"Fuck." Aidan knew this meant his timeline was closing. He needed to get this done by the next morning. "Okay, so I can't stay here once this is out. They know where I live, and while I did nothing illegal, we see what they already did to me, attempting to get my camera. They probably know you came here and you're on the tape, too. You need to go somewhere safe. If I send this in the morning, it may go live shortly after. How soon can you go?"

Mia nodded, chewing her fingernails. "I already spoke with my family. We dropped out of summer classes this morning and are heading there until the next school year, anyway. This has all been too much, we need to get away from here. I guess we can go home and pack, leave in the morning. I don't think anyone is paying us any attention, right now. Or yet."

Aidan nodded and looked at Zeke. "I have friends, family honestly, in North Carolina. I'm sure we can stay with them. You up to leave tomorrow?"

"I go where you go. Are you fit to travel, though?" Zeke asked gently, knowing sitting for hours in the Jeep would not be the best for Aidan's recovery.

"Looks like I don't really have a choice."

Chapter Sixteen

After a tearful goodbye, Mia and TJ headed home to pack. TJ came over to Aidan to remind him they'd been friends their whole lives, nothing would change that. They embraced for a long time, aware they might not see each other again for a while. They always circled back, though. Mia gave Aidan a threaded bracelet she wore, slipping it on his wrist. He didn't have anything to give her, so told her to go to his room and pick one thing. She came out with one of his favorite t-shirts and he acquiesced.

After they left, Aidan went to lie down for a bit, knowing it was going to be a long night. They still had to pack anything they were bringing. Just personal items, things they'd need for the trip. The furniture could be left for the landlord to either use or dispose of. Aidan also had to get on the camera and laptop to pull off the clip to send to a news station. He wasn't emotionally ready for that, yet, and climbed into bed.

He was surprised when he woke up and realized he'd slept through most of the day. He couldn't remember any dreams and hadn't been jolted awake. He made his way to the bathroom and his urine was still red, but it wasn't getting worse. Hopefully, getting better. Chris and Zeke had begun sorting and packing, loading the Jeep as they went. The apartment already felt empty and Aidan felt a pang of regret. He sat on the couch after Zeke waved him away from helping.

"I don't figure we need all of the dishes or anything like that. Just packing sentimental items, clothes, a few dishes to eat off of, toiletries, stuff like that. Your landlord won't freak will they?" Zeke asked.

Aidan shrugged. He'd lived there almost three years, always paid rent on time, and rarely had parties. "Whatever. I paid a hefty security deposit, so they can keep it. Least of my concerns is their feelings."

It came out harsher than Aidan intended, but he was tired of always trying to do the right thing. Zeke watched him and nodded.

"Hey, I know this is hard. No one could have seen this coming," he said gently.

"Everyone has seen this coming. This country is built on oppression, turning people against each other by using false belief systems and bigotry," Aidan replied with bitterness.

Zeke could see Aidan was in a mentally dark place and let it drop. Chris cleared his throat, sitting down.

"Aidan, you know, you *are* right. When I was younger, my very conservative parents told me how we lived in the best country in the world, how other places lived under oppression. Then I went to those places to 'free' them, and it came to mind that people living in war zones know they're being oppressed and adapt or fight. People here are so subliminally being oppressed, they do exactly what the oppressor wants and turn on each other, instead of fighting back. It's corporate oppression; decimate all resources, tap into deep-seated beliefs like religion, get the people to blame each other, and sit back reaping the rewards, while the people tear each other apart."

Aidan listened and shook his head. His world had always been his bubble. He carried his own suffering, he thought no one understood. When he met Zeke, he saw Zeke had a different bubble of suffering, and they shared it with each other. Seeing the police kill Enrique, and meeting Chris, opened up the world that everyone had their own bubble of suffering. The best way to control them was to convince them they had it worse than other people, or that other people were causing their suffering. Divide and conquer.

It had been hundreds of years in the making. The way to control people was to have them not unite, to create systems to keep them apart. Race systems, class systems, gender systems. Use the media as an all-knowing voice, control it with corporations, and convince people of free press. Now, Aidan was wanting to become part of this system through filmmaking. Or so he'd thought.

Maybe that's why he didn't take any of the jobs offered. He didn't want to perpetuate other people's beliefs. He wanted to share the truth, and the only way he knew to do it was on his own. He'd secured hours and hours of footage; interviews from people baring their souls and telling their truths. But he had no one to give it to. If he took any of those jobs, he'd be behind the scenes, helping tell versions of stories he didn't necessarily agree with. Even him being behind the camera filming wasn't changing anything. He should've put the camera down and stopped the police from killing Enrique.

As if he read Aidan's mind, Zeke spoke. "Aidan, that's why you need to keep recording what is going on. You won't sanitize it. We all see it happening but can't stop it."

"I can't stop it either, Zeke. I watched Enrique die and didn't do a damn thing to change it!" Aidan spat enraged.

Zeke flinched, never having seen Aidan angry like this. "Aidan, none of us could. We all tried and had no way of preventing the police from doing what they did. You wouldn't have made any difference. I know it sucks, but maybe now you *can* with the video. We can't bring Enrique back, but that video will bring to light the brutality the police have been getting away with."

"You don't fucking understand," Aidan seethed. "You can say you tried. I can't. I stood in the goddamn shadows, hiding behind a screen."

"You weren't hiding. You were exposing the truth," Zeke replied.

"At what cost? At the cost of a man being shot in the middle of the street, doing nothing wrong?" Aidan felt the spiral coming on but couldn't stop it. Rage had turned his chest hot and he couldn't focus. Shame racked his body as he saw Enrique falling over and over in his mind.

"Aidan, you have to stop blaming yourself," Zeke said firmly, seeing Aidan was spiraling out.

"What the fuck do you know, Zeke? You run from every problem, anyway!"

The words sliced through the air and the room fell dead silent. Chris knew there was nothing he could say. He got up and walked outside. Zeke stared at Aidan, red spots forming on his cheeks. He put down the box he was packing, rubbing his nose as he glanced away. He looked back, his eyes hard.

"You know what, Aidan? Fuck you." Zeke went to their bedroom and shut the door quietly.

Aidan knew better than to try and follow. He sat alone in the living room, trying to justify his words but knew he was wrong. Zeke had been nothing but kind to him. Zeke had stayed through all of this and didn't bow out when things got hard. He'd held him during his panic spirals, bringing him back to the surface. Fresh shame washed over Aidan and he put his head in his hands. He heard Chris come in and sit down. He glanced up at Chris, who was watching him.

"Zeke's a good person. He wears his heart on his sleeve and doesn't turn anyone away. He didn't deserve that," Chris said, his words firm but kind.

"I know. It's me. It's my shame."

"Well, some of it is also your concussion, not that I'm making excuses for you. But right now, you need to be listening to Zeke. Your brain has an injury and it's making you irrational. You can't see it because it feels like the truth, but I promise you some of how you're feeling is because you're suffering physically and emotionally. Punch a pillow, yell in the shower. But don't take it out on Zeke."

Chris said this with an air of finality. He wasn't requesting or guiding. He was telling Aidan what to do. Aidan met his eyes and nodded.

"You're right."

"I know I am."

Aidan picked up the camera and went to the table in Mia's old room. He moved slowly, pausing by Zeke's and his bedroom door. It was quiet. He thought about going in but shame got the better of him, and he headed on to Mia's room. He pulled out his laptop and connected the camera to it. He needed to set up folders to sort all the footage he'd collected, so he could clear the camera. It would take hours, but at this point, he couldn't face Zeke, anyway. Chris brought him some juice and a sandwich.

"You missed dinner. You gotta eat."

"Thanks, Chris. I mean, for everything."

Chris headed to the living room and clicked on the television. Aidan opened his online storage account, creating folders as he broke down and dragged different clips over. He found the one of the night Enrique was shot and dropped it in. After a couple of hours, his eyes were getting blurry, but he had almost everything categorized. He found the email for a reporter, known for exposing corruption, and created a separate email account. He sent the reporter a quick message.

"I have video from the night Enrique Graza was shot. Do you want to view it to see the truth? Will I keep my rights if shared?" He signed it AO.

Within less than a minute a reply came back. "Yes and yes."

Aidan responded, "I'll send it over in the morning. I'm afraid for my safety and am leaving town tomorrow. I'll send it then. Can you promise to distribute to bring justice if you feel it warrants it?'"

"Yes. Will you stay in contact with me after you send it?"

"Yes. Thank you." Aidan took a deep breath. It was in play.

He shut the email and went back to make sure the footage was in the folder. It was and he clicked out, seeing the folder from their surfing trip. He opened it and watched TJ's proposal to Mia.

He attached it to her email and sent it, realizing he'd forgotten to before. He then watched the video of Zeke surfing. He was beautiful, cutting in and out of the waves, laughing and looking back at Aidan on the beach. Aidan thought about how they'd sat on the boards and kissed, how at that moment he didn't think there could be anything wrong in the world. He watched the video again, knowing it was time to go crawling back and ask for forgiveness. Chris came into the room to lie down. Aidan turned to face him.

"I was thinking when we leave, you can stay here for a bit if you want. I still have one more month paid on the lease, it might be good if it looks like someone is around. You can come and go, but I can leave you the key, so you can be here when you want."

Chris watched him, considering the offer. "You know I'm homeless because I sort of chose to be. I tried being part of regular society, but it just doesn't work for me. Eventually, I just walk away and leave everything. Like really, lock the doors and disappear. I don't want to be this way. Or maybe I do, I don't know. I just feel like I went through eight years of mind altering, then came back to a place that refuses to recognize the horrors around it. I guess what I'm saying is, being homeless isn't who I am, it's the current state I'm in. I'm hoping it doesn't last forever. Talking to you and Zeke has made me realize, maybe I *can* find a place where I don't feel so surreal."

Aidan listened and leaned closer. "Chris, you're one of the smartest guys I've ever met. Maybe you need to elevate who you're around. Not in reference to the encampment, but in reference to the jobs and places you tried when you got out. Wash everything away and start over. Who do you want to be?"

"I could ask you the same question."

"Fair enough."

"Yeah, I guess I have to think about it. As a kid, I liked being in nature, I was obsessed with animals and bugs. I'd carry a little notebook around and chart info on them. I liked drawing them. The military was my parent's idea. Serve my country and all. I don't even believe in this country. I mean, I love the physical land, animals, some of the people, but not the government and all that shit."

"You and me both," Aidan agreed. "Anyway, the place is yours for the next month. I'll give you my key. Last day just take what you want, sell what you want, and drop the key in the drop slot."

"Aidan, Zeke is right though. We don't control this. Your voice is your best weapon."

Aidan nodded and headed to his bedroom. The lights were off and Zeke was turned facing the wall, with his back to Aidan. Aidan climbed in, ignoring the pain, and slid up next to Zeke, wrapping his arm around him tightly. Zeke relaxed and laced his fingers through Aidan's.

"I'm an asshole," Aidan said apologetically.

Zeke rolled over to face him. "I know this is a lot and you also are dealing with physical trauma, but you can't speak to me like that. I'm hurting, too, and attacking me on things I've shared with you is unfair. I trust you and that didn't come easy."

Aidan felt his face get hot with shame, he was glad Zeke couldn't see him. "You're right. That was a shitty thing to do. I didn't mean it, either. You're the most stable, loving person I know, and you don't run from things. You only run to things. You ran to survival."

Zeke sighed. "I ran to you."

Aidan reached out and placed his hand on Zeke's face in the dark, feeling the coolness of his cheek. He leaned in until he met Zeke's lips and held them in his own. Even in the dark, Zeke was his light.

"Now, we have to run together."

Chapter Seventeen

The alarm went off at four in the morning, and Aidan woke up in so much pain he couldn't move. Everything inside of him was on fire, and he was running a high fever. Zeke helped him to the bathroom but the room was spinning so much, Aidan couldn't stand by himself to pee. He was delirious, swaying violently back and forth. Zeke braced Aidan so he could use the toilet, gasping when the urine came out. It was bright red and had clots in it. Zeke called out to Chris for help. Chris rushed in, took one look, shaking his head, and met Zeke's eyes with a level of seriousness Zeke hadn't seen before.

"He has to have an infection somewhere, and the kidney bruise isn't healing. He needs antibiotics at a minimum, he has to see a doctor. Like now."

Aidan tried to shake his head no but started to lose his balance. Despite their best efforts, he went down, smacking his head on the sink. The last thing he remembered was Zeke standing over him, calling his name as he blacked out.

Aidan woke up in a hospital with an IV attached to his arm and no idea what happened. He couldn't talk and was too weak to lift his arm. Zeke was sitting in a chair beside him and glanced over when Aidan opened his eyes. He jumped up, placing his hand on Aidan's forehead. The fever had broken. A fever Aidan didn't even remember he'd had. Aidan tried to ask what happened but nothing came out. His voice didn't work.

"Your injuries were life-threatening, Aidan. You had internal bleeding, a ruptured kidney, and an infection. They have you on antibiotics and had to scrape out your knee. They did emergency surgery to repair your kidney. You should be okay now, however, you have a long recovery ahead of you."

Aidan tried to ask how much time had passed, but his throat was raw from being intubated. He motioned for paper and pen, using his hand to draw in the air. Zeke opened the drawer beside the bed and found a pad.

Aidan wrote, "What day is it?"

"It's been two days in the hospital since we brought you. You had surgery when they brought you in."

"What about the police?"

"I don't know. We got you out through the back, and TJ was waiting in the alley. An ambulance met us about halfway and took you from there. I didn't see any police in that time."

Aidan nodded. "The video?"

Zeke appeared uncomfortable and chewed his lip. "We sent it. I got into your laptop and found the folder. The reporter you'd emailed had written to follow up when he didn't hear from you. Your email was still open, so I attached and sent it, explaining what happened to you. That you were hospitalized from injuries caused by the police. Are you mad?"

Aidan shook his head no. He'd been worried it hadn't been sent and they'd missed the window. Zeke clicked on the television, switching over to the news. Aidan's video was plastered everywhere. They watched it for a few minutes before Aidan motioned to turn it off. He didn't need to see anymore.

"Did they use my name?" he wrote.

"They haven't said your name. I asked them to keep that out of everything since we were waylaid from leaving. The reporter wants to speak to you."

Aidan nodded. He didn't know how he'd speak, but he wanted to make sure he had a say in how it was handled. A nurse came in to check his vitals. His temperature was back to normal. She encouraged him to sip on ice chips to stay hydrated and help his throat. His mouth was sore and dry, so he gratefully took the cup of ice chips. He tried to sit up in bed, but pain shot through him. She shook her head, showing him how to raise and lower the bed, so he could sit up. She handed him a device he could press to give himself morphine. When she left, Zeke dragged up a chair next to him.

"They had to drain pooled blood from inside you and remove some dead tissue from your kidney. They saved the kidney though. Doctor said it's going to hurt for a while. You can leave a few days if you feel up to it, and they clear you. I told them we were going on vacation and you'd be relaxing."

"Tomorrow," Aidan wrote.

"Aidan, you don't want to rush this. You almost died, you were septic."

"Tomorrow," Aidan wrote again, underlining it this time.

"Fuck, fine. But I call all the shots. We can't go back to the apartment now that the video is out. Chris said since it was released, the police have been circling. TJ and Mia left this morning. They waited as long as they could, but they were afraid. No one, except them, knows you're here."

"My parents?"

"Well, they'll know when they get the insurance bill I'm sure, but no. I told the staff I was your next of kin, and they were too under the gun to get you into surgery to question it."

"You *are* my next of kin," Aidan scribbled.

Zeke smiled, resting his head against the large plastic bed guard. "Good to know."

A doctor came in shortly after and went over Aidan's chart. Zeke mentioned Aidan wanted to be discharged the next day. The doctor frowned and looked back at the chart. She shook her head.

"He just got out of surgery two days ago. No fever and his vitals are good. But I doubt he can even walk. He still has a catheter."

Aidan raised his eyebrows, staring hard at Zeke. Zeke cocked his head and mouthed, "I know" back to him.

"Yeah, he needs to be discharged tomorrow. We'll make it work."

The doctor seemed unconvinced but sighed. "If he wants to go, we can't keep him here, however, you'll be basically caring for an invalid."

Zeke glanced at Aidan, his eyes nervous. Now, they didn't even have a home to go back to. Aidan wrote something down and waved towards Zeke to read it.

It simply read, *"Please."*

Zeke nodded and turned to the doctor. "I understand. Anything you can do to help us would be great."

She shrugged, noting the chart. "He'll have his catheter removed shortly, then you'll have to help him to the bathroom when he has to go until he's discharged. In case you want to change your mind."

She walked out, letting the door slam behind her. A little while later, a nurse came in with a basin to remove the catheter. She eyed Zeke.

"You can leave if you'd like. It's not the most pleasant."

Zeke shook his head. "Nope, here to stay."

The nurse lifted Aidan's sheet and the hospital gown. She readied the basin to drain the catheter and drainage bag. She instructed Aidan to exhale as she pulled the tube out of his penis. He exhaled and she carefully withdrew the catheter. He winced and Zeke squeezed his hand, wincing as well. She disposed of the catheter and urine bag into the basin, then cleaned him up.

"You'll still probably see blood in your urine for another week or so. It should get less over time and more clear. If not, you'll need to come back."

Aidan nodded, feeling the burning from the catheter removal. The nurse stood up and gathered all of her supplies. She glanced at Zeke.

"I hear the doc has said you are going to help him to the bathroom tonight? Call if things get rough."

Zeke gave her a thumbs up, though not convincingly. After she left, he turned his attention to Aidan. "You owe me."

"No shit," Aidan wrote back.

Since Aidan was still on IV fluids, it wasn't long before he needed to pee. He glanced at Zeke to let him know. Zeke sighed tensely and got up. He dropped the arm of the bed, helping guide Aidan's legs over the side. They made sure the IV pole was on that side, and Aidan placed his hand on it, his other hand on Zeke's arm. He shifted his weight down to his feet and buckled as soon as he tried to stand. He'd forgotten about his knee. They'd debrided the tissue and stitched it closed, but it didn't feel like it could bear any weight. He bit his lip and tried again, this time shifting the weight to the opposite leg. He was able to stand, so they started the slow, painful crawl to the bathroom, only a few feet away.

Once they got to the bathroom, Aidan moved his hand from the IV pole to the metal handrail on that side and braced himself. Zeke continued to support his other arm and Aidan realized he didn't have a free hand to move the gown to use the toilet. Zeke reached over, pulling the gown back as Aidan urinated. It burned like hell and was bright red. His kidneys ached, he felt like he might vomit. Once the wave had passed, he nodded to Zeke, who braced his waist, helping him turn around. They made it back to the bed, and Aidan prayed he wouldn't have to go again anytime soon.

Unfortunately, this was repeated every couple of hours all night, which made Aidan question himself on leaving the hospital the next day. By the next morning, they had the routine down, even though Aidan realized he wouldn't have the IV pole or the handrails to hold onto once he left the hospital. He had Zeke ask the nurse about crutches, she said she thought she could find him a pair.

Aidan tried out his voice again after the morning run to the bathroom and although faint and raspy, it was coming back. He got Zeke's attention.

"I love you," he whispered. He wanted those to be the first words he said when he could speak again.

Zeke grinned. "Well, I think it's obvious I love you, too. But fuck, you scared me."

"I'm sorry, Zeke. Thanks for not listening to me and getting me here."

"I suppose I proved I'd take a bullet for you, huh?" Zeke teased.

He had. Zeke had proved that what he felt for Aidan was more than a relationship built on attraction. Aidan nodded.

"Everything."

"What do you mean, Aidan?"

"You're everything to me," Aidan raspily got out.

Zeke watched him, his eyes replaying a memory. "You know when I was a kid and left my parents home, part of me didn't know what I was fighting so hard against them for. Why I didn't just give in and marry that girl to make them happy. Now, I know," Zeke said and eased into bed next to Aidan. "It was so I could know what it was like to be loved by you."

Aidan leaned against Zeke and whispered it again, "I love you."

Though the doctor agreed to discharge Aidan that day, she held off as long as she possibly could, waiting until after dinner to sign the discharge papers. In that time, the reporter came by to talk to Aidan. He knocked lightly on the door and showed his press pass. He appeared to be in his late forties, with a short, unkempt beard and glasses.

"Hey, I'm John Peterson, the reporter you've been emailing with?"

Aidan waved him in and pointed to a chair.

"Aidan had surgery and is just getting his voice back," Zeke explained, sitting down next to Aidan.

John nodded and sat down. "Sorry to hear about your injuries. Those were from the police?"

Aidan nodded and spoke painfully, his words fractured, "They saw me filming...chased me. Threw me down. Smacked my head on the door frame when they arrested me...put me in the back of their car...pretty much massive dicks."

John made some notes and glanced up. "They didn't get your camera, though?"

"Stashed it. Homeless guy got it...brought it to me. Long story. Anyway, got it back... video sent to you."

John bobbed his head, staring at Aidan for a moment. "Because of this, a full-scale investigation is being initiated on the police department. The family of Enrique Garza is intending to file a lawsuit. Most importantly, you brought to light policies and procedures which are strictly against the desires of the people of Seattle. The mayor has finally spoken out against this type of heavy-handed policing. This will change how things are done. This went national; Seattle is under deep scrutiny. You should be proud of yourself. That was a very brave thing you did."

The last thing Aidan felt was proud. He felt ashamed for not saving Enrique. He nodded and looked away, then shook his head vehemently. "I didn't stop them."

"No, but I doubt anyone could have that night. You're stopping them, now. I know you want to stay anonymous until you feel you're safe, but I'd recommend talking to a lawyer and standing up against the department over your injuries. They're well documented. And obvious. I hope you got pictures of them." John stood up, handing Aidan his card. "If you need anything, call me.

You have retained the rights to your footage, I won't do anything else without your permission. Bear in mind, you may get subpoenaed when, or if, charges are filed against the officers involved."

Aidan took the card and held it. He hadn't thought about that. About having to go to court. John gave a small wave as he left, and Aidan stared at the door for a long time. What had he gotten himself into? The police had already gone after him over the camera, almost costing him his life. What would they do if they knew he was going to testify?

He looked at Zeke with alarm. They needed to go...now. The window of safety had closed, the further they got from Seattle, the better off they'd be. The risk was higher to stay than for him to leave with his injuries.

Zeke went out and pushed the issue at the nurses' station. He refused to move from the desk and finally got the discharge papers handed to him. The nurse who'd been in earlier removed Aidan's IV, assisting him to get his clothes on. She guided him into a wheelchair and had him sign the discharge papers, taking their copy to legally release them from any liability. She snagged some crutches from a supply closet and told him he could keep them. Another nurse came in to wheel him out. He was a tall, quiet, mocha-skinned guy, hunching over as he pushed the chair. When they got to the doors, he leaned in to say something to Aidan, his voice soft in Aidan's ear.

"I overheard you talking to that reporter earlier. That you filmed what the police did the other night. I saw it on the news. Thank you for standing up for that guy who was shot. He didn't deserve to die like that. No one does. It takes people like us to stand up against people like them. Otherwise, they will always win."

Zeke drove the Jeep up and jumped out to get Aidan in. He helped Aidan out of the wheelchair, his arm braced around Aidan's waist, and to the passenger's seat. Aidan was able to slowly slide himself in and buckle his seatbelt. He glanced at the nurse, who nodded, giving him a thumbs up. The nurse turned and headed back inside, pushing the now empty wheelchair. Zeke hopped in and started driving, trying to use as much of the day left to make headway. They wound through the streets away from the hospital and got onto the interstate out of the city limits. As they left Seattle, Aidan glanced back in the mirror and thought about what the last nurse had said to him. His words echoed in Aidan's mind.

Otherwise, they will always win.

Chapter Eighteen

They stopped when they hit the northwest Oregon border to stretch and go to the bathroom. It had been a few hours and Aidan slept most of the time. He offered to drive, to which Zeke just laughed. Zeke woke him up as he filled the tank, then went into the gas station to get snacks. Aidan peered around groggily, checking the time. He could take more pain pills and dry swallowed a couple. Zeke got the bathroom key and asked Aidan if he needed to go. Unfortunately, he did. Zeke drove around to the bathroom, getting as close as he could. He checked the bathroom first, surprised to find it wasn't disgusting. He came around to help Aidan but was waved off.

"Just let me try. This is humiliating enough as it is," Aidan insisted.

Zeke grabbed the crutches and set them up, so Aidan could move on to them as he got out of the vehicle. Had Zeke not been holding the crutches firmly, Aidan would've pitched forward onto the ground. Aidan grunted as he tried to adjust the crutches under his arm, cursing under his breath. Once he was balanced on the crutches, he couldn't figure out how to move forward.

"Now what?" Zeke asked, trying not to laugh.

"Fuck if I know. I guess I'll just stand here forever," Aidan replied, exasperated.

"Okay, let's try one crutch with me helping." Zeke slid one crutch out from under Aidan, slipping under him to catch him before he fell.

It was like a three-legged race. If they could get down a pattern, they could move. If not, they stumbled around each other. By the time they made it to the bathroom, they were cursing and laughing, Aidan soaked in sweat. Aidan leaned on the wall by the toilet and handed Zeke the crutch, so he could slip down his shorts. One step back in the dignity direction. After he was done, he pulled his shorts up, reaching for the crutch. The toilet was filled with red liquid, so Zeke flushed it down. That might scare the shit out of the next person in there if he left it.

They made it back to the Jeep, and Aidan was able to get himself in without much help. It was awkward and ugly, but he did it. Zeke handed him a bottle of water, which Aidan gratefully chugged before he thought how it would just start everything all over again. Zeke started the engine, heading back to the highway. Aidan watched the trees fly by his window, illuminated by the headlights. He needed to call his parents in the morning. And Sam, she had no idea they were on their way. He dozed off, listening to Zeke sing along softly to a song on the radio.

By the time they made it past Twin Falls, Idaho, Zeke was exhausted from driving all night and needed to sleep for a couple of hours. They pulled into a rest stop, which Aidan was relieved to see was empty. He didn't want people staring while he struggled to the bathroom. Zeke helped and this time they'd figured it out, going twice the distance in half the time. Once back to the vehicle, Zeke kicked his seat back, falling asleep almost immediately. Aidan checked the time on his phone, it was just before five in the morning. It was almost seven on the east coast, so he dialed Sam's number, hoping she wouldn't be mad he was calling so early.

"Hello? Aidan?" A groggy voice answered.

"Hey, Sam."

"Are you alright? What's going on?" Aidan never called, so she knew something was wrong.

"Look, I, um...I'm coming out there."

"To the Outer Banks? When?"

"Now. We're driving there. In Idaho at the moment. It will probably take a few days, but I have nowhere else to go."

The line was silent for a moment. He could hear noise in the background and another voice came on the line. A voice Aidan needed to hear

"Aidan, what's going on?" Smitty asked, concerned.

"So, I don't know if you're watching the news about Seattle. About the guy the police shot?"

"Yeah, I've seen it. It's fucking horrible to watch."

"I took that footage," Aidan whispered, hearing the fear in his own voice.

"Jesus, Aidan."

"I took it that night, the police saw me. They chased me and arrested me. I'd hidden the camera, so they had nothing on me, but they roughed me up pretty good. I was just released from the hospital."

"Okay, Aidan, I can tell this is a lot of work for you. Your voice sounds weak. Just get here and we can figure it all out. We have an extra room you can stay in. Sam said you said *we*. Are you alone?"

"No, coming with my friend Zeke. He's driving. I can hardly walk, on tons of pain pills. He's sleeping now. He won't let me drive, so it's going to take a few days." Aidan was out of breath from trying to speak.

"I got you. Look, be safe and let me know when you're a day out. I'll take some time off from the restaurant. I can't wait to see you but am worried as hell for you. Just get here, Aidan."

They hung up and Aidan let his voice rest. He texted TJ to thank him for taking him to the hospital.

TJ texted back, "halfway", making Aidan laugh.

He responded, "Thanks for getting me *halfway* to the hospital."

TJ asked about the surgery and how he was recovering. Aidan was hesitant to let him know he'd basically checked himself out but knew it was better to get it over with. He texted TJ the whole deal to which TJ replied, "Jesus, Aidan."

He'd been hearing that a lot lately. TJ let him know they'd made it to California and were staying with Mia's family. Aidan told him he'd let Sam and Smith know he was coming their direction. TJ asked him to let them know he was thinking of them. They'd all known each other at different times, forming a ragtag extended family. Aidan began to feel tired and signed off. He rested his head against the glass, only briefly opening his eyes when Zeke woke back up to start driving.

The next time he woke up, they were parked, and Zeke was staring at a church they were near. Aidan had never seen the look on Zeke's face before and reached out to touch his arm.

"Hey."

Zeke glanced over, smiling faintly. "Hey. You slept a bit. I took a detour."

Aidan peered around, having no idea where they were. Zeke's eyes were fixated on the church, and Aidan felt ill as it dawned on him where Zeke had brought them.

"Is this where you grew up?"

Zeke nodded. "This is my parents' church."

Aidan was surprised. The church was small and run down, not the big shiny church he'd imagined. One which had the power to control people's lives. These people were the radical religious group that spewed hate, and made their children marry into their cult? It almost looked quaint. Aidan was confused why they were there.

"Zeke?"

"You know how you said you should've changed things, to not have filmed what happened? How you told me I run from things?"

"I didn't mean it," Aidan tried to explain.

"Aidan, just listen. These people have beaten and married off their children for generations. The only way out is to either be exiled from your family and everything you know, while being beaten for it...or to kill yourself. I considered both." Zeke let tears roll down his cheeks. "By the time I was twelve, I thought about killing myself every day until I finally left."

Aidan listened in horror. He hadn't known this about Zeke. Zeke, who saved everyone and seemed so okay with who he was, now. Zeke turned to him.

"There are kids in there still going through that. Because while rushing in might save one, it won't save all. The only way to change things, Aidan, is to expose them. What you did that night, was to change things, to expose such deep corruption that even had we saved Enrique, we would've lost the rest. Do you understand?"

Aidan nodded. For the first time, he did. In order to take down the system, someone had to show it existed in the first place. He was that someone. He took Zeke's hand in his and held it, feeling the blood pulsing between them. Zeke had run because if he hadn't, he would've died. Either by his father's hand or his own. He knew he was only saving himself, but at that time it was all he could do.

Aidan had to piss and pushed the door open. He slid the crutch out, positioning himself on it. Zeke came around and helped him to a place by the woodline near the church. Aidan felt some satisfaction urinating on the church grounds, watching the red stream leave its mark. He turned on the crutch, glancing around.

"Zeke, can you get my camera?"

Zeke frowned and bobbed his head. He didn't want to stay around too much longer. The church was empty, but people could show up at any moment. He went to the Jeep and grabbed the camera out. Aidan couldn't hold the camera and the crutch, so he moved to lean against a tree.

"I'd like to film you with the church behind you. I want you to tell your story. You couldn't save anyone then, but you can now."

Zeke seemed unsure and glanced back at the church. "Aidan, I don't know if I can. I've put it behind me."

Aidan adjusted the camera, focusing in on Zeke. "You're just telling me your story. Tell me about the first time you knew you didn't fit in. Tell me what happened, how it made you feel."

Zeke started to speak and before long, the gates broke open. He told everything. How he was beaten regularly by the time he could walk. How his siblings were married off, and if anyone challenged the church, they were physically tortured by the elders of the church. Beatings, burnings, even rape. Zeke talked about knowing he was gay and was beaten almost to death by his father. He spoke about how the church forced children as young as nine into conversion therapy. By the time he'd gotten everything out, Aidan had almost an hour of footage and they were both crying. It was the most terrible thing Aidan could imagine a child going through.

"Zeke, come here, please. I can't get to you."

Zeke walked over to Aidan and they held onto each other, allowing the pain and shame wash away from them.

"You did nothing wrong," Aidan whispered. "These people, they're sick...demented. You were just a kid, you needed love and support. I promise for the rest of my life, I'll make this right for you."

Zeke drew back and stared at Aidan. The abused and tormented boy flashed across his face, making Aidan wince. He wrapped his arms around Zeke again, holding him as close as he could. Zeke helped him back to the truck, and they gave the church one last look. It was one of many, using religion to control people and abuse children. Aidan committed to figuring out a way to expose it.

Zeke drove slowly through the town and turned down a side street, pulling up near a small, faded, yellow house. It was nondescript; no flowers, shutters, or windchimes. Nothing. Aidan knew immediately this was Zeke's childhood home. The curtains were drawn and there were no signs of life. Aidan almost wished he *would* see Zeke's father, so he could beat the hell out of him. It dawned on him, he'd about as much chance of doing that as taking a leak by himself. The house stayed lifeless, and Zeke let out a shaky breath. He put the truck in gear, but not before Aidan had taken footage of the home. It was as hideous as the people inside were.

As they drove out of town, Aidan reached out and rested his hand on Zeke's thigh. Zeke peered at him and smiled sadly, placing his hand over Aidan's.

"Thanks, Aidan."

As they drove away from Zeke's past and towards Aidan's, they knew it was on them to change the game.

Chapter Nineteen

By the time they'd made it halfway across the endless flat stretch of Kansas, it'd been almost a week since Aidan had last showered, and he could hardly stand the smell of himself. Brushing his teeth and baby wipes weren't cutting it anymore. His ass itched like crazy, and he needed to roll down the window just to get fresh air away from himself. He wasn't allowed to shower until the stitches were removed and that was still about a week away. He eyed Zeke across the Jeep, contemplating a way to actually bathe.

"Damnit, Zeke, I can't take another day of smelling myself all day. I need to fucking actually get clean."

Zeke glanced over and grinned. "Yeah, you're pretty ripe. I wasn't going to say anything, but damn."

Aidan started laughing, which pulled at his surgery incision. He gripped it, as he couldn't stop the laughter and it was hurting like hell. Zeke glanced at the map and nodded, heading off the interstate. He skirted it, using back roads. Before long, he pulled off the back road onto a dirt road, driving down it for a bit into empty fields. He turned off the road and peered around. They were out in the middle of nowhere, with nothing in sight. Zeke leaned in the back, grabbing a basin and medical supplies.

"We have to change those bandages, anyway. It's been over thirty-six hours, and we're supposed to change it every day. Hold on a sec."

Zeke got out to pull blankets from the back and a few jugs of water they'd packed for the ride. He gathered soap, razors, towels, washcloths, and a couple of changes of clothes. He spread the blanket out in the field they were next to and set up the supplies on it. He came back around to Aidan's side and opened the door, handing him a crutch. Aidan was moving better but still required Zeke to brace him, so he didn't fall. They made it to the blanket, and Zeke helped Aidan get his shirt off while he was standing. The bandages were oozing through on both his knee and kidney surgery incisions.

Aidan eased onto the blanket, lying down. Zeke peeled the bandage off, revealing a long wound running across the skin above his kidney. The stitches were stretched with swelling and the skin was sewn together neatly. Zeke rinsed the wound with antiseptic the hospital had given them and let the wound air out, while he changed the knee bandage. The knee was neatly stitched together as well, and the doctors said the butterflying had helped it keep from becoming a bigger issue. They needed to go in and debride tissue because when Aidan had repeatedly torn it open, bits of dirt, rocks, and debris had gotten embedded, causing infection and necrosis. Now, it looked like a clean, healing line with only a little swelling.

Zeke rinsed it but left a bandage off, per doctor's orders, unless Aidan was going to be doing anything which might get it dirty.

Once he'd cleaned the wounds, Zeke assisted Aidan in removing his shorts and underwear, then filled the basin with water. Aidan felt exposed but was in no position to protest. Zeke came around and poured water into Aidan's thick black hair, completely soaking it, lathering it up with soap. Aidan liked the way Zeke hands felt scrubbing his scalp and shut his eyes, focusing on the sensation. Zeke ran his fingers over Aidan's full, black eyebrows and chuckled.

Aidan opened his eyes, peering into Zeke's face. "What?"

"Your eyebrows were the first thing I noticed about you at the skatepark the day we met. I saw you across the bowl and your eyebrows were epic. They made you look so intense."

Aidan laughed, having heard it before about his eyebrows. Casey also had the same eyebrows, but his eyes had been crystal blue.

"That was the second thing I noticed," Zeke murmured. "That freaking beautiful smile."

Aidan thought about what he first noticed about Zeke, and it was hands down how comfortable Zeke was in his own body. How he skated so fluidly and had complete control of every movement. Next, he noticed his striking, pale eyes that seemed to be reading Aidan's soul. He thinks he knew then, around the table that first night with Mia and TJ, what he felt was more than friendship for Zeke. He just wouldn't let himself admit it. Or didn't know where to start.

Zeke rinsed the soap out of Aidan's hair and dipped a washcloth in the water basin, lightly coating it with soap. He went to start washing Aidan's body, but Aidan stopped him and took the washcloth.

"I can do this," he said quietly, feeling self-conscious. Aidan sat up and tried to wash himself but kept yanking at the incision, causing him to suck in his breath sharply.

Zeke took the cloth. "Aidan, just let me do this."

He scrubbed Aidan's back and arms and rinsed them, being careful to not get the incision wet. He cleaned the cloth and wiped down Aidan's chest and waist with only water since those couldn't be rinsed. He put his hand on Aidan's chest to have him lie back down. Aidan flushed from head to toe, realizing what Zeke needed to do.

"Jesus, Aidan, I've been helping you to use the bathroom, I think this is okay."

Aidan lay back and closed his eyes, feeling vulnerable. Zeke washed his legs, working his way up and started to wash Aidan's genitals. Not being able to help it, Aidan felt himself get hard as Zeke's hands moved over that area. His face got hot.

"Sorry," he muttered, attempting to quell his body's messages.

Zeke didn't reply but finished rinsing the area and his legs. He got up and went to the Jeep to get another blanket since that one was soaked. He helped Aidan shift to the dry blanket, lying down next to him.

"Never apologize for me turning you on," he whispered in Aidan's ear.

He'd grabbed oil from the vehicle, rubbing it between hands and began to massage Aidan's shoulders and chest. He worked his way down, placing his hand on Aidan's still hard penis. Aidan moaned and leaned into Zeke, not being able to resist the sensation. Zeke moved his hand up and down slowly, gradually increasing the speed. As Aidan let go and came, he forgot the constant pain he'd been in for the last week. He sighed and opened his eyes, meeting Zeke's cool eyes. Zeke kissed him softly, wiping his body off with the washcloth.

Zeke got up, taking off his shirt to wash his own hair. He stepped away and poured water over his head, scrubbing his scalp with soap. He rinsed his hair clean and shook it, spraying droplets everywhere. He slid off the rest of his clothes and began to wash his body. Aidan watched with admiration at how beautiful Zeke was. Zeke rinsed himself, catching Aidan staring at him. Zeke's desire was apparent and Aidan motioned to him.

"Zeke, come here."

Zeke came to lay next to Aidan, their naked bodies touching. Aidan reached down, wrapped his hand around Zeke's penis, gently stroking it. Zeke rested his head against Aidan and sighed. Aidan took his time, wanting to feel Zeke's desire for him as long as he could. When he could feel Zeke getting close, he kissed him hard, letting his lips stay there as Zeke shuddered and released. Zeke moaned, grasping Aidan's arm. He placed his face on Aidan's neck, breathing heavily.

"Damn, I needed that," Zeke said, his voice low and husky.

"Me too," Aidan replied and held Zeke close to him.

They lay, staring at the huge, blue, Kansas sky. Zeke rolled over, placing his arm across Aidan's chest and dozed off. He'd been driving almost non-stop, and Aidan could see he was exhausted. He ran his fingers up and down Zeke's spine until he fell asleep as well.

When they woke, it was early evening. They'd slept for hours. Apparently, no one had come by, or if they had, they didn't notice the two naked guys lying in the middle of the field. Zeke got dressed, brought Aidan clean clothes, and covered the kidney incision with a fresh bandage. Aidan felt great to be clean and in fresh clothes. Having been intimate with Zeke was a bonus he wasn't expecting.

He needed to pee but wanted to do it on his own. He rolled over onto his side, pushing himself up onto his good leg. Zeke handed him the crutch and started to get up when Aidan stopped him.

"Let me try."

Aidan took the crutch, hobbling over to a fence line. He leaned on the crutch and was able to get his shorts down with his other hand. His urine was a lighter red and it didn't hurt as much to pee. He finished and yanked his shorts back up. He turned around with the crutch, shuffling back over to Zeke, who was grinning.

"Show off," he teased.

Aidan was stupidly proud of himself and accepted Zeke's help to sit back down. Zeke went to gather a cooler and bag of food. They made sandwiches, ate chips, and drank bottles of tea. The sky started to change colors with the sun setting and not having anything to block its view, turned the world around them into magnificent shades of red and orange. With the surfboards on top of the Jeep in the background, it reminded Aidan of growing up at the beach. For the first time, he looked forward to going back to North Carolina. Aidan and Zeke stayed to watch the complete sunset, reveling at the moment in their little piece of the world.

When the sky was dark, Aidan made his way to the Jeep as Zeke collected everything up. He slid in grateful for the seat back, so he could take pressure off the incision. He popped a couple of pain pills and took a swig of water. Zeke packed everything up and slid into the driver's side. He peered at Aidan.

"You're the best thing that has ever happened to me."

Aidan blushed and took Zeke's hand, not knowing how to respond. Zeke pulled out onto the dirt road, heading back out onto the interstate. They drove through the night, neither tired since they'd slept all afternoon. Aidan plugged his phone into a little speaker they'd brought since there were few towns and no radio stations. He played music from his phone as they joked and talked through the night. It almost felt like two friends just taking a cross country road trip, without a care in the world. They knocked out the rest of Kansas, Missouri, Illinois, and the tip of Indiana, only stopping to get gas, snacks, and use the bathroom.

At one point, when the conversation fell quiet, Aidan watched Zeke in the light illuminated from the headlights and dashboard. He was the most incredible person Aidan had ever met, living with such openness, despite what hell he'd been put through. Aidan thought about what Zeke said about wanting to kill himself every day as a child. Even planning it out, but being too scared to go through with it. Feeling like he was worthless and shameful. It made Aidan think of Casey, how he just couldn't hold on any longer. What if Zeke hadn't been able to hold out any longer? What if as a child, he'd ended his life and never met Aidan? Aidan couldn't bear the thought. He loved Zeke as much as he loved Casey. Even though he never would've known Zeke if he'd killed himself, Aidan believed he would've felt Zeke's absence even so.

He chewed his lip, considering how empty his life would've been without Zeke. Zeke caught Aidan watching him and smiled, raising his eyebrows.

"Everything okay?"

Aidan nodded. "Yeah, I was just thinking."

"About what?"

"If we'd never met. If you hadn't had the strength to make it through the shit of your childhood and made it out to find me."

Zeke met his eyes. "But I did."

"You did. I guess I was thinking how fucking lonely I'd be without you in the world. Like, even if we'd never met, I would've spent my life searching for you, but not knowing what it was I was looking for," Aidan said, his voice filled with emotion.

"Aidan, for years I'd lie in bed and wonder who was out there for me. Who would be my person, you know? My family. At times I resigned myself you didn't exist, but something always told me you did. The first time I saw you, part of me told me you were it, but you didn't even know you were gay. I'd waited that long to find you, I knew I could wait until you found yourself."

Aidan thought about that. He needed to find himself to even know he was searching for Zeke, but he hadn't been able to find himself without Zeke. It hurt his brain to even think about. There was one thing he knew for sure. He rubbed his thumb across the top of Zeke's hand.

"No matter what, I was going to figure myself out to be with you," Aidan whispered, then repeated the words Zeke had told him earlier.

"You're the best thing that has ever happened to me."

Chapter Twenty

Aidan's phone started blowing up midday the next day. The first call was from Mia, and she was frantic.

"Aidan! I'm glad I reached you. Have you seen the news?"

"No, we're still on the road. What's going on?"

"They leaked your name as the person who shot the footage. They've put your picture on every news station."

Aidan felt panic seize his chest. He hadn't told his parents anything yet and knew they'd freak out. He wasn't safe, now. Every police officer and radical police supporter in America knew his name, and what he looked like. He had a target on his back. He started to hyperventilate, and Zeke quickly pulled off the road. Aidan could barely get words out.

"Mia, I need to call my parents."

"Be safe, please. Get somewhere," she insisted. "Aidan, wait. They've said Zeke was your partner, too. Like your romantic partner. They're exposing a lot of your life. I don't know how they're getting this information, but they're trying to make it seem like you aren't a reliable source."

"Fuck. How could they possibly know that? Okay, I gotta go. Love you, Mia." He hung up the phone and stared at Zeke with fear in his eyes.

"What, Aidan?"

"My name and picture are all over the news, tying me to the video."

Zeke's mouth dropped open. "How?"

"I don't know. They know about us, too, our relationship. It was leaked. I'd better call my parents and the reporter to try and head this off." Aidan shakily dialed his parent's house phone.

His mother immediately answered, having seen the news. "Aidan! What is going on? Your picture is all over the news. They're saying the footage of the police shooting that man was taken by you?"

"It was, Mom. I've left Seattle and am heading to North Carolina to stay with Sam and Smitty for a bit."

His mother was silent; Aidan worried the call had dropped. Finally, she spoke, "I'm worried for you. People have been calling here. Reporters, other people who seem to be trying to find out where you are. They're saying all kinds of things about you."

"What did you tell them?"

"Nothing, I hung up. I tried calling you but it went to voicemail. I was waiting for you to call me and tell me you're okay."

"Mom, I have things to tell you and Dad. I'm pretty much going into hiding. I was roughed up by the police and arrested, but they let me go because I hid my camera. I ended up in the hospital, needing surgery on my kidney and knee from it. I have a reporter who is a safe contact and will only talk to him. Don't talk to anyone."

"We won't. Aidan, what about this Ezekial Overby they are talking about? They have said things about you both."

Aidan sighed. He certainly hadn't planned on coming out to his parents like this. "Mom, Zeke is my boyfriend."

"Oh."

He waited for something further but the line went quiet. "Mom?"

"Alright. Is he with you?"

"Yes, we're driving to North Carolina, now. We're currently in Kentucky."

"Be safe, Aidan. You and Ezekial both," she said, her voice gentle, giving her acceptance as best she could.

"I love you, Mom. Tell Dad everything. I'll let you know when I get to Sam and Smith's."

They hung up, and call after call kept coming to his phone. He let them all go to voicemail to get his bearings, resting his head against the back of his seat. He was fucked. Zeke had given Chris his phone before they left, so they could stay in contact. When a call came in from him, Aidan just handed the phone to Zeke to answer. Zeke talked to Chris for a bit and from what Aidan could hear, it wasn't good. People had figured Aidan's address and had left death threats in the mailbox, smeared shit on the door, and thrown rocks at the window. Chris went back to the encampment for his own safety.

Aidan called John, the reporter, to try and figure out what happened. John picked up on the first ring, much to Aidan's relief. John sounded apologetic.

"Likely the police leaked your information to try and discredit and intimidate you," John told him. "Maybe pulled hospital records as well."

"Well, it worked."

"You still did the right thing, Aidan. While they can try to discredit your name, experts have confirmed the footage is valid, not altered in any way. Are you somewhere safe?"

"Right now, we're sitting on the side of the road in Kentucky...so, no."

"Look, get somewhere safe as soon as possible. Your face is out there, as is Zeke's name. Needless to say, you're easy to spot."

"Thanks, John. Okay, I'm going to go. We've got to keep moving. I'll let you know once we're safe."

"Aidan, you did what most people are afraid to do. It doesn't come without a cost, but it's the only way things change."

They hung up and Aidan glanced at his voicemails. There were over twenty, and he didn't recognize any of the numbers. They'd leaked his number, too. He tried listening to a couple, but they were the most vitriolic words he'd ever heard. Not only had he gone against the police, but he was gay to boot. People wanted to torture and kill him. And Zeke. The calls kept coming in, so he dialed his phone service and had the number changed as Zeke drove. They were in cop country and couldn't afford too many more stops.

Once his number was changed, he texted everyone who mattered on his contact list the new number and left a message on his parents' voicemail. He was shaking uncontrollably and felt the urge to puke. He motioned to Zeke to pull over, opening the door in time to spew all over the ground. Zeke made sure he was alright, then continued driving. They still had about eleven hours straight driving time and needed to push on. They'd be driving all night again.

Aidan called Sam to give her a head's up they should be there by early morning. They'd seen the news, too, and were ready to hide them for as long as needed. Zeke and Aidan began searching for gas stations run by people who weren't white, figuring that was their best chance to be left alone. They looked to see if changing their route would matter but no matter what, they were passing through the rural south. By evening, Aidan could see Zeke was running on fumes, having driven all night and the whole day before. Aidan had been able to sleep before the calls came in and was aware he needed to get Zeke a break.

At the next gas stop, Aidan got himself to the bathroom, while Zeke went in for snacks. As Aidan came out, Zeke went to the bathroom, and Aidan took the chance to override Zeke's wishes, sliding himself into the driver's seat. Zeke came out and shook his head.

"Aidan, you can't. You need to keep weight off your incision."

"Zeke, it's not an option. I can adjust to lean off of it, while my foot is on the gas pedal. I'm not going to have you pass out from exhaustion; we have to keep moving. Just a couple of hours, you sleep and when you wake up, you can take back over. Besides, I don't want you driving us off the road," Aidan kidded.

Zeke knew Aidan wouldn't budge and handed him the keys. Aidan peered at the map and got them on the highway. Zeke fell asleep almost immediately, as Aidan focused on the road. His incision burned, but once he was able to get them up to speed, he shifted his weight the other way and rested his foot on the pedal. It was uncomfortable but doable. Zeke slept for four hours and sat up, blearily glancing around. Aidan had to piss like crazy but he'd known he'd wake Zeke up if he stopped. They were in West Virginia, about an hour from the Virginia border. They pulled off at a rest area to use the bathroom. When he came back out, Zeke had his hand out for the keys.

They got back on the road as fast as possible, trying not to make contact with any people. Gas was getting low, but both of them wanted to get out of West Virginia before stopping again. They gassed up in Virginia and Aidan dozed off, sleeping until after two in the morning. When he woke, he kept his eyes closed for a bit, listening to Zeke sing along to the music playing. Zeke's voice was soft, but low, and had a soothing effect on Aidan. He knew if he sat up Zeke would stop, as he only did it when he thought Aidan was sleeping. Finally, he wanted to talk to Zeke, so he sat up and looked at passing road signs. They were just a few hours out.

Zeke glanced over at Aidan and smiled. "You were sleeping heavily. That's good for healing. We should hit the North Carolina border in about two hours. Then another hour and a half to their place."

Aidan nodded as nerves overtook him. He hadn't been back to North Carolina since his family moved out west after Casey died. He made mindless chatter with Zeke, attempting to take his mind off it. As they came to the *Welcome to North Carolina* sign he couldn't contain it anymore, letting tears slip down his cheek. Zeke noticed and veered off to the Welcome Center.

"Hey, you okay? I know this has got to be a lot to process. I went through the same when we passed into Utah."

Aidan gave a half-smile. "Yeah. It's like stepping back to being fifteen and losing Casey. I guess you understand, though. Sorry I wasn't there for you when you drove into Utah."

"You're always there for me. Just seeing you next to me when I passed that sign, made me strong enough to face the past. Even if you were sound asleep," Zeke teased.

They got out to stretch and use the bathroom, knowing the last stretch was in front of them. Aidan texted their location to Sam and Smitty, who immediately responded they'd have breakfast ready for them. Neither of them had eaten more than snacks in a while and were grateful for a real meal.

The last bit was driven in silence, each in their own worlds, thinking about what came next. When they drove up to the address listed on the map, Smitty was sitting on the front steps waiting for them, barefoot in jeans and a t-shirt. He stood up to his full height of six-four, taking Aidan's breath away. The last time he'd seen Smitty had been after Casey died, and right before Smitty went to prison. Smitty had been twenty-seven then, in the throes of addiction. So thin, every bone had poked through his skin, with dark circles under his eyes and hair much shorter. Smitty had been sober since prison, now standing filled out with broad muscles, his bleached out, light brown hair down to the middle of his back. He smiled at Aidan, in the way only someone who has cared about you your whole life can. Lines crinkled around his eyes, and he stepped towards the Jeep.

Aidan pushed the door open, so driven to get to Smitty he forgot his crutch. He almost pitched forward on the ground before Smitty caught him and enfolded him tightly, his arms strong and sturdy. Years earlier, Aidan had taken ketamine to try and connect to Casey after his death, and Smitty had found him behind the gas station so fucked up out of his mind, he could hardly stand. Then, like now, Aidan had pitched forward and Smitty had caught him before he hit the ground. He'd stayed with Aidan through the night until Aidan came out of the k-hole and slept off the effects of the drug. This memory made Aidan start to bawl, soaking Smitty's shirt as Smitty held him to his chest.

"Hey, little dude, it's alright," Smitty murmured into his hair. "You're here now and safe."

He'd always called Aidan little dude when they were kids, and Aidan tried to keep up with Casey and him. Casey was seven years older than Aidan, and Smitty three years older than Casey, so he'd always seemed like a god to Aidan. He still did. Aidan glanced up at Smitty, into his compassionate amber eyes and hugged him as hard as he could, ignoring the pain on his incision. He noticed Smitty was wearing Casey's prayer beads, which Aidan had given to Sam before his family left the town. He reached up and held them in his fingers briefly.

"I fucking missed you so much, Smith," Aidan whispered, calling him by the name he'd known him by his whole childhood. Smitty had been the nickname Sam had given him and while it stuck, he'd always be Smith to Aidan on some level.

Smitty chuckled, sighing. "Now, that's a name I haven't heard in a long time."

"Sorry, I guess it's who you are to me still."

Smitty let go and smiled down at Aidan. He ruffled his hair gently. For a moment Casey was standing there with them and no time had passed. Smitty gave him a quick wink.

"You can call me an asshole, as long as I get to see you again."

Chapter Twenty-One

Sam came out and gave Aidan a hug. She was a sight for sore eyes, not having changed much. Her hair was lighter and she smiled more, however, she was still the tough-as-nails, but gentle, woman Aidan remembered being friends with Casey. Aidan hadn't known her long before his family left, but reached out to her after Casey's death on a couple of occasions. He'd first met Sam when she stood up to a table of locals at the restaurant where she bartended. They were bad-mouthing his mother over Casey's drug use and death. She hadn't known Aidan was in the restaurant at the time, but from the moment she went toe to toe with one of the guys, to defend Aidan's family, he knew Sam was important to him. They'd stayed in touch since. She'd stood by Smitty during his prison time for selling ketamine, and they'd moved to the Outer Banks after he was released.

Sam walked over to Zeke, who was watching from the front of the Jeep and wrapped him in a big hug. She treated him like family or a friend she hadn't seen in some time. He wasn't a stranger. "You must be Zeke. Welcome to our home."

Zeke smiled sheepishly and hugged her back. Smitty went over to him, sticking his hand out.

"Thanks, man, for standing by Aidan. I know you all went through a lot."

Zeke took Smitty's hand and shook it, appearing a little star-struck. Smitty had that effect on people, now that he'd matched his weight to fit his height and was head to toe muscles. His long hair gave him an intimidating rugged appearance, but as soon as he smiled, his face softened into a slightly goofy guy who'd done his time in this world. Zeke let go of Smitty's hand and went to Aidan, making sure he could make it inside. Aidan was wavering, and Zeke got to him just in time to grip his waist.

"Can you get his crutch?" Zeke asked Sam, pointing at the back seat.

Sam grabbed the crutch and helped slide it under Aidan's arm. "They really did a number on you, huh?"

Aidan nodded and moved slowly forward, grunting from stiffness and pain. "To say the least."

"Hey, I've got to rinse his wound and change out his bandage. Is there a place I can do that?" Zeke inquired.

"I made up the bed in the spare room if you want to do it there. Just lay a beach towel down to catch the runoff," Sam replied.

Once they got Aidan inside, she showed them to the room and the bed. Singular. Full-sized, but only one. Aidan met her eyes, and she shrugged with a mischievous grin. Like Mia, Sam just knew. Not that it wasn't all over the news, now. Smitty came in and pulled a beach towel out of the closet. He spread it on the bed and helped Zeke ease Aidan down on his back. Zeke ran to the car to get the supplies, sitting down next to Aidan on the bed when he returned. He peeled the bandage back. The incision was inflamed and oozing pus.

"Fuck," he murmured, slipping the antiseptic from the bag.

Smitty watched quietly from the door, as Zeke cleaned the wound. He needed to put pressure on the wound to draw out any pus, which made Aidan wince in pain. Pushing through and not stopping had set Aidan back, he risked further infection. Zeke dug in the bag, handing Aidan antibiotics and pain pills. Their hands brushed and Aidan grinned at Zeke appreciatively. If Sam and Smitty hadn't known they were a couple by then, they would've seen it at that point. They moved with such familiarity around each other, their connection was obvious. Zeke rinsed the wound well, leaving the bandage off. He checked Aidan's knee, which was healing nicely, and gave it a quick rinse.

Smitty came close and peered at Aidan's kidney surgery wound. He lifted his shirt to expose a wound on his side, he'd gotten from being knifed in prison.

"Looks like we'll have matching scars," he teased.

Aidan looked at the ragged line of Smitty's scar and knew it probably had done some serious damage. Zeke took the dirty bandages out to dispose of them, and Smitty sat down next to Aidan on the bed. Sam left to show Zeke where the trash can was.

"You used to look at Casey like that," he said quietly.

"Like what?" Aidan asked, shifting up to sit with his back against the headboard.

"Like he hung the stars and moon for you."

Aidan thought about that. He did feel that way about Casey. He felt that way about Zeke, too. "Casey did, and Zeke does."

Smitty smiled. "Aidan, I'm glad you have Zeke. You obviously love each other. I'm also glad you're here. I know we've written and talked over the years, but seeing you again means the world to me. Not a day goes by, I don't think about you. About Casey. I know you were angry at me at first, and I deserved it. But if you hadn't let me back in your life, I'd have served a sentence much worse. I love you. You're my little brother like Casey was. I'm so glad you came home. Well, back to North Carolina. Our home is your home for as long as you need it to be."

Aidan watched Smitty's face as he poured his heart out. He'd never forgive himself for selling Casey the ketamine, but they'd all come to know that Casey was on a path of self-destruction none of them could have stopped. Zeke came to the door and was waiting, listening. He had no family, certainly no one who wanted him around. Except for Aidan.

Smitty turned to Zeke. "That goes for you also. We all learned through tragedy and love, a different kind of family grows. Zeke, you're also our family. Aidan trusts you with his life and that says a lot. Aidan takes a while to let people in."

Zeke blushed and stared at his feet. It was unfamiliar and would take time. Smitty, recognizing his own lonely childhood in Zeke, switched gears.

"Hey, let me help you unload the Jeep. I made space in the garage for anything you don't need now, and we can bring the rest in here. Think of this as your room. I'll make Sam take care of the patient," Smitty said, winking at Aidan.

Zeke required guidance and support, raw emotion from strangers was too much for him at first. They headed out to unload the Jeep and Sam poked her head in.

"Hungry? We have breakfast."

Aidan was famished and nodded. "Yes, please! I think for the last day and a half, all we ate was chips and peanuts."

Sam disappeared and came back with a plate of food. Pancakes with whip cream, fruit, and hashbrowns.

"Smith went all out?"

"Hey, I helped. But, yeah. Since Smitty knew you were coming, he's been beside himself getting ready. He took the next week off work. He bought out the restaurant, so he has that prerogative. Eat as much as you can, there's plenty."

"Thanks, Sam. I missed you both. It's been too long."

Sam paused at the door, smiling. "You have no idea. You may never get to leave."

After Aidan ate, a wave of pure exhaustion washed over him. He set the plate on the bedside table, then put his head back to sleep. As he started to doze off, he could hear Zeke talking with Sam and Smitty in the kitchen as they ate. He felt all the tension that had been driving him fade away. Zeke came and checked on him regularly, ensuring he made it to the bathroom safely, but as soon as Aidan could lay back down, his eyes closed again. Sometime after dark, he felt Zeke climb in bed with him, slipping his arm around him. He kissed Zeke on the forehead and fell back into a deep slumber.

By morning, he'd slept twenty-four full hours and Zeke had gotten a solid nine. They woke up and stayed in bed, not wanting to move until they smelled food cooking in the kitchen. Aidan sat on the edge of the bed, standing to see if he could balance without the crutch. He swayed but was able to keep his footing. He edged his way to the bathroom and successfully accomplished going without anyone's help or crutches. He was still too weak to do much, so by the time he got back to the bed, he was out of breath. But it was something. Zeke reached over and rubbed Aidan's back, while Aidan regulated his breathing.

"That's progress."

Aidan smiled at him. "Baby steps. Literally."

Zeke got up and dug out clothes for them. Everything was still in bags, scattered around the room. Zeke peered around and shook his head. "Now that you're awake, I can make sense of all of this."

Aidan slid on a tank top and shorts, catching sight of himself in front of the closet mirror. He'd lost weight and his face appeared tired, pale. His lip wasn't swollen anymore and the black eye had started turning yellowish-brown. He looked like the loser in a boxing match. He lifted his shirt, staring at the incision. It was purplish-red and ugly. They'd stitched it together well, but it would never be not visible. Zeke came up behind him, wrapping his arms around Aidan's waist.

"It's your battle scar," he whispered.

"Yeah courtesy of the government of the greatest country in the world," Aidan responded bitterly. "Our own friendly police state."

Zeke hugged him, kissing him on the neck. "We're going to change that."

Aidan turned to put his arms around Zeke, resting his head on Zeke's shoulder. At least they were safe, and no one knew where they were. It gave them time to work things out; figure out what they were going to do. They made their way to the kitchen,

Aidan measuring each step. His knee was holding better, and if he didn't make any sudden motions, he could traverse the floor. While Zeke grabbed them plates, Aidan called his parents and let them know he'd made it safely to Sam and Smitty's. They were relieved and said they were getting so many calls day and night, they'd turned the phone off until they saw it was his number calling.

A quick text to TJ and Mia, let them know he and Zeke were safe. He left a message with John, asking if he could recommend a good lawyer, then texted Chris to give him a head's up they were on the east coast. He realized it was still really early west coast time, no one was probably up moving around yet. Except for his parents, who were always up at the crack of dawn, if not earlier.

Zeke brought him a plate of food, and they sat on the front porch. Aidan breathed in deeply, smelling the salt air and sighed. Although it wasn't where he grew up, it was close enough to make him feel nostalgic. Smitty joined them on the steps and stretched his long legs out, reaching from end to end. He eyed Aidan carefully.

"I'm glad you got some rest. You both looked like you were knocking on death's door when you came in yesterday. Aidan, I know you need to rest up but, Zeke, Sam was wondering if you wanted to come to the surf shop with her today? She has a couple of surfboards on order, and she has to get them knocked out. If you want to help?"

Zeke's eyes got big, lighting up. Aidan could see Zeke definitely wanted to go with Sam to help, but he was worried about leaving Aidan. Aidan reached over and touched Zeke's hand, squeezing it.

"Go. I can hang here with Smitty. We have years of catching up to do. Plus, Sam is awesome, you should get to know her better. She doesn't take any shit," Aidan assured.

"No, she doesn't," Smitty concurred, chuckling.

Zeke grinned. "That would be fucking awesome! I'd love to learn how to make surfboards."

Sam came out a little bit later with her keys. "Hey, Zeke, you ready? We'll take my car, so we can get back home quickly if needed. I usually walk, but I imagine you're worried about being gone?"

Zeke bobbed his head and glanced at Aidan, not wanting to leave him stranded. Aidan waved him off.

"Go. Seriously. I'm in good hands, and all you've done for over a week is be my nurse. Go make something awesome."

Zeke leaned over and kissed Aidan firmly on the mouth. Aidan's hand naturally slid up behind Zeke's neck. They met eyes and smiled. Smitty walked Sam to the car, holding her for a moment before she got in. She placed her hand on his cheek as a silent message passed between them. Their spark had never dulled. Zeke caught up and jumped in the passenger side, giving Aidan a thumbs up. He was like a kid at Christmas.

After they left, Smitty grabbed Aidan and himself coffee as they sat on the porch to catch up. They talked about how Sam and Smitty ended up in the Outer Banks and Smitty becoming the head chef of his own restaurant. They spoke about Aidan's schooling, about his desire to change things through film. Aidan told Smitty how he met Zeke and all that transpired since. How he loved Zeke more than anything.

The conversation turned and they talked about the night Enrique was shot, how Aidan had run from the police. He told

Smitty about his injuries, that he held firm until the police department had to let him go. He spoke about Chris, how he'd saved his camera and they'd become friends. How Chris had been in the military and now didn't fit in anywhere. Smitty nodded, familiar with the feeling.

Lastly, he told Smitty about how he was getting death threats. He admitted how he regretted not putting the camera down to step in, even though he knew he couldn't have stopped it. Smitty listened, asking questions as Aidan told him everything. They finally fell silent as Aidan grappled with his own guilt. Smitty watched Aidan and reached out, putting his hand over Aidan's.

"This world isn't fair. Good people die, bad people rule. Going to prison, I learned that the one thing you have on your side is your voice when you can use it. Once other people realize you have a voice, they'll do everything in their power to silence you. You used your voice. Despite the risk it put you in, you did it anyway. Casey would be proud of you. Aidan, *I* am proud of you."

Those words resonated on a level in Aidan he'd never felt, and he knew he'd come full circle.

He had indeed come home.

Chapter Twenty-Two

The next few days proceeded about the same. Zeke went with Sam to the surfboard shop, and Aidan hung out with Smitty. Each day brought more ability to move, and his kidney healed enough that his urine started to become clear. His incision settled into a less angry, but still very apparent, line. John sent him the name of a lawyer who'd worked on cases for clients suing the police department. John said she was tenacious and wanted to speak with him, knowing Aidan had filmed the video of Enrique's murder. Aidan sent her an email but asked for a week to get himself sorted and feel like he'd healed. She immediately wrote back, saying she was at his disposal, giving him her direct line.

Aidan also had an email from one of the film studios, following up on their job offer. They mentioned they'd seen his name on the news in conjunction with the video and were interested in talking to him more. He closed the email without responding, not ready to cross that bridge yet. Part of him insisted he needed this process to unfold before taking on anything else. His brain and his body had suffered so much trauma, he couldn't think about anything new.

Smitty made sure he was taken care of during the day. They spent their hours getting to know each other again, filling in blanks on the past. By the end of the week, Aidan felt like they'd never been apart and wondered how he'd manage to ever leave again. Zeke and Sam bonded quickly. She was helping him develop a prototype for a skateboard, based on her skills making surfboards. The owners of the shop had semi-retired, handing the reins to Sam. They were old hippies and had shifted more to design, spending their days at the beach. Sam ran the shop and surfboard company, her designs now being internationally known. She and Smitty surfed almost every morning before work. With Aidan recovering, the three of them rotated who'd go surfing, one of them always staying back to be with Aidan.

Aidan was mentally over requiring a nurse, so he began pushing himself to do more. Finally, being frustrated being the patient, he took a pair of scissors and snipped out the external stitches from both the kidney surgery and knee incisions at the two-week mark. He took tweezers and dragged each thread out through the incision, being half fascinated and half disgusted by the scraping sensation they made as they moved under the skin. Once they were all out, he rinsed the tiny holes they left with antiseptic and put that chapter being him. More or less.

Sam had a couple of days off before Smitty needed to return to work at the restaurant, so the four of them took a day trip to the ocean. Aidan knew he was still not able to surf but at least wanted to get in the water. That morning he and Zeke made love, then held each other in the bed, ready to start considering their future.

"Have you thought about staying here?" Zeke asked, running his finger up and down Aidan's arm, as Aidan leaned back on his chest.

Aidan had, but there were so many factors involved. "Yeah. But if I want to pursue filmmaking as a career, I need to be on the west coast. I'd rather be here, but that's where the action is. I've got to be able to network and make connections."

"True. I suppose you'd have to travel a lot. I love it here. I never felt any connection out west, but there is just something about here that feels like home. Sam said Jim and Marie were open if we stayed to take me on, to help make surfboards and maybe design skateboards. They said I have natural talent."

Aidan flipped over onto his stomach, staring at Zeke. "Really? That's fucking amazing!"

It was but certainly didn't make decisions any easier. He didn't want his career to impede on Zeke's, but he was also madly in love with Zeke and didn't want to be away from him. Zeke seemed to be called to the east coast, Aidan to the west coast. Or was he? He used to think so, however, being back in North Carolina with Sam and Smitty felt so natural. Like he belonged. But TJ and Mia were out west, and they were also family to him. He chewed his lip pensively.

"Let's not think about it yet. Keep letting Sam be your mentor and when the time comes, let's hope it will all make sense. The one thing I know is, we have to be together," Aidan said firmly.

Zeke bent down and kissed Aidan, his lips soft and warm. "That's not even up for discussion. I'd live on the streets to be with you. We'll figure it out."

They ate breakfast and packed up for the beach. They followed Sam and Smitty in their car, and Aidan felt a joy bubble up in him as they got close enough to see the waves. No matter where he moved, the coast of North Carolina would always call to him like a mother. This is where he grew up and became who he was. Until he met Zeke and found a part of himself, hidden deep inside. They parked and Aidan stared out at the waves, which were like a cross between the calmer waves from the small town he was raised in, and the rougher waves of the west coast. Since the Outer Banks stuck further out into the Atlantic Ocean, the waves were bigger than a lot of places on the east coast.

Zeke grabbed boards off the top, knowing although Aidan had weeks before he could officially surf, it at least gave him the option to paddle out on the board. Aidan was still weak but wanted to sit on the board in the water. The saltwater might do him good. They set up a place on the beach and Aidan wandered to the shoreline. He stepped in and walked until he was chest-deep, adjusting his moves with each wave. It was like coming home. They didn't have to wear wet suits like in Washington, and he enjoyed the sensation of the water hitting him gently in the chest. Once he was chest-deep, he crouched down to put his head underwater, letting the silence call to him.

Being under the water had always been a place Aidan's head stopped spinning. It calmed to a buzz and he felt like even though he couldn't breathe underwater, he could breathe mentally. Like a long, deep sigh for the mind. He stayed under as long as he could, every muscle in his body relaxing. He used his arms, waving out beside him, to stay under and allowed his mind to fall into a kind of numbness, which felt like hallucinating. Since he was a child he'd do this, first freaking his mother out, thinking he was drowning. Until she realized he was fine. Then seeing how long he could stay down for. Before long, it was minutes. It was the only place he felt like his soul and body combined.

He came up for air and peered around. Zeke was paddling out towards him with Aidan's surfboard in tow.

"You were down there awhile, I was starting to get worried," Zeke said, shifting Aidan's board towards him.

"Sorry, I should've told you I do that. The first time I ever did it, my father dragged me out by my hair, while my mother was screaming from the shore that I was drowning. I wasn't. It's my therapy I guess," Aidan explained as he hoisted himself on the board.

"Good to know. You just disappeared and didn't resurface. Smitty said he thought you used to do something like that as a kid."

Smitty and Sam were surfing out past them, and Aidan sat as the waves rolled by him. It was soothing and surprisingly good for his recovery. He could feel his stomach muscles adapting to the changes of the water, and though he was weak, he could tell it was loosening them up. Zeke eyed him to make sure he was alright.

"Go surf, this is what I need, right now. My body is still trying to figure itself out," Aidan insisted.

Zeke slid over to kiss him, reminding Aidan of the first time they surfed together. When nothing seemed to be standing in their way. Aidan reached up, running his fingers through Zeke's hair, grateful he stood by Aidan and came out east with him. Zeke smiled in a way that said everything and paddled out to where Sam and Smitty were. Aidan spent the rest of the time paddling out a bit, then allowing the waves to carry him back in. The sound of the gulls flying overhead, and the waves hitting the beach, brought him back to when he was little when the whole world was in front of him. In a way, it was again but without the carefree beliefs of childhood.

He let the water move him back to shore and got off the board, dragging it slowly behind him. When his feet hit the sand, his knee buckled and he fell forward. Being out on the water had a way of doing that, and his knee was still not strong enough to compensate. He got on his hands and knees to turn over, sitting on the edge of the water. The waves washed over him up to his waist, as he sat watching Zeke surf with Smitty. They were laughing and for a moment Aidan felt left out, on the outside looking in. Zeke caught his eye and reading Aidan's face, touched his chest above his heart, pointing at Aidan. Aidan did the same back, reminding himself how much Zeke had given up to be with him.

Aidan got up and carried the board to their area. He lay back on a beach towel, exhausted. He knew it was temporary, but he wanted to be riding the waves with Zeke, not observing from the beach. He stared up at the sky, watching the clouds move at their own pace across the sky. It didn't matter how long it took, they got where they were going. He needed to give himself time. He'd always pushed himself hard and wanted things to come fast. He had to learn to let things happen in their own time, so they happened right.

He could hear Sam, Smitty, and Zeke come out of the water up the beach towards him, laughing and chatting. Sam and Smitty had set up an area close to them, and they'd made a cooking station between the two areas. Smitty promised fine beach dining by his own hands and began to prep. Zeke came over to where Aidan was lying and sat down next to him, toweling off. Aidan put his hand over his eyes, peering up at Zeke.

"You're so fucking beautiful to watch out there," he said honestly.

Zeke smiled at him and leaned in. "Is that so?"

"It is so. I could stare at you all day," Aidan replied.

"Hmmm, why watch when you can touch?" Zeke whispered, lying down next to Aidan. He pressed his body against Aidan's.

That did it. Aidan quickly grabbed a towel to put over his crotch, hiding the blood rushing there. "Fuck, Zeke, stop," he said, laughing.

Zeke grinned and sat up. Sam and Smitty were only feet away, he knew what he was doing to Aidan. Aidan sat up, making sure the towel completely covered his groin until the blood moved on.

"In all fairness..." Zeke whispered, motioning between his legs. Aidan was having the same effect on him.

Aidan shook his head and chuckled, trying to think about anything other than Zeke. Once he'd successfully redirected the urge, he got up and snagged them drinks out of the cooler. Smitty was sober, so there was soda, water, tea, and lemonade. Aidan got himself tea and Zeke lemonade. The beach was busy but they had their own area, and Sam had set up a couple of large umbrellas to give them shade. Smitty was focused on cooking, using a two-burner propane stove on a small metal folding table. It smelled amazing. Zeke joked Smitty should have business cards to hand out for the restaurant because everyone on the beach was peering over to see what that aroma was.

Sam came over to sit with Aidan and Zeke while Smitty finished his masterpiece. Smitty handed them each a plate of food. He'd grilled flatbread in oil, adding sauteed vegetables, marinated Gigante beans, fresh avocado, sliced tomato, and greens. He made a homemade tzatziki sauce to drizzle over the top. It was fine dining with just a touch of sand. Smitty sat down across from Aidan, crossing his long legs and scarfed down his plate of food so fast, Sam shoved him.

"Slow down. No wonder you always have indigestion. You'd think you'd take time to appreciate eating the food as much as you do making it," she teased.

Smitty grinned and slid his arm around her waist. "My talent is in cooking, not eating."

"Obviously," Sam replied, focusing her attention on Zeke and Aidan. "So, we were thinking. We seriously love having you around. Aidan, now that you're here, we don't want you to go. We missed you so much, the idea of not seeing you again for years is too much to think about. Would you consider staying if we gave you the extra room? Zeke has a guaranteed job with me, and Smitty can always use help in the restaurant. You could live with us for free as long as you needed and work only when you wanted to, leaving you free to pursue film."

Zeke and Aidan looked at each other.

"We appreciate the offer and want to stay, but the west coast is where the story is. Besides, Mia and TJ are also out there, I love them, too. My parents are in Washington state and you know how they are. I have to see them on the regular. We want to be here, but have to be there as well. Zeke and I'll need to have a place of our own at some point, and we can't afford two places. Not to mention, we can't be two places at once," Aidan explained. He wanted to be near Smitty and Sam, but he didn't know how to swing it.

Smitty was gazing out at the ocean, lost in thought. He started grinning and met Aidan's eyes. "But what if you could?" he asked.

"Could what?" Aidan replied, furrowing his brow at Smitty.

"Be two places at once."

Chapter Twenty-Three

Recreational Vehicle. RV. The thought had never crossed Aidan's mind. Smitty suggested they invest in an RV to live in, so they could travel back and forth between coasts and have their own place to live. Additionally, it would allow Aidan to travel to where the story was to film. They could keep the vehicle at Sam's and Smitty's property when they were there and move it around as needed. Zeke's eyes lit up as they discussed the option.

"Wherever you are, Aidan, I am, and home is," he said thoughtfully.

"This could be a home base for you, allowing you to travel as much as you have to. It even allows you to be on-site filming wherever you need to be. Zeke can work with Sam when he's here and act as a traveling liaison when he isn't," Smitty explained.

Everyone was staring at Aidan for his opinion on the idea.

He couldn't think of a downside except one. "Money. We don't have the money to buy an RV, and we'd still need Zeke's vehicle."

"Okay, so get one which can be towed by the Jeep. That's not hard," Zeke offered.

"Still puts us back to money. I have very little and we're burning through your savings pretty quickly."

Sam cleared her throat. "First, I'm paying Zeke for any work done, and he'll get to keep the rights to any prototypes and designs he creates. Second, you're family. We can spot you for it."

Aidan shook his head. "Sam, you guys are already doing enough for us. Hiding us, supporting us. You don't need to do any more."

"We don't need to," Smitty interjected. "But we want to. If it meant keeping you in my life and getting to see you even for part of the year, I'd cut off my arm and throw it in the ocean."

"Not sure how that would help," Aidan said, trying not to laugh.

"See? How could I live without that dark sense of humor?" Smitty chuckled, raising a brow. "Seriously though, I own the restaurant and investors have already asked me about opening another. Money is good for us, but we have no family here. We aren't going anywhere and would love to have you both around."

Aidan chewed his lip, deciding if he should let them take the risk on him. It would solve Zeke's and his issues, and allow him to be with everyone he loved. Zeke was all in, it would be his first actual home. Aidan owed him that. It would give them both space of their own, no matter where they went. He could see TJ and Mia regularly, too, which was a huge bonus. He missed them every day and the life they'd shared together.

"We *will* pay you back," he said firmly, meeting Smitty's eyes.

"I know, Aidan. You've always been fighting to make your own way. I respect that. There's no rush. We own our cottage and some land. We have a lot of equity. Let me do this for you. For Casey, okay?"

Aidan nodded. Smitty had served his time but still felt he owed Aidan. "Smitty, you're my brother. You don't owe me anything. We both have Casey as part of us forever, you helped bring that back to me. I accept your offer but not out of obligation. Out of love."

Smitty reached forward, grabbing Aidan in a hug. "Thanks, little dude. I fucking needed to hear that."

Zeke jumped up and whooped, making Sam laugh. She started to gather up their dishes and pack away the food to keep the encroaching gulls at bay. Zeke helped her and for the first time, Aidan noticed they looked like they could be related. Blond hair, light grayish eyes. He'd been drawn to both of them immediately when they first met, how each of them lived their lives with a cool observation. They were the steady flow in constant chaos.

Smitty saw Aidan's eyes watching them and read his mind. "I know. Eerie isn't it? If Sam had told me she had a little brother, I would've pictured Zeke. What's his story?"

"It's not a good one," Aidan replied.

"It usually isn't." Smitty sighed, not hiding the bitterness in his voice. "That's why we make our own."

Aidan had told Smitty about how he and Zeke met, and some basics about Zeke's life, but felt it wasn't his place to share the gory details. He observed Zeke with Sam and a deep need to protect Zeke came over him. Zeke turned and met his eyes, cocking his head in question. Aidan shook his head and smiled. Zeke smiled back as he carried trash to the car.

"Does he have any family?" Smitty asked.

"He has me," Aidan replied, watching Zeke walk away.

Smitty nodded, completely understanding. His parents had written him off well before he'd gone to prison, then prison had been the nail in the coffin.

"It's why people like him and I, find people like you and Sam," Smitty muttered, almost to himself.

Aidan glanced over to see what Smitty meant.

"Those of us, who are convinced by the world we're worthless, believe it and shut off the possibility of anything different, surviving on moments. Then we meet people like you and Sam, who insist we believe in our worth and let us out of that prison. There is no sentence worse than believing you don't matter," Smitty said, staring out at the ocean.

Aidan looked from Smitty to Zeke, absorbing Smitty's words. What if that was the base of everything? All of society's problems? Drugs, prisons, violence, mental illness. What if the people in charge knew this, and used it to control people? Convince them they're unworthy, useless, lazy, stupid, predisposed. Then they don't even have to lock those people up. The other part of society that is convinced they *are* worthy, do it for them. They perpetuate the belief, and thus the policy that people's value was based on others' opinions. What if the best way to control people was to imprison them by imposing arbitrary standards? Standards that can be changed, depending on who they want to control? Then use the media to repeat the narrative until it's so familiar, the viewer doesn't even know it wasn't their belief to begin with. It's what abusers do. Devalue, breakdown, control. The church used

Zeke's parents to do it to him. The government used the police and media to do it to those they currently deemed unworthy. Smitty's parents did it by withholding their love and acceptance.

All people want to feel like their existence matters. If they don't, they sit in a prison cell holding the key in their hand the whole time, not knowing it. Because everyone has value. All babies are born with exponential potential if the right people are there to guide and support them. That's where the system starts to break down. Parents, school, society, religion, media...all start to come in and try to mold that child into a belief system. This matters, that doesn't...they do, they don't...you do, you don't. A series of mind fucks for ultimate control.

Zeke came back and sat next to Aidan, resting his head on his shoulder. "Today's been a good day."

Aidan put his arm around Zeke and sighed, content. "Yeah, it has. I love you."

The ride home was quiet, Aidan lost in his thoughts. Zeke reached out and held his hand, knowing Aidan had to work through things at his own pace. Aidan glanced at Zeke and watched him focus on the road. Zeke had been his key. He hoped he'd been Zeke's.

"If we hadn't met...where do you think you would've ended up?" Aidan asked.

"We were going to meet, Aidan. Maybe not then and there, but we would've found each other eventually," Zeke responded matter-of-factly.

"How can you know that, though?"

"How can you not?" Zeke replied.

Therein was the difference. Aidan spent his life believing things were a series of events that happened to him, whereas Zeke lived his life believing he was a catalyst to his own future. Aidan was waiting by the door, while Zeke was jumping out the window. Aidan considered this, how it impacted his life.

"I don't know, I guess I think of things in factual or practical terms. Like, if I'm driving and turn left, I'll have missed what would've happened had I turned right. It passed me by."

"But are you always going to turn left? At some point, you'll have to turn right and maybe the thing you missed also made a different turn, and you run into it then. If it's meant to happen, factors will come into play. Maybe not that day, but the next," Zeke replied.

Aidan smiled to himself. Zeke saw the world in such a simple, yet complex, way. "This is why I love you."

Zeke grinned. "So, your question is moot."

Aidan laughed. "Indeed it is."

By the time they got home, Sam and Smitty were already on the porch.

"Come sit with us," Sam offered. "Smitty is already scouring the paper for RVs. Dog with a bone."

Smitty glanced up and shoved her foot off the bannister with his hand. "They're all shit, anyway. May need to go new. You don't want leaks in the seams. It will rot the walls and grow mold."

Aidan knew as much about RV's as he did flying an airplane and shrugged. "I mean new has to be pretty expensive. How bad can the older ones be?"

Smitty eyed him. "Yeah, good thing I'm helping. We can go look at some new ones tomorrow if you're up for it. I'm sure Zeke wants to go along."

Zeke nodded. "I do. I'm the one who'll be keeping it clean and organized, anyway, so storage is a must. Aidan is like a tornado."

Smitty laughed and leaned back, thinking about something. "Oh yeah! My god, when he was little, his floor was such a mess, you couldn't actually see the floor. Shit strewn about everywhere. He wore dirty clothes half the time because it was all one big heap."

"Not much has changed," Zeke teased.

"You do know I'm sitting here, right?" Aidan asked, perturbed.

Zeke squeezed his hand. "Sorry, but it's true. I'd say it was endearing, but I'd be lying."

Aidan snickered at the call out. "Fair enough. It used to drive Mia crazy, too."

"Mia? That's TJ's girlfriend?" Sam asked.

"Fiancé, now. He proposed a couple of months ago," Aidan said.

"Our TJ is engaged? How did we not know that?" Sam exclaimed.

"I remember him being a little kid, maybe six or seven, begging me to teach him how to surf. So, I did," Smitty reminisced.

"And he taught me," Sam added.

"Wow, you're all seriously interconnected then, huh?" Zeke asked.

"Small town. Now you're sucked in, too, Zeke. No way out," Smitty joked.

Zeke didn't reply but blushed and grinned. He wasn't trying to get out.

"I made a decision I wanted to discuss with you all." Aidan cleared his throat. "I've already emailed a lawyer, she said she'd represent me."

"About the police?" Zeke asked.

Aidan nodded. "Let me backtrack a minute. I want to start my own film studio. Documentaries, exposés. I don't want to spend the next ten years trying to get my name out there, creating other people's movies. I spoke to one of the film studios that offered me a job. They wrote again after seeing my video on the news and said it was professional quality, upping their offer. I'd still be working on other people's ideas. Getting that validation from them, though, helped me appreciate my skills. I have to do this on my own."

"That's a good idea. So, what's your plan?" Smitty asked.

"Well, the RV would help because it would give me freedom of movement to go where the story was, to do interviews. I need more equipment, so that's an expense. I also have to register and start putting out feelers on ideas I have. I'd like to have a place here, where I can store things and work for final edits. A film studio of sorts." Aidan paused to read the room, but everyone was listening intently.

"Alright, so the lawyer. Before I move forward with the film studio, I need to put some things behind me. I'm suing the Seattle police department over my injuries. First, to pay my parents back on my hospital bills. Second, to hold them accountable for falsely arresting and detaining me, causing severe injuries. If I win, and after the bills are paid, I'd roll any money into the film studio to get it off the ground."

"Damn, Aidan. I'm in awe of your strength and determination," Sam said, kicking back in her chair. "You've clearly thought this through."

"The lawyer said if it goes to court, I'll have to go back to Seattle for that, but she thinks with all of the national attention, they'll push to settle out of court."

"Whatever you need, little dude. We're here for you," Smitty agreed.

Zeke reached out to take Aidan's hand and shifted forward, meeting his eyes. "See? All along you had it in you. You just needed to believe in yourself. The ability to see your worth and not take people's shit. I'm so fucking proud of you."

Like that, the heavy door clicked open, swinging wide. Aidan mentally stood up, walking out of the prison he'd been holding himself in since Casey died.

Chapter Twenty-Four

The three guys headed out in the morning to secure a travel trailer for Aidan and Zeke. Smitty pushed for new, so it was wired for computers and equipment. Aidan was reluctant, but not because he didn't agree, simply not wanting to put so much on Smitty and Sam. As he was fighting Smitty on the issue, when he saw the prices of new trailers before they left that morning, Sam cut in and set him straight.

"Look, Aidan, Smitty and I decided early on we didn't want to have kids. We don't have family to worry about, and we make good money. Like, we have a ridiculous savings account. We don't need much and love our little cottage, which we bought outright. We have very few expenses, and as Smitty said, business is booming. We donate so much to charity, especially Casey's Fund. Let us do this. It is as much for us, as it is for you. If you want to pay us back fine, though I imagine Smitty will never cash the checks. We love you. Besides, it obligates you to visit us."

Aidan laughed. "No need for obligation there. I'd never leave if I had a choice. I want to thank you for Casey's Fund in person. It means the world to me and my parents."

Smitty ruffled Aidan's hair and smiled. "Us too. It's helped a lot of kids in Casey's name. So, if you try to pay me back, it will probably just go there, to be transparent. I know you have your pride, and I honestly get that, but we try not to hoard money, giving a lot of it away to people who need it more."

Aidan considered what he said. They still shared a car, lived in a two-bedroom cottage with about an acre and a half of land, and weren't lavish about anything. With Smitty owning the restaurant, and Sam making commissioned boards that sold for thousands, they lived well below their means. Smitty told him it allowed them to stay off the radar for the most part. No debt, no payments, and no one knocking on their door. It was a simple life, all Smitty had ever wanted.

Aidan stopped fighting them and instead tried to appreciate their generosity. He knew they had their reasons for wanting to help, but he assured them they couldn't get rid of him if they tried. So, they headed out and checked out RV lots. The Jeep had a weight limit it could tow, but neither Zeke nor Aidan wanted anything bigger than that. They were practically on top of each other wherever they went, anyway, so space wasn't an issue.

They finally found a twenty-foot trailer that would suit their needs. Queen bed, small but fully applianced kitchen, shower, toilet, and a table with recliner style chairs. It had decent storage underneath and inside, not that either of them had much in belongings. As Smitty hoped, it had USB ports, a place to hook up solar panels, a rechargeable battery, water tanks, and a propane tank. It had an option for a large screen mounted television and microwave. They skipped the microwave but said yes to the tv. Both Aidan and Zeke liked to watch movies, and the tv could swivel to be viewed from the recliners or the bed. It was nicer than Aidan's apartment in Seattle, in some ways.

Aidan balked at the price tag, but Smitty didn't bat an eye. He didn't give Aidan a chance to resist, letting the salesperson know they were taking it. Smitty did some wheeling and dealing to get the price down by a few thousand. They knocked off another thousand when he said he could pay in cash. Aidan and Zeke watched in awe as Smitty worked his magic.

The maintenance person on the lot showed them how to hook the trailer up to the Jeep, giving them tips and tricks on hauling it, backing up, and things to watch out for. When it came time to leave with the trailer, Zeke and Aidan stared at each other, deciding who would be first to drive it. Aidan pulled the *I'm still recovering* card and Zeke shook his head, knowing he was being played. He took the keys and fired up the Jeep. They eased out of the parking lot, onto the main road. Since they'd driven a distance to find the trailer, Zeke got plenty of experience on the ride home. Mainly to start braking sooner, taking wider turns, watching out for people who cut too close, and backing up, which wasn't easy because the trailer liked to jackknife.

They finally made it back, and Smitty hopped out to guide them to a shaded area behind the cottage. Once they drove in and decided the trailer was in a good place, they got out to truly admire it. Sam came out and whistled. They could hook up electricity and water while they were stationary for a bit, then rely on the water tanks, propane, and solar when they were traveling. Smitty showed

Sam all the bells and whistles, to which she was rightfully impressed. Aidan liked that it was designed for modern technology since he planned to be able to edit film in there when they were on the road.

Sam ordered pizza from a local pizzeria for dinner, allowing them to all chill and spend the evening listening to music outside in the backyard. They'd strung lights over a small patio to a tree in the yard and had wired speakers out onto the patio. The patio had a large wooden table and chairs, which appeared like they'd been handcrafted. Zeke recognized the handiwork.

"Sam, you made these?" he asked, though he knew the answer.

"I did! I couldn't find anything I liked and used scraps from the shop. Jim helped me with the chairs though, since I didn't get the logistics and didn't want us falling on our asses."

Smitty put on some Motown and they dug into the pizza. The lights above gave it a cafe feel and a breeze blew through, keeping the bugs down. After they ate and cleared the table, Smitty put his hand out to Sam. She took it, their eyes locked, and they stepped out in the yard to dance. They swayed together under the lights, Smitty's arm around Sam's waist, with her hand resting on the back of his neck. They smiled at each other in such an intimate way, Aidan was touched. They'd fought to get there. Although Aidan had been a teenager, he'd been aware of Smitty's addiction, how it almost tore him and Sam apart. But it didn't. They'd found their way back, despite everything.

Zeke touched Aidan's arm. "I'm not much of a dancer, but would you like to?"

Aidan nodded. He'd only ever danced with girls at school dances, which was at best awkward and stiff. He stood up and they headed to a patch of grass under the tree, where the lights met the branches. Both were bashful, but Aidan stepped in and put his arms around Zeke. Zeke moved in and kissed Aidan, making it less awkward. His hands slid around Aidan as they leaned into each other, not matching their movements to the music, but it didn't matter. They matched their movements to each other. Aidan breathed in Zeke's scent, a smell he knew as well as his own now, and he sighed. If it could just be like this. Nobody hating them, no police brutality, no world where some people matter more than others. Just this. The music, the lights, the trees. The breeze blowing the tang of saltwater through the air. It was perfect.

Zeke pulled back and met Aidan's eyes, his own hooded with desire. "You want to sleep in our own home tonight?"

"Sleep?" Aidan teased, brushing his fingers across Zeke's soft lips.

"Well, eventually," Zeke replied, his voice low.

Aidan nodded as he felt heat rise in his body.

They hung out with Sam and Smitty for a bit, then excused themselves to go check out their new home. Sam took the meaning and led Smitty inside. Everyone needed some alone time.

Aidan and Zeke went inside and closed the door behind them. It was small, but they could move around each other easily. The bed was tucked in by the front, making it so one of them would have to climb over the other to get out of the bed, but neither minded. They stood in the middle between the kitchen and the table and chairs, kissing fervently. They helped undress each other and ran their hands over one another's bodies.

Zeke paused at Aidan's scar and furrowed his brow. "I thought I was going to lose you. I was devastated," he whispered, tracing the scar with his fingers.

Aidan had never felt so loved by anyone. He never had to chase Zeke, he was just present in his life. "I never want to be away from you, Zeke. We just make sense. We fit."

Zeke nodded and pushed the hair from Aidan's face, kissing him softly. He kneeled, running his fingers down Aidan's thigh and took Aidan in his mouth. Aidan thought his mind would explode and he grasped onto the counter. His knees started to buckle, so Zeke stood up, leading him to the bed. Aidan fell back on the bed and Zeke finished bringing him to climax. Once he could catch his breath, he turned to face Zeke and pushed him back on the bed, his hand on Zeke's chest.

"I want to taste you," he murmured and made his way down on Zeke.

Afterwards, they lay in their new bed, their arms and legs intertwined. Within minutes, Zeke was fast asleep. Aidan chuckled, watching the most beautiful man he'd ever seen. Zeke could stay up as long as was required, but the moment sleep was presented as an option, he was out like a light. Aidan slipped out of bed and dressed to go inside to get his laptop. Zeke didn't stir and Aidan paused at the door to admire Zeke's long, lean body. He stepped out into the night, cutting off the lights to look up at the stars. The night was clear and the stars were bright. He leaned against the trailer and watched silently. They could just stay, put it all behind them. He knew it was a lie he was telling himself, but it was a lie that made the night perfect.

He wandered inside to grab his laptop and saw Sam was sitting at the table, drinking a cup of tea.

"Do you want a cup? It's supposed to help with sleep. I don't know if it works but it tastes good," she offered.

"Sure, Zeke is out."

"Smitty too. I have trouble falling asleep most nights. The brain, you know?"

"I do. The spiral right?"

"Exactly," she sighed in agreement as she got up to make a cup of tea. "Here you go, the water was still hot."

Aidan sat down and they sipped their tea.

"You know, Aidan, Smitty talks about you all the time. I don't know if you've ever truly understood how much you mean to him. When you didn't want to speak to him after Casey died, he wanted to die. Your forgiveness was everything to him, and when you forgave him, he began to live again. It was the missing piece. We both love Zeke, how much happiness he brings to you. I know the world won't be as kind, but you always have a safe place here."

"Thanks, Sam. We've been attacked before, and the phone calls I got after my name went public were pretty hateful; very anti-gay. I know it's going to be tough on us at times, but I'd do anything for Zeke."

Her pale gray eyes stayed on his face, and she nodded. "I understand. I would've done anything for Smitty. I always will."

The person being mentioned came to the doorway in boxer shorts, rubbing his face. "Hey. What are you doing up?"

"Sleep tea," Sam said, holding up her cup. She drained the cup and put it in the sink. "I'm coming."

Smitty nodded and watched Aidan. "You okay?"

"Yeah, I couldn't sleep. I came in to get my laptop. Figured I'd do some film editing for a bit."

Smitty walked over and kissed Aidan on top of his head. "I'm so glad you came back to us, little dude."

After Sam and Smitty went to their room, Aidan grabbed his laptop. He didn't want to wake Zeke up, so he sat on the front porch and opened his laptop. The lawyer had written, waiting for his go-ahead with the lawsuit. The only way he was going to be able to move forward was to put the past behind him.

He hit reply and thought about what to say. Finally, he settled on a single word. "Proceed."

Chapter Twenty-Five

The next few weeks were a series of lawyer's meetings over the phone, and updates in the Enrique Garza case. Manslaughter charges were brought against the officer who shot Enrique, based on witness reports, Aidan's video, and forensics. Mostly Aidan's video. The other officers on the scene were charged with lesser offenses, though John told Aidan it was unlikely those would stick. They'd probably get a slap on the wrist, looking at past history in these types of cases. The city and state were considering banning certain police procedures which had been allowed to ride for too long, such as chokeholds and holding officers accountable for not interceding when they saw excessive force. Seattle had been put in the national spotlight, and the city government was not happy about it.

Aidan's lawsuit against the Seattle police department moved forward, bringing him back into the news. His parents were prepared this time and changed their phone number, aware the threats would start to roll in. Chris was back at the encampment, volunteering with the assistance group to try and do something to better the lives of the residents. Zeke kept his old phone bill paid, so they could talk to Chris. Chris told them tensions had increased with the charges being filed against the police officers, and groups of citizens in vehicles were coming to harass the residents of the encampment. The police turned a blind eye. Even when a woman reported she'd been raped by a member of one of these groups, the police did nothing more than file a report.

Aidan was healing physically, but mentally was getting dragged back down by the news he was hearing. He wondered if he'd made things worse for the people of the encampment, however, Chris assured Aidan his action was necessary.

"Dude, things are what they are. The police here have always been this way. We don't matter. Growth only comes with busting some seams. They'll push, we'll push back, and so on. It will matter who is stronger. We're stronger in the long run if we stick together. What you did was shine a light on an already existing situation, so we aren't fighting it alone."

"Thanks, Chris. I guess you're right. It's just hard to grasp from so far away. I wish we were there to help."

"No, you don't. They're out for your blood here. You're better off fighting from an undisclosed location. Some of these radicals here want to kill you, your family, anyone you love."

Aidan knew it, but hearing it still shook him to his core. People who didn't even know him would shoot him in the street, simply because he filmed something which was happening. He didn't make it happen, he just exposed it. But those people wanted things to stay the same, the way they'd always been. They liked their racist, classist, homophobic society. It gave them someone to blame and feel superior to. Aidan took a walk after talking with Chris to clear his head. Zeke was working with Sam, and Smitty had run to the restaurant to order supplies. Aidan was alone and didn't want to be.

He headed for the ocean, cutting through a few streets of the town. It reminded him of Crestview, the town he grew up in, but less poor and tourist-focused. Tourists still paid a lot of the bills here, but the locals made sure they were seen and heard. There wasn't an invisible line between the town and what the tourists wanted to see, as there had been in Crestview. As he walked, a small Beagle looking dog started following him and he tried to shoo it away. It would dart off, but before long he'd see it again, following him. He didn't want it to get too far away from home, so he stopped and checked for a collar. There was no collar and it was thin. He pulled out some chips he'd brought and gave them to the dog. Now, it was never going to leave. He figured he'd continue to the beach and if the dog was still with him on the way home, he'd go back the way he came to try and find its home. In the meantime, it was nice company.

Aidan sat on the beach for a couple of hours, mulling over everything that was going on. He felt pretty safe with Sam and Smitty, but while he was sitting on the beach a couple walked by and did a quick double-take. They started whispering between themselves, watching him. He'd forgotten to put anything on which might hide his identity and was pretty sure they recognized him from the news. They started to approach him when the dog came out of nowhere, snapping at them. This threw them off their guard, but they were still staring at Aidan in an accusatory manner. He began commanding the dog in Hebrew, the little he remembered from growing up. This made the couple falter, now not sure they did recognize him. Aidan looked them dead in the eye, talking to them in a mixture of Hebrew and mostly gibberish, real friendly-like. They glanced at each other and shook their heads, sure they'd been confused. The dog continued a low growl at them until they were a distance away.

Realizing he'd put his location at risk, he got up and started the trek back home. The dog stayed at his heels, and even though he passed all the same houses, it never once stopped like it belonged anywhere. At one point, the dog stopped to poop, and Aidan saw it was riddled with worms. He sighed, knowing he'd have to explain why he was bringing a dog back with him.

Smitty was on the porch when he came back and waved as he saw Aidan approach. "What you got there?"

"Fuck if I know, he has been following me the whole way," Aidan said, plopping down on the steps.

"*FuckifIknow*, is that what you're calling him?" Smitty teased.

Aidan chuckled and shrugged. "I haven't called him anything yet, but he did chase off a nosey couple on the beach. I think they recognized me."

"Damn, Aidan, that's not good. They seem like locals or tourists?"

"Tourists, I think. I started speaking Hebrew to them and they scurried away, so I think I'm good. For now."

"You have to be more careful. You're recognizable. I mean, they're using a school photo and you're shaggier than that now, but you have a pretty specific look."

Aidan nodded, he'd fucked up. "I won't do it again. I just needed to step away and think. I guess I got lucky."

"That's what you should call him. Her?" Smitty joked.

"It's a boy. Call him what?"

"Lucky."

Aidan laughed. While it seemed fitting, he'd no intention of keeping the dog. Life was complicated enough. Not that he had any clue what to do with it. When Zeke got home, the decision became even harder when he peered out and saw Zeke rolling around the grass with the dog, cracking up. He stepped out and shook his head. Zeke sat up, brushing the grass off his arms.

"Where did he come from?"

"He followed me to the beach. And back."

"He's cute. What are we doing about him?"

Aidan eyed Zeke, seeing he'd already made up his mind. "I don't know. Smitty said I should call him Lucky."

Zeke called the dog over to him, saying Lucky over and over. They were stuck with the dog, now. At least he didn't look like he'd get too big. He appeared to be a Jack Russell and Beagle mix. Maybe something else thrown in there, it was hard to tell. The dog was cute and *had* defended him on the beach. Maybe having something to alert him about unexpected visitors would be a good thing. Zeke was already attached, and it was the least Aidan could do for the man who gave up everything to follow him across the country.

By evening, Zeke had run to the store and bought everything they had for a dog, plus some. He told Aidan how growing up the church didn't allow the church members to have pets. Animals were strictly functional. Food, clothing, work. Aidan's family had a cat but never a dog. But he'd grown up around them, as there was always at least one kid whose dog was in tow when they hung out. Casey had loved dogs and begged their parents for years, but they'd never buckled. They just weren't dog people. Eventually, Casey quit asking.

Zeke dewormed and overfed Lucky, which led to an evening of a bloated dog with diarrhea and worms coming out of his rear end. It wasn't pleasant but Zeke cleaned up after him, never complaining. Aidan watched with a mixture of horror and amusement. Finally, he was tired enough to go to bed. Zeke had bought a bed four times the size of Lucky and put it beside their bed. Lucky chose to lie on the floor next to it.

Aidan confessed to Zeke while they were lying in bed, how he'd screwed up and almost been recognized at the beach. Zeke turned on his side and propped his head on his elbow, staring at Aidan.

"That's scary. You have to be safe. We can't hide forever, though. Does John give you any idea when this might blow over for you?"

"He said until after the court case it probably won't, but that people have short memories and may not know why they're recognizing me. I just need to be careful and try to change my appearance from the picture that's been shared."

Zeke bobbed his head, reaching out to touch Aidan's hair which was getting longer. He hadn't cut it since graduation and it was almost to his shoulders.

"This helps, you don't look like the fresh-faced young boy in the photo they're showing. This makes you look older, tougher."

Aidan laughed. "Older maybe, but I'm still pretty soft."

Zeke moved in and kissed him. "No, you aren't. Over the last few months, I've watched you go from quiet schoolboy to construction worker, running from the cops, getting beaten, and healing from a surgery that would knock most people on their ass for months. You're tougher than you give yourself credit for. You have scars. Take a look in the mirror. You aren't a boy anymore."

Aidan furrowed his brows and got up to use the bathroom. He paused by the full-length mirror on the door, made to make the space look bigger, and understood what Zeke was saying. He was leaner, his face more defined with lines, and now his intense brows made more sense with the rest of his face. His hair was a little wild, and overall he had the impression of being slightly pissed at all times. The photo they were using was so clean-cut and innocent-looking, most people wouldn't put the two together. The tell was in his eyes. They'd always appeared haunted and slightly puzzled.

He slid into bed and put his arm around Zeke, pressing his face into Zeke's back. The fine blond hairs on Zeke's back tickled his nose. He rubbed his face against Zeke's skin and sighed as he heard Lucky let loose a long, squeaky, wet fart. It was going to be a long night. He could feel Zeke shake with laughter as Aidan buried his head under the sheet to try and stave off the smell.

By morning, Zeke and Lucky were already up, and Zeke had left the door open to try and air out the trailer. Aidan boiled water for coffee and poured it into a French press. He let it steep, enjoying the smell of something other than dog farts. Once it was brewed, he poured two cups and brought one to Zeke, who was throwing a ball for Lucky. Zeke grinned at him.

"Sorry. I don't know how dogs work," he confessed.

"Not like that, that's for sure," Aidan replied, laughing.

Lucky bounded up to them and sat at Aidan's feet with his tongue hanging out of his mouth. Aidan bent down and rubbed his head. Lucky rolled on his back and farted.

"Jesus, Lucky. Still?" Aidan covered his nose.

Zeke threw the tennis ball and Lucky took off after it. He was good at chasing it, but not so good at bringing it back. He took the ball to lay with it halfway back, ripping the fuzz off. Zeke ran to get the ball from him, and Aidan sat on the patio watching them play. Sam came out, joining him with coffee in hand.

"How's life with a dog?" she asked, putting her feet up on an extra chair.

"Not like it is on television," Aidan said.

"Rarely is."

Zeke came up and sat with them, gulping his coffee. Lucky ran around the yard, chasing his tail and barking. They were enjoying the morning, feeling almost normal when Smitty came to the door. His face was serious and worried, his gaze landing on Aidan.

"Uh, Aidan. You may want to come see this. All hell has broken loose in Seattle."

Ⅹ

Chapter Twenty-Six

All hell had most definitely broken loose in Seattle. From the news, the groups of radical police supporters had breached the encampment and were beating residents, tearing down tents, and setting things on fire. The police didn't get involved until protesters got wind of what was happening and descended on the scene. The media tried to go into the area to film, but many were thrown down and their equipment destroyed by the police or their supporters. Aidan watched horrified, as a place he knew well was turned into a war, with only half of those fighting having weapons. His phone rang and he saw it was TJ.

"Hey, TJ," he said, not taking his eyes off the television.

"Aidan, you see what's going on?"

"Yeah, those fuckers. I need to go back," Aidan replied.

Zeke heard him and met his eyes. He knew. They couldn't keep hiding while vulnerable people were having their lives destroyed in the face of the world. He nodded at Aidan. It was time.

"Okay, Mia and I were discussing that, too. When are you leaving?"

"Today. If we drive straight through, taking turns, we can get back to Seattle in a little over two days. Maybe less, but since we're towing a trailer, I doubt it."

"It's only going to take us a day. We'll head up by the end of the day and let you know where we are. We can meet up when you get here. They aren't letting the press in, and if they manage to get close, they're pushing them back."

"I saw. We know the back alleys and may be able to get close. I'll talk to John and see if he has any intel which will help."

"See you soon, Aidan. Missed you, brother. Sorry it's under these circumstances."

TJ hung up and Aidan stared at Zeke. "You ready for this?"

Zeke tipped his head in agreement. Sam overheard the conversation and went to the kitchen to pack them food and drinks. Smitty watched quietly, torn between knowing they needed to go and wanting to keep them safe. He got up and left the room. Aidan was hurt but knew Smitty was struggling with it because he loved him.

They packed as fast as possible and brought the trailer around front. Lucky bolted in the door as soon as they opened it, not wanting to be left behind. Sam filled their fridge with premade food and embraced each of them tightly.

"This is so hard. Like sending your sons off to war," she whispered with tears in her eyes. "Please be careful."

Aidan went to find Smitty, determined to make things right before he left. Smitty was sitting on the edge of his bed with his head in his hands and looked up, his eyes lined with concern when Aidan came in.

"Smith, I have to go. This is what I've dedicated my life to." Aidan sat on the bed next to Smitty, leaning his head against Smitty's broad shoulder.

"I know you do, and it's the right thing to do. I just am scared of losing you, like I lost Casey. I didn't stop him and have regretted it ever since."

"I'll be careful. We know those streets and alleys, we're going in incognito. The goal is to expose them and not get caught or beaten."

Smitty stared at Aidan, wrapping his arm around him in a hug. "You and Sam are my only family. Zeke now, too. I need you to come back."

Aidan bit his lip, not wanting to make promises he couldn't keep. "I have every intention to."

"You know with your hair growing out like that, and you getting older, you look more and more like Casey. But angrier," Smitty teased, rubbing Aidan's head.

They walked out to the Jeep and trailer. Zeke was already behind the wheel for the first round. Smitty went over and hugged him hard.

"I want you to know we consider you family and want you back as much as Aidan. We love you, too," Smitty said honestly.

Zeke stared at Smitty and nodded, trying to not tear up. Aidan climbed in beside him, releasing a deep breath. Smitty reached across Zeke and slid something over Aidan's head. Aidan looked down and saw Casey's prayer beads swinging against his chest. He put his hand on them, meeting Smitty's eyes. Smitty nodded.

"You can give them back when you come home. They got me through some of my toughest days. Maybe they'll give you some protection."

Smitty stepped back and shut Zeke's door. He went around to Sam and put his arms around her, so they could hold each other up while their boys drove away. Aidan choked back tears, holding on to Casey's beads as they pulled off. Zeke put his hand out and Aidan took it. They didn't know exactly what they'd be going into, or how they'd get in, but this was their calling.

They drove almost non-stop for two days, only pausing for gas, to use the bathroom, and to grab food out of the fridge. Aidan took the second leg on straight highway to get used to driving the Jeep with the trailer in tow. It wasn't as hard as he thought and made sure to give himself time to react in any situation. Zeke slept next to him peacefully as Aidan laid his hand on Zeke's leg. At least they were together, he wasn't facing this alone.

On the morning of the third day, Aidan called John to get updates and things weren't any better. If anything, they were worse. The police had started using tear gas, bean bag rounds, and rubber bullets against the protesters and the homeless, indiscriminately. The city government was vacillating between supporting the police and condemning any acts of excessive force. It sent mixed messages, bringing out radicals on all sides. The protesters were protesting peacefully but had been infiltrated by trouble makers, wanting things to escalate. Stuck in the middle, were the residents of the encampment, including the disabled, children, and people with medical conditions. Chris had not been reachable since it all started, which worried Zeke and Aidan. John said there had been serious injuries, some life-threatening.

"Aidan, I appreciate you coming back, but we have to be careful. They're preventing reporters from getting into certain areas. If you're wearing a press pass, you have a target on your back."

"We won't be wearing press passes and will be on foot. We used to move around the city sometimes by rooftop, so we're planning to use alleys, fire escapes, and roofs to get through. We're going to use skateboards to get as near as we can, then duck into the alleys. I have my camera and will film what I can. Oh, hey, can you watch our dog, Lucky, when we go in?"

"Alright, let's meet up when you get to town and go over some things. If we can figure out a way to live feed from your camera to my computer, I can get this transmitted immediately. In case you get caught and they destroy your camera. Bring your dog when we meet up. I'll keep him at my apartment."

"Will do, John. Thanks. We're parking the trailer at a campground outside of town, then driving in closer. I'll text you a meetup location and time." Aidan hung up and stared out at the road.

If they destroyed his camera. That's not all they'd do if they caught them. He had the scars to prove it. Zeke stirred just about the time they pulled into the campground and peered around.

"Are we here?"

"We are. Talked to TJ and Mia, they're already in town. We need to meet them in about an hour."

Zeke rubbed his eyes and nodded. "I've got to piss, but then we can unhook the trailer and go."

Neither wanted any downtime to think. The sooner they met up with TJ and Mia, the sooner they could make a plan. Aidan texted John the meetup location and checked his camera was fully charged with a backup battery. He'd moved all stored footage to his laptop, so he had ample space in the camera. Zeke drove into the city and parked a few blocks away from the meetup location. They'd be on skateboards and foot from here on out. They skated over to the coffee shop they'd agreed to meet up at, seeing TJ and Mia waiting outside. Aidan jumped off his board and hugged Mia as hard as he could. Mia put her hands on his face and frowned.

"You look tired."

"We just drove straight across the country, then came right here. I am tired," Aidan responded.

"How are you healing, you look different?" Mia asked, concerned.

"Healing. A little slow but not too bad. On my feet."

"I like your hair, it makes you look intimidating."

Aidan laughed, shaking his head. "Nope, same old goofy dude."

He embraced TJ, and Zeke hugged Mia. Lucky bounced around at their feet, sniffing TJ and Mia up and down. They moved to a back corner of the coffee shop's covered patio to figure out what to do next. They all had face coverings, goggles, and pepper spray in case they got cornered. They worked out a couple of escape routes and meet-up points in the chance they got separated. The goal was to keep Aidan and his camera away from the police, as the footage fed live to John. He'd control it from there.

John came in and Aidan waved him back. He introduced everyone as John sat down. His face was serious and exhausted.

"First, I need to say you all understand the risk you're taking here? Reporters have been thrown to the ground and hit in the face. We're supposed to be protected but are targets, right now. I don't want you going in thinking otherwise," John explained firmly.

They all nodded, glancing at each other nervously. John showed Aidan how to log into his live feed account and connect his camera to it through his phone. Once Aidan logged in and started filming, it would feed to the account and John would activate it to go live on the news station website. From there, they could get it on the television news.

"I want to be clear that while I'm here with you, the station won't take any part of any action for or against you. I'm doing this of my own accord because there doesn't seem to be another way."

"John, we're all here by our own volition. We understand the risks and appreciate you doing this to give us a platform. People need to know what is actually going on down here," Aidan said.

John got up to leave and paused. "It's your generation who will change things. The rest of us sat around thinking there was another way, waiting for politics to change. For those in charge to evolve. You all are the true leaders of this country. You have my admiration."

He took Lucky's leash, giving him a rub on the head. Lucky glanced back at Aidan and Zeke but followed John out the door. The group went over the plans one more time. They'd go in on skateboards to get as close as possible without being noticed. From there, they'd move into the alleys, winding through those and over rooftops to get into the center of what was happening. Zeke would stay with Aidan to let him keep his focus on filming. TJ and

Mia would work their way through the crowd, keeping Aidan apprised of where he needed to go to film. Zeke tried to contact Chris, but it went straight to voicemail.

They headed out, skating through the streets until they could see where the cops were, preventing people from getting through. They ducked into an alley, moving on foot to make a circle around the police line towards the encampment. Most alleys were blocked by police cars, so they climbed a fire escape onto a roof to get a better view. The encampment was surrounded by police and their cronies. Protesters and others were standing just outside of the line of tents. Bottles were being thrown and the police responded by firing rubber bullets into the crowd, despite not knowing where the bottles were coming from.

Aidan was already filming, but they needed to get closer, so faces could be identified. A few of the rooftops had police stationed on them, so they moved over the ones which didn't, having to jump from rooftop to rooftop. Most were close together, but there were a few where Aidan questioned their sanity as they leapt across. They peered down and saw a way in, going down the fire escape, then past a parked car in the alley.

They all stared at each other, not knowing what was going to happen next, and made their way to the roof's edge. Mia and TJ were heading down first to get into the crowd. Zeke and Aidan had marked out a spot tucked into the shadows, to start filming from ground level. They'd wait until TJ and Mia were out of sight before heading down. Aidan looked at the best friends he'd ever had and smiled, his mouth wobbling.

"I love you all. See you on the other side."

Chapter Twenty-Seven

The crowd absorbed TJ and Mia into their folds as some of their own. Aidan and Zeke climbed down the fire escape and moved along the brick wall of the alley. It would be harder for Aidan to not be seen carrying the camera, so he moved behind Zeke, who acted as a barrier between him and visibility. Once they were at ground level and could see what was going on, it was unreal. Protesters were trying to form a protective line between the police and the encampment. Police supporters were starting fights with the protesters and if the protesters fought back, the police would immediately use force against them. Behind the protesters, medical tents were set up to treat the injured.

The air had a thickness of previously sprayed tear gas, making Aidan and Zeke cough, even though their noses and mouths were covered. Zeke had his goggles down over his eyes but

Aidan hadn't put his on, afraid it would make it harder to see through the camera lens. He slid them over as his eyes began to water and close.

They stayed in the shadows and filmed, the footage going directly to John. A couple of protesters saw Aidan filming and came around to create even more of a wall of protection for him. They slipped into the crowd, closer to the police. Aidan caught on camera police supporters shoving and punching a protester, as the police did nothing. A few protesters moved in to help, and the police shot them with rubber bullets. The only time the protesters fought was to protect someone. This wasn't what was being presented to the world.

Zeke checked the phone to see where TJ and Mia were. They'd moved to the other side of the encampment, to a medical tent where resident children were being treated for injuries. Zeke and Aidan made their way methodically through, filming as they went. The violence was being perpetuated by the radicals on the police side, then backed up by the police if anyone tried to stand up against them. It was surreal and rage filled Aidan. The police supporters used weapons and were allowed to move freely, while the protesters were attacked if they did anything. Aidan filmed a cop spraying an unarmed woman directly in the face with tear gas, while she stood peacefully chanting. She buckled to the ground, and he sprayed anyone who came close to help her.

As they moved through, they spied a familiar figure and headed towards him.

"Chris!" Zeke yelled, embracing their friend with relief.

Chris nodded at them, keeping his mouth and eyes covered. He pointed towards what appeared to be one of the police supporters, setting fire to a police car. Aidan zoomed in and caught the person setting the fire, simultaneously talking and joking with police. Clearly, they were doing things to make it seem like the protesters were being destructive. Chris put his hand on Aidan's shoulder in silent support, not wanting to disrupt the filming. Zeke and Chris stepped away to talk, Chris telling him how bad it had gotten. The police had smashed him in the head a few days before and broke his phone. Knowing he couldn't use it, but not wanting the sensitive information stored on it, he'd stashed it.

No one had been exempt from the brutality, and the protesters had come to protect the encampment. People from all over the country. They tried evacuating children and anyone who wanted to leave, but the police had formed a line all around the encampment, preventing escape. Volunteer groups and media were prevented from coming in. What the end goal was, no one was sure. Suffering and punishment for standing up against the police department seemed to be their primary motivation. The police department had gone rogue with their radical supporters, creating an army. The residents and protesters wouldn't be able to hold off for much longer.

Zeke checked the phone and handed it to Aidan. A message from John from earlier simply read, "streaming."

No matter what, the world would at least see what was happening down there. Other protesters were using their phones to try and capture video, but as soon as they were seen the police supporters would attack them and take their phones. Very little had made it out and what had, was being discredited by radicals through social media saying it was fake or staged. Aidan's footage was going directly through the new station website, being aired nationally.

They made it to the medical tent where TJ and Mia were. With their parents' permission, Aidan filmed the children's injuries. Some had been hit with rubber bullets or sprayed with tear gas, all were traumatized. One little girl was holding her knees and rocking back and forth with a blank stare. Aidan couldn't understand why no one was helping. Why were the police being allowed to treat people this way? It had to go deeper, someone higher up wanted this to happen. The police were just cogs in the machine. Often dumb, violent cogs, but they were being used to do the bidding of the powers that be.

A text came in from John which read, "Keep moving! Otherwise, they'll figure out where you are."

Aidan hadn't thought about that and signaled to Zeke, but it was too late. Radicals rushed the protesters and made their way towards the tent. Protesters slowed them down, giving Aidan time to cover his camera and move. One of the police supporters saw him and ran in his direction. Zeke stepped into his way and the radical hit him in the head with a metal rod. Zeke went down. Aidan went to help, but Chris pushed him away, shaking his head as he went to Zeke. Aidan had slipped out of view, and a group of protesters surrounded him. He could see Chris helping Zeke up, blood was gushing from Zeke's head. Aidan wanted to go to him, but Chris was guiding him to the tent. The radicals were searching through the crowd for Aidan and he was getting cornered. He continued filming in case they attacked him to make sure it was seen, glancing around for an escape route. If he could be invisible for a moment, he was close to an alley and might be able to get there. It was about twenty-five feet away, but he'd have to run in the open to get there, risking being seen and caught.

Mia, realizing he had no way out, snagged a megaphone and scrambled on top of a car. She clicked it on and took a deep breath. She released her voice into the megaphone, singing *Ave Maria* from the opera Dialogue of the Carmelites, written during the French Revolution. Her voice ringing out above the crowd, caused a momentary pause on all sides, in which she met Aidan's eyes during a breath and mouthed, "run!" He took off, hunching down and running, making it to the alley just as a police officer hit Mia in the knees with a baton and sprayed her with tear gas. She fell off the car and TJ ran to protect her, but he was knocked to the ground being hit with rubber bullets.

Aidan kept filming as he ran and scaled up a fire escape. Police were firing bean bags and rubber bullets on the protesters openly, and Aidan had been spotted by a group of radicals, who were running down the alley from both sides. He realized he was trapped. Even if he got to the roof they'd still corner him. Cops were on too many rooftops nearby. He couldn't go back down because they'd be there at the bottom by the time he did. He kept the film rolling, while he whispered, "shit" over and over to himself.

All of a sudden, a window he was crouched by opened, and he was dragged in as the window slammed shut before he even registered what happened. The curtains closed over the barred windows and he was in darkness, hearing the sounds of people chasing him up the fire escape. They didn't know where he went and were trying to open the windows. He held his breath as hands tried to force the window up. The window remained closed and the group moved on. They went to the roof and then back down. Aidan sat in the dark, figuring out what to do. Once it had fallen quiet again, a faint light clicked on and he could see a man crouched by the window, looking out at the street. He was old and glanced at Aidan with his fingers to his lips, motioning for Aidan to come over. Aidan went to the window and saw it had a clear view of what was going on below.

The man nodded, pointing at his camera. Aidan picked it up and began filming from the corner of the open window. Down below was chaos. Protesters were being attacked by the radicals and police, trying to fight back. While they had the numbers, the police had the weapons. From the corner of Aidan's eye, he could see movement and saw one of the radicals get into a car and start to drive towards the crowd. The car picked up speed and Aidan realized it was going to run the protesters down. Knowing he would give away his location, he needed to get their attention. He saw Chris on the edge of the crowd, close to where the car was coming.

"Chris! Chris!" he yelled at the top of his lungs. Chris glanced up.

Aidan motioned excitedly towards the car coming at them. Chris followed Aidan's motions, his mouth falling open. The soldier in him kicked in, and he began throwing people out of the path as he ran towards the moving car. Aidan saw the kid, who joined the army, thinking he was defending his country, turn into the man, who put himself in the line of danger, fighting for the people he'd intended to protect all along. He moved fluidly, getting people out of the way as the car bore down on him. All Aidan could do was film horrified, as he watched his friend get mowed down by the car he was running towards.

Chris's body was thrown into the air, and he fell crumpled to the side. The person driving the vehicle was dragged out by the protesters and pinned to the ground. People went to help Chris, but he lay motionless. Aidan felt tears streaming down his cheeks as he kept filming. He felt his phone buzz and took it out. John messaged:

"NATIONAL GUARD WILL BE ARRIVING MOMENTARILY. FOOTAGE NATIONAL. GOVERNOR ORDERED NATIONAL GUARD TO STEP IN AND HELP PROTESTERS TO DIFFUSE SITUATION. HOLD ON."

Aidan stared at the message. The National Guard was coming to help *them*? He tried to see where Chris was, but he'd been moved by gurney to the medical tent. As Aidan watched from his perch, his friends were fighting for their lives. But without him filming, the National Guard wouldn't have been sent in to help. The old man next to him reached out, placing his hand on Aidan's shoulder. He'd saved Aidan to save the others. Within minutes, the National Guard descended, pushing back the radicals and the police. Enemies *domestic* and foreign. Behind them came the media, rescue groups, and ambulances. Aidan clicked off his camera and fell against the wall, trembling.

"You did good, kid," the old man whispered.

Aidan started to shake violently with all of the stress he'd been bottling up inside himself. He was hyperventilating, so the old man gave him a paper bag to breathe into. He slowly drew his breath in and out until he felt himself settle and glanced at his phone. He had numerous messages, but none from TJ or Mia. Zeke didn't have a phone because he'd given his to Chris.

He wrote Smitty and his parents a short message. "I'm okay."

He texted Mia but she didn't respond.

He peered back out as the National Guard quickly made sense of the chaos, and the injured were transported out. Aidan had to go down and find his friends. He stood up, reaching out to shake the old man's hand.

"Thank you. You saved my life. I'm Aidan."

"Carl."

"Thank you, Carl. I need to go find my friends and see if they're safe."

The old man nodded, rubbing his face. He got up and showed Aidan to the door. Aidan headed down to the street, which appeared like it had been ravaged by war. The military was everywhere, armed to the hilt. They eyed Aidan but saw him carrying his camera and let him pass. He stumbled through, trying to recognize anyone. He got to the medical tent, but everyone had been moved out. Gurneys were on their side, supplies scattered everywhere. A guy came in who'd been treating the injured. Aidan got his attention.

"Where did the injured go?"

"They're being transported to local hospitals."

"The guy, Chris, who was hit by the car. Is he going to be okay?"

The guy stopped and stared at Aidan, shaking his head. "No, man, I'm sorry. He didn't make it. That guy was a fucking hero."

Aidan felt like he'd been punched in the gut. Dazed, he stumbled back out into the area where so much blood was shed, by people that shared the same country. It didn't even look like a city in America. Growing up he saw warzones on the news but never thought he'd see something so close to him. People who were told they mattered but clearly didn't.

Ultimately, none of their lives had any value beyond the money trail. They were all expendable. They were used against each other, all scrambling for the few meager scraps thrown to them. Stray dogs, fighting to survive. Aidan fell to his knees and leaned forward on the ground, Casey's beads hitting him in the face.

He buried his face in his hands and cried for everything they'd lost.

Chapter Twenty-Eight

John picked Aidan up with Lucky in the back seat. The area was closed off, so Aidan walked a few blocks to meet him. There'd still been no sign or word from Zeke, Mia, or TJ. They may have been on the move or had their phones off. Aidan climbed in and glanced at John, who was visibly shaken up about all that transpired. Lucky jumped up into the front and sat in Aidan's lap, licking his face. John nodded, clearing his throat.

"I knew it was bad down there, but seeing your footage feeding through... it was all too unreal."

"Trust me, it was real. I saw our friend Chris get run down. They hit Zeke in the head with a metal bar. They shot TJ with rubber bullets. They hit Mia and tear-gassed her. I couldn't do anything," Aidan replied, his voice just above a whisper.

"I saw. I'm sorry."

Aidan realized of course John would've seen because anything Aidan was seeing, the world was seeing through his camera feed. His eyes became everyone else's.

"I need to find them. The guy at the medical tent told me Chris was killed. I don't know about the rest of my friends."

John nodded and eased out into traffic. "Most of the injured were taken to the nearest hospital. Let's start there. Aidan, I know what you saw was traumatizing. I'm here if you want to talk."

Aidan stayed silent, the images replaying over and over in his mind. Chris lying lifeless on the ground. Blood gushing from Zeke's head. TJ falling as he was hit by rubber bullets. Mia singing so beautifully, as the police smashed her in the back of the legs, spraying her in the face with tear gas. His friends, like him, standing up against tyranny. Paying the price for being better people. His friends protected him, so he could make sure to show the world the truth. He was desperate to find them.

They parked near the hospital and wound through rows and rows of cars, ambulances, and reporters. It was madness, Aidan started to feel himself go numb. John led the way into the emergency room, and they scanned the people there. People were bleeding and crying, some sitting as they rocked back and forth, holding broken limbs and contusions. Still, no sign of any of his friends. Where had they gone? They were all injured but hopefully able to leave on their own accord. Aidan racked his brain, trying to think. Lucky was at Aidan's feet, but no one seemed to care. They asked the nurse if any of those names had been admitted, and she shook her head after scanning the sheet. Aidan started to panic. What if something happened to them?

They left the hospital, heading back to John's car. No one lived in Seattle anymore, so there wasn't a home to go back to. Their designated meet-up points had been blocked. TJ did have his car, but they wouldn't have left Aidan. He knew that. *The rooftop.* He turned to John.

"We need to go back. We started at a rooftop before coming into the area. We ended up on the other side by the medical tent, but maybe they went back to the roof to regroup."

They drove back down but were stopped by the National Guard. John flashed his press pass and they let him through. When they got there, Aidan was confused as to which roof it was, as all the markers they'd used were gone. He retraced his steps, coming to an alley he thought was the right one. He asked John to wait with Lucky and went up the fire escape, but when he got to the top no one was there, and it didn't look right. He went back down and to the next alley, which appeared almost the same. He looked at the fire escape, and tied to the bottom was Zeke's bandana he'd been wearing over his face. Aidan went and untied it, peering up. *Please let them be up there*, he thought. He waved at John to wait and ran up the fire escape.

As soon as he got to the roof, he caught a glimpse of Mia's long, dark hair blowing in the wind. She saw him and ran straight into his arms.

"Aidan! We didn't know where you were or if you were safe! What happened to you? Our cell service is down."

Her eyes were red and puffy from tear gas or crying. Or both. TJ was sitting with Zeke and got up. He hugged Aidan tightly. Zeke smiled up at them with a nasty gash on the side of his head. Aidan kneeled, putting his fingers near the wound. It required stitches. Zeke's eyes were slightly unfocused, but he kept them on Aidan.

"Love you," was all he said.

Aidan sat down in front of Zeke, slipping his arms around him. "I was so scared when I couldn't find you."

Zeke nodded and Aidan felt him shaking before he realized Zeke was crying. He sat back to meet Zeke's eyes. Chris.

"I saw that guy run Chris down. I was trying to follow him, but I was dizzy and lost my balance. When I stood up, I saw Chris in front of that car with nowhere to go. Then he just landed; I knew he was dead."

Aidan sighed. He saw it, too. Their friend. The person who was a catalyst to ending this all was gone. A soldier extinguished by hate on his own soil. Aidan sat beside Zeke and slid his arm over his shoulders. Zeke leaned his head against Aidan and bawled. It was too much.

Zeke fell silent, his tears dried up. He stood up, reaching down for Aidan. "Let's go. I don't want to be here anymore."

The four of them made their way down the fire escape to where John was waiting with Lucky. Lucky wagged his tail when he saw Zeke, but Zeke didn't seem to notice. Aidan gave TJ and John the address to the campground where the RV was. Aidan helped Zeke to the Jeep and drove them out to the campground. TJ, Mia, and John came shortly after. Once they all met up, they built a fire and sat outside, trying to process everything.

"Chris Huber," Zeke said.

Aidan peered at him and nodded, understanding.

"John, can you make sure our friend Chris is identified, and that he is recognized as a hero, not as some homeless guy they'll try and discredit? He was a war veteran and a hero. And a resident of the homeless encampment. It all matters," Aidan requested.

John bobbed his head and wrote Chris's name down. He asked about any other info they may have, so he could make sure the family was notified. They only knew that and he was from a small town in Oregon. He was private about his life.

"Can you maybe see if he had any belongings at the encampment, too?" Zeke asked.

"I can do that. Let me make some calls and see what I can track down," John replied, then stepped away to use his phone.

"Mia, you shifted consciousness with your voice today," Zeke said quietly. "If even just for a moment. Everyone stopped to listen. I was in awe."

Aidan remembered Mia pouring her soul into that microphone and the beauty which came out. It was so brave of her to risk herself like that, knowing they'd take her down. Zeke had stood in front of Aidan to protect him, Mia had climbed on a car to give him time to run, TJ had fought the police. No matter what was said about their generation, the four of them risked everything to expose the truth. And for each other.

John came back and sat down. "I have someone going through the encampment to search for Chris's tent. Once they do, they'll box it up and get it to me. I think I may have found his family, the hospital is reaching out to let them know what happened. He lived his life with such strength and bravery. I found him in the system and he was highly decorated, having saved his crew over in the Middle East from a roadside IED. They were ambushed, but he kept it under control and held off the insurgents until help arrived."

Chris had done the same today. He'd made sure to get people out of the way, even though it cost him his life. Would the government care? Probably not, considering he was a homeless veteran, and they hadn't cared up until this point. Aidan scrolled through his phone until he found a picture of Chris from the day Zeke cut his hair. He sent it to John's phone.

"Please use that one and tell the world what he did. Don't let him be faceless and forgotten," Aidan said once it was sent. "He was...he *is* our brother."

Tears started to roll down Zeke's face again as he stared at the ground. He'd lost so much in life, he couldn't afford to lose any more. John went to his car and grabbed a first aid kit. He sat down beside Zeke and began to clean his wound. He butterflied the gash closed, dabbing it with gauze. Zeke didn't flinch, he just kept staring at the ground. TJ went to the campground office to see if there were any cabins to rent for the night. There were, so he and Mia went to clean up. They all agreed to meet back for a late dinner, as it was already almost midnight. John offered to go get pizza and no one refused.

Aidan guided Zeke into the trailer to the bed. Zeke went to lie down but kept staring off. Aidan knew he needed to bring him back somehow before he stayed away too long. It was a deep hole to get out of. He lay facing Zeke, placing his hand on Zeke's chin.

"Zeke, look at me."

Zeke's eyes flitted up to meet Aidan's. He smiled but didn't mean it. Aidan tried again.

"You're the most compassionate person, you wear your heart on your sleeve. It's what I love about you, but it means you have no armor. Nothing to protect your soul. You've been through more than most people, yet kept your belief that the world was a better place than it is. People suck. Not all, but a lot. A staggering amount. But there are the *TJ's*, and *Mia's* of the world, who are fighting to keep the balance. There are the *you's* and the *Casey's* of the world, who are the heart. There are the *Smitty's* and the *Sam's* of the world, who are the protectors. We aren't alone. Chris, he was a protector. He knew that from a young age. You could tell him how it all ended, and he'd still make the same choice. You'll never stop loving with all your heart. It's alright. This is going to hurt for a while, but Chris will always be part of us. I learned that after Casey. I still feel him around sometimes."

Zeke listened, his eyes watching Aidan. He smiled, real but sad this time. "I love you, Aidan."

"I love you, Zeke."

They lay together for a bit, Lucky joining them, licking each of them until they couldn't help but laugh. A knock came at the door and they got up. John was back with pizzas and TJ and Mia made their way over. They sat around the fire, bruised and battered, but had won the battle. The war was much larger than them, it would need to be faced another day. Lucky managed to get pizza from everyone and came to lie at Zeke's feet, completely bloated. Zeke leaned down, rubbing his belly.

Even though everyone was tired, no one wanted to go to sleep, so John pulled out a bottle of aged scotch, handing it around. It passed a few times as they talked about the world and their place in it. Aidan knew he needed to keep filming. Finding the hard, untold stuff and exposing it. It was the only way people would believe it was happening. If even then. There were those who discredited everything that didn't back up their rhetoric. The deniers. The same type of people who'd say the Holocaust never happened. Aidan had family who were directly affected by the Holocaust, but the deniers would accuse him of lying if he told them, or even showed proof. Their minds wouldn't be swayed. The ones he needed to reach were the apathetic, the misinformed, the fence riders. Those were the ones he had to show the realities to. They were the vast majority, opening their minds would change the tide.

"Hey, Aidan," Zeke spoke, drawing Aidan out of his thoughts. "You know how you said Casey and I are the heart of the world, TJ and Mia are the fighters, and Smitty, Chris, and Sam are the protectors?"

Aidan nodded. "Yeah?"

"You know what that makes you?" Zeke asked, meeting his eyes.

"What?"

"The truth."

Chapter Twenty-Nine

John kept his word and made sure Chris was presented to be the hero he was. The media shared his enlisted photo and the one Aidan had sent to John. His bravery, both in the military and during the protests, was highlighted. It was mentioned that he'd been a resident of the encampment, which brought to light the lack of support for veterans returning from war. A local citizen group came forward with an offer to put a plaque in the area with his name, and what he'd sacrificed to save so many lives. Both home and abroad. He died at thirty-one years old, having spent his life putting others first. His family couldn't be reached for comment but his body was sent to be buried in the family plot. John made sure the belongings Chris had at the encampment were boxed up and brought to him. He showed up at the campground a few mornings after the National Guard had taken control of the area. Aidan and Zeke were outside with Lucky when John drove in.

"Hey John, what's the news?" Aidan asked as he threw a tennis ball for Lucky.

"I have something for you. It's Chris's stuff," John said, reaching into the back seat to grab the box. He handed it to Zeke as Lucky came to circle his feet.

"Wow, thanks. You want coffee?" Zeke offered.

John nodded, his eyes lined with exhaustion. Aidan poured him a cup from the French press they had on a small table outside the trailer. John motioned them to sit down with him, so they could talk. He rubbed his beard and sighed.

"I've been gathering info on what is going to happen, now. There is serious talk of defunding the police since, after the last incident, they didn't stop breaking policies and pretty much took this on themselves. Defunding, as in withholding or redirecting funding until they can determine where it would be best served. The question is to defund the police department and assess a new system altogether, or reform the existing one? At this point, most of the current leadership has either resigned or been put on administrative leave. Anyone proven to be involved has been placed on probation while an external investigation is being completed. The National Guard will stay in place until further notice. There are police, both in the city and from other areas, condemning the action of the police involved. Not sure that means much, but good to see they're breaking ranks."

"What does this mean? Like for now?" Aidan asked.

"I'm not a hundred percent, but it looks like the National Guard will act as the police until decisions are made. They're diverting non-crime based calls to social workers, and anything with risk of violence will be handled by the National Guard or police officers from other areas who've volunteered to come in. The thing is, there is some darker shit tied to all of this."

"What do you mean?" Zeke responded as he rubbed Lucky's ears.

"Well, there are those saying this has ties to white supremacy groups and is being funded by some pretty well-known corporations. A modern-day cleansing, if you will."

Aidan and Zeke stared at each other. What the fuck had they stumbled into?

"Are we in any danger?" Aidan felt a knot form in his stomach and took a deep breath.

"Not necessarily, or no more than you already have been," John explained. "This time the feed went through my account through the station, so your name isn't directly connected. It's still your footage and you own the legal rights to it. Just remember, I've been doing stuff like this for years and have received so many death threats, I've lost count. But I'm still here. The majority of people like to spew hate from the sidelines. The big guns have political, religious, and corporate ties, so don't go after individuals per se. Their goal is more mind control for financial gain."

Aidan nodded and chewed his thumbnail. Nothing was really for the people or by the people. From children starting school on up, the brainwashing began. Everything was presented for the great buy-in. Literally. Buy in mentally, buy in financially. Keep the system churning. He glanced at Zeke playing with Lucky, then back to John.

"I heard from the lawyer this morning," he said, his voice low.

"You did? What did she say?" John inquired.

"They're offering a settlement. Two hundred and sixty thousand."

John whistled. "Means they know you could get a lot more, but don't want it in the press. Are you taking it?"

"I think so, yeah. My parents are in the hole at least twenty thousand from my surgery and hospital bills after insurance. I'd like to pay them back. Then lawyers fees, taxes, etc. The rest I'd like to invest into my film company, give Zeke and me a fresh start. I'd also like to help the encampment in Chris's name. He fought so hard for their rights."

John nodded. "I forgot to tell you. The city is going to make the encampment a protected area, overseen by a board made up of the volunteer and assistance groups in the area. Maybe that's who you can work with to help."

Aidan smiled. That would make TJ and Mia happy. They were planning to stay in Seattle to finish their schooling, and TJ had already been asked to stay on full-time with the assistance group they'd been working with. It didn't pay much, but it was his life's goal. Aidan had already planned to give them some of the settlement money to get a better place while they finished school. TJ would resist, wanting to do things on his own, but Aidan knew he could figure out a way.

"Alright, thanks for the coffee. I've got to head on back in, to work on some things for the station. How long are you in town for?" John asked and stood up.

"I think we're heading out in a couple of days. We're having dinner with TJ and Mia tonight, tying up some loose ends tomorrow. We'll be back soon, though. At this point, we'll make North Carolina and my parents' house our main home bases, and travel across the country making documentaries."

"Yeah? That's cool. What next?" John replied, coming over to look at Zeke's wound. It had sealed together nicely and wouldn't need stitches.

Aidan met Zeke's eyes, nodding. "We're taking on the religious, anti-LGBTQ, conversion therapy establishment."

"Damn. Be careful. Believe it or not, they are hands down the most vicious and vindictive system to take on," John warned.

"I believe it," Zeke mumbled.

"Yeah, so we've heard. I'm using a service which diverts calls and mail through a dummy box, so my location and direct info won't be out there," Aidan assured.

"Smart." John stepped over to shake Aidan's hand. "There are a lot of ways to be a soldier, like Chris. You and your friends are heroes. Never doubt that. In a country of apathy, hate, and delusion, you're an arrow through the bullshit. I'm proud to have worked with you. Anytime you need me, you have my number."

"Thanks, John. For everything. You're one of the good ones," Aidan said.

John took a small bow, grinning, and walked to his car. He raised his hand in a wave as he left.

Zeke opened the box of Chris's things and began pulling them out. There was a canteen, camp stove, metal cup, and bowl. Wrapped in a blanket was a tattered copy of Aldous Huxley's *Brave New World,* and letters from his high school sweetheart, who broke up with him when he enlisted. At the bottom of the box was a stack of clothes Zeke had given him, rolled up in some socks was Zeke's old phone, now shattered, and a pack of cigarettes. There was a small wooden box containing his military awards and his dog tags, along with a picture of his parents. Last was a journal. When

Zeke opened it and started reading, he burst into tears, then handed it to Aidan.

There was handwritten poetry and profound thoughts. Pages about when he met all of them, and how they'd become friends. How much they meant to him. How he missed them when they left. Notes on botany and insects. Parks all over the country he planned to camp at. Drawings, really good drawings. Portraits of people from the camp, and of Aidan, TJ, and Zeke. One absolutely stunning one of Mia, capturing both her timeless beauty and impish personality. They were better than ones Aidan had ever seen, using just a ballpoint pen and unlined journal paper. Chris could've gone to school for art, but he went into the army to fight for a country that saw no value in his breath. He'd sacrificed everything. On the last page, Aidan held his breath when he read what Chris had written.

"All is not lost in the company of friends."

Aidan wiped away the tear rolling down his cheek. This hurt. Chris had waited for them to come back and when they did, he fought beside them until his dying breath. War is a concept sold to the public as on foreign lands, against unfamiliar people. War can happen anywhere, against people you live amongst. Chris was killed by someone he may have sat next to on the bus. Someone who he might have shared the paper with, on the bench seat between them, and talked about the weather. Someone who looked like him, but whose beliefs were so radically different, they saw no problem murdering a fellow citizen in the name of whatever leader they were following. A silent war with the smiling face of deception.

Aidan shut the journal and stared at Zeke.

"I know," was all Zeke said.

Later, when they drove down to meet TJ and Mia for dinner, they passed by the encampment. Other than the National Guard at their posts, it appeared like nothing had happened. The streets had been cleaned and barriers removed. The encampment was surrounded by temporary fencing and there were a plethora of assistance groups on-site, working with the residents. Children from the encampment were playing on a closed-off street, with toys that had miraculously appeared.

They arrived at the restaurant before TJ and Mia, finding an outside table since they had Lucky with them. Aidan sat with his back to the wall and watched as people walked by. It was as if it all had been a dream. A nightmare. No one seemed affected. He heard another table of patrons talking about Chris, and how they wouldn't have done what he did. They would've let people get run over. Aidan shook his head. Fucking people. Zeke held his hand under the table and met his eyes. The world was a different place for them.

Mia came up behind them and put her arms over both of them, kissing them each on the cheek. "My guys."

TJ came around and sat across from them. "Hey, you hear what's going on with the police and the encampment?"

"John came by today and filled us in. Crazy, right?" Aidan replied.

"Yeah, I'm working with a group that builds tiny houses for the homeless. They already have an area in another part of the city, but they'd like the chance to come in and do some work here. We're looking into funding for materials. We have an influx of volunteers wanting to help. Sad that it took this, but still."

Aidan smiled. "I may be able to help you with that."

TJ cocked his head. "What do you mean?"

"I'm getting a settlement for my injuries. I'm paying my parents back, paying Sam and Smitty for the trailer, investing in film equipment and studio space in North Carolina, but I want to do something in Chris's name. I can donate a chunk for the tiny homes. How much do they cost?"

"About two thousand, or so, for raw materials per home. Since the land is already designated by the city, we'd just build where the tents are."

"So, if I donated fifty thousand, that would build what, like, twenty-five homes? Do you think if I did that, they could name it after Chris?"

TJ smiled. "I think they'd be fine with that. They've already talked about doing something in his memory there. I think they'd totally sign off on the Chris Huber Village. Aidan, I can't express how much this would mean. This would allow us to do it before winter."

The waiter came and they paused their conversation to order their food. After the waiter left, Zeke slid two frames upside down to Mia and TJ. They turned them, staring in silence at the pictures. They were the drawings of them Chris had done.

"Thought you might want these. Chris drew them," Zeke explained.

"He did? These are insane," Mia whispered.

"He caught you perfectly, "TJ murmured, peering at Mia's portrait.

"You too. Look, in your picture, you're gazing off lost in thought. Probably trying to figure out how to save the world," Mia teased.

"Aren't we all?" TJ asked honestly.

The waiter brought their drinks and set them down. Once the waiter departed, Aidan raised his glass, fighting back tears as he spoke.

"To our brother, Chris."

"To Chris!" They replied in unison, clinking their glasses together.

Chapter Thirty

On their last day together, the four friends headed to the skate park where most of their lives had intertwined. Their first commonality as a group. Aidan didn't film, wanting to capture the memories in his mind. They took over a bowl near the far end and skated until they were drenched in sweat, laughing so hard they could hardly stay balanced. It was a perfect picture of their life before. No worries, no responsibilities to the outside world. Just four friends, doing what they loved most.

Aidan paused at the lip of the bowl to watch the other three move fluidly past each other, aware of each other's existence but moving to their own inner voices. No camera could capture that moment for what it truly was. He dropped in and sped past TJ coming the other way. As they passed, they touched hands and grinned. TJ had been his first real friend. Mia, the one who made him accountable. Then Zeke, the one who helped him face the truth about who he was. How could he let any of them go?

One by one, they hopped out of the bowl and came to sit down next to each other. Aidan couldn't fight the sadness, knowing even though they'd be friends for life, it'd be in different realities. TJ and Mia were getting married and starting jobs. Aidan was forming his film company with Zeke and wouldn't have a permanent residence. At least, not for some time. The country had too much they needed to uncover, too many dark secrets. They'd have to stay on the move. He glanced at Zeke, smiling to himself. He had Zeke. The most beautiful soul on earth chose to do this with him. Zeke caught his eye and grinned. It would be okay.

They ordered lunch to go, then it was time to go their separate ways. Aidan stood up off the wall where they'd eaten their food and threw away his trash.

"Zeke and I need to head out to get ready for dinner with my parents."

"Zeke, have you met them before?" Mia asked.

"Nope, first time," Zeke replied, not hiding his nerves.

"They will love you!" Mia exclaimed.

Aidan knew better. They were unhappy when they thought he was straight and living with her. It was almost scandalous. Being gay, and living with Zeke was probably blowing their minds. But it had to be done. He loved Zeke and wanted to spend his life with him. It was non-negotiable, so if they wanted Aidan in their lives, Zeke was part of the deal.

"TJ knows my parents. They're old school. This will be less a coming together and more of a meet and greet, so they know who I'm in love with."

TJ nodded. "Good luck, man. Your parents are a tough sell. Nice, but set a high bar."

Zeke seemed even more nervous. "Not helping."

Aidan kissed him and met his eyes. "It doesn't matter what they think. I'm doing this more for me, than them. You're part of my truth and if they don't like it, that's on them. *I* love you."

Zeke nodded, not completely convinced but smiled at Aidan. "I never get tired of hearing it."

They unhooked Lucky's leash as he stretched and yawned from the shade he was sleeping in. The four friends knew it was time. They'd see each other again, but now it was time to begin their new journeys. They all embraced, taking countless pictures together. Aidan paused with TJ.

"Come back to North Carolina sometime. I want to surf with you again out there. The Outer Banks are insane."

TJ put his arm over Aidan's shoulder and nodded. "You know it. I need to see my mom, anyway. Mia and I are talking about getting married in California, then honeymooning in North Carolina in the spring. I'll let you know."

"You better. We wouldn't miss your wedding."

Once the goodbyes had fallen to silence, they all smiled sadly and waved as they headed their own directions. Mia and TJ had secured a place to live in Seattle to finish school and work. Zeke and Aidan headed back to the campground to get ready for dinner with his parents. They were leaving straight from his parents home to get on the road back east, so decided a nap might be in order first.

Aidan climbed in closest to the wall with his arm behind his head. Zeke lay next to him, placing his head on Aidan's chest, yawning. Aidan ran his fingers through Zeke's hair and sighed contently. It was just dinner. They'd be on the road by nightfall, then alone again. Zeke slid his hand up under Aidan's shirt, resting it on his stomach and dozed off. Aidan breathed in the moment and closed his eyes. Sleep came easily.

When Aidan woke up, Zeke was already up, dressed, and pacing off nervous energy. The campground area had been packed and cleaned. Zeke had even hooked the trailer to the Jeep and was biting his nails. Lucky was sitting, watching Zeke pace back and forth across the small kitchen area. Aidan sat up and rubbed his head, shaking off the last bits of sleep.

"Hey, come here," he said gently to Zeke.

Zeke came and sat down. "I'm seriously fucking scared about tonight. Parents aren't something I've had to deal with in a long time. And last time, it didn't go well."

Last time he'd been beaten near to death and lost the only family he'd ever known. Aidan wanted to make it better but didn't know how. He slid over and put his legs on either of Zeke. He rested his head against Zeke's back, wrapping his arms around Zeke's chest.

"I'm sorry. They aren't mean, just really set in their ways. They may be awkward, but they'll be polite. I can almost promise they won't throw rocks at you in the driveway."

Zeke shook with laughter and put his hand on Aidan's arm. "Well, that's something right?"

Aidan squeezed him hard. "Rite of passage is all. Get everything out in the open, then head out into the night, okay?"

Zeke sighed. "For you? Anything."

Aidan's parents' house was about forty minutes away, just outside of Tacoma. They pulled the Jeep and trailer into a side driveway and snagged the flowers they'd brought. They put Lucky in the RV to sleep and turned to face the house. Aidan felt his palms get sweaty when they walked up to the front door. He took a deep breath as he knocked. Zeke was pale and didn't know where to direct his eyes. Aidan held his hand tightly as the door opened. *Just a rite of passage,* he thought, as his parents smiled weirdly from him to Zeke, then down to their clasped hands.

"Aidan! Your hair is so long," his mother said, touching his hair. "More like Casey's."

His dad reached out to shake Zeke's hand. "Welcome. You must be Zeke. Aidan has told us about you. Come in."

They headed in and much to Aidan's relief, they'd already set the table and were putting food on it. No awkward small talk around the kitchen. Zeke stood unsure what to do by the table, so Aidan took his hand to show him pictures on the wall, while his parents finished getting the food out. The pictures were mostly of Aidan and Casey. Zeke smiled at a picture of little Aidan, grinning up with ice cream around his mouth. There was one of Casey holding Aidan, where Aidan was staring at Casey with such admiration and love, it was almost painful. Zeke touched the photo and smiled at Aidan.

"You have such a big heart. Look at how you're staring at Casey."

Aidan peered at the photo and smiled, even though it broke his heart. He didn't think Casey ever truly knew how much he held the world for Aidan. Casey didn't know his own value. Aidan turned, watching Zeke.

"I look at you that way, now," he said honestly.

Zeke touched his face and nodded. "I know."

His parents let them know dinner was served, so they headed towards the table. Zeke paused, staring back at the wall.

"Do you think they'd let us have copies of those?"

Aidan nodded. His mother had a box of duplicates he could rummage through. She'd been keeping them for him, for when he started a family. That was now. They sat down across from his parents, Zeke pressing his fingers into Aidan's leg to calm his nerves. Aidan shifted his leg and rested it against Zeke's. The warmth between them calmed them both. Aidan's mother made small talk while they ate, avoiding any heavy topics but kept eyeing Zeke. Aidan could see her brain was trying to understand how her son could love another man.

"Mom, let's just talk about it," Aidan said firmly. "I love Zeke. He makes me happy. I'm gay. I'm never not going to be gay. Zeke didn't make me gay. I just had to be honest with myself. I want to spend my life with Zeke. He's the love of my life. Does that about cover it?"

"Aidan," his father said sharply. "That is not how you speak to your mother."

"No, he's right," his mother replied, her voice gentle. "I was being rude. I don't mean to stare. I just, just..." she trailed off struggling to find the right words. "I want you to be happy, Aidan. You're my only child left, I want to see you thrive and follow your dreams. I wasn't raised this way. With this mindset. My family was very traditional. I like you, Zeke. You seem kind and caring. You remind me of my Casey in a way. Soulful. I can't say I understand, and I admit it makes me uncomfortable, but it's not my place to say who anyone should love. I love you, Aidan, that's all that matters."

Aidan felt Zeke's fingers wind around his own and relaxed. He'd been ready for a fight, to defend Zeke, but wouldn't need to.

"This is new to us, but we recognize the world has changed. You are welcome here, Zeke. If Aidan chooses to spend his time with you, we will open our doors," Aidan's father added.

It wasn't a gushy, beautiful moment and was stilted, but more than Aidan thought they'd offer. They went back to eating in silence. After dinner, they cleared the plates and moved to the living room for coffee. Zeke wandered around, looking at the pictures. Aidan came up behind him, wrapping his arms around Zeke tightly. He saw his mother flinch and his father glance down quickly, embarrassed. This wouldn't come easy. He turned around to face them.

"Hey, Mom, can I go through that bin of old photos? We'd like to take some to put in our home," Aidan said, not allowing a diversion. He put his hand on Zeke's waist. It was something they'd have to get used to.

His mother nodded and opened a cabinet by the fireplace. She pulled out a plastic tote filled with pictures, all organized by date. Aidan led Zeke over and they sat down to go through them. Seeing pictures of Aidan growing up brought Zeke out of his shell, and soon he was laughing hysterically. Aidan's parents filled in backstories on some of the photos. By the end of the evening, they'd bridged a small gap, having shared intimate family history. Zeke had a stack of photos in his lap, holding them like a prized possession.

It was getting late and they wanted to get on the road to make as much time as possible. Aidan kissed his parents goodbye, thanking them for the dinner and photos. They each shook Zeke's hand and smiled. They offered the side driveway for when Aidan and Zeke were back in the area, and Aidan assured them he'd take them up on it. Before he left, he handed his father a check for part of the hospital expenses. It wasn't much, however, Aidan needed to show he intended to pay them back. His father tried to refuse but Aidan shook his head.

"Dad, I need to. It's part of growing up and being a man. I'll get the rest to you once the settlement comes through. You don't have to take care of me anymore."

"We always will, Aidan."

Aidan nodded, grateful for his parents. Although the world was changing too fast around them, they were at least making an effort. He hugged his dad tightly and headed out. Zeke was down by the RV and had let Lucky out to use the bathroom. Aidan walked up to them, winding his arms tightly around Zeke.

"Rite of passage."

Zeke laughed. "Hey, and I got pictures of little Aidan to cherish."

Aidan watched him and wondered what Zeke had looked like as a kid. Obviously blond. It made him sad that part of Zeke had pretty much been erased.

"I wish I could've seen you as a child," he considered out loud.

Zeke stared off lost in thought. "Well, when I was little, before I became discarded, my parents had pictures of me. Then there were also school photos. I mean, I don't know if those were all destroyed or not."

Aidan drew up the memory of that tiny plain house they'd parked outside of. He couldn't imagine pictures of Zeke being displayed in there. "They did?"

Zeke nodded and shrugged. "As long as you abide, they do some things like other families. Pictures, holidays. As long as it doesn't go against the church. So, no Halloween, no secular music, no tv, no world outside of the church. But other than that, they like to pretend they're normal. To some extent. Like, I didn't know other kids outside of the church weren't beaten for every infraction until I was out on my own. I thought everyone did that."

Aidan's parents had never so much as raised a hand to him. Zeke's world was so encapsulated, he grew up thinking the whole world was the same, and he was the only one who was different. How isolating that must have been.

"School pictures? They let you go to school?"

Zeke laughed. "Well, sort of. There was a church-run school. All approved textbooks, only what they wanted us to know. The first time I stepped into a library after I left, my mind was overwhelmed. I know it sounds ridiculous, but I didn't know the difference between nonfiction and fiction. It all seemed like make-believe. I haven't stopped reading since."

Aidan was floored, Zeke had pretty much been raised in another country. In an alternate reality. He thought of the book they found in Chris's belongings, *Brave New World*. He'd read it for school but couldn't remember it completely. Something about a controlled utopia, and a man coming to it who had been raised as a "savage" as the citizens called him. He was actually called *The Savage* in the book, even though in a way he was the most civilized. How he came to this new world and couldn't comprehend it. Aidan was curious to read the book again, now that it had been of importance to Chris. Maybe it would mean more as an adult to him.

Aidan peered at Zeke with a whole new understanding. He didn't just lose his family. He'd been thrust into a completely different world he didn't understand, yet figured out his way against the odds. Aidan reached up, placing his hand on the side of Zeke's face.

"You're the most determined, true to yourself person. You know that?" Aidan whispered.

Zeke chuckled, the tips of his ears turning red, and shrugged. "I suppose."

"Still wish I could see you as a kid, though."

"You know, if we time the journey right, there just might be a way."

Chapter Thirty-One

They timed it right. They drove into Provo, Utah at just after eleven the next morning, which was a Sunday. Zeke eased the Jeep and trailer onto a side street. They went the rest of the way on foot, staying in the least visible areas as they moved. They didn't want to be seen or able to be identified. They rounded the corner and saw Zeke's childhood home, sitting in all of its dilapidated glory. Zeke froze, staring stone-faced. Aidan reached out and put his hand on Zeke's back.

"You sure about this? No one is home?"

Zeke nodded. "It's Sunday. Services started over an hour ago. They would never miss a church service. They go for a few hours, followed by a potluck. The family will only come home around three to freshen up and get back for the evening service. We're safe until then."

"How are we going to get in?"

"They leave the back door unlocked. Not like there is much to steal. Would you break into that shithole?" Zeke asked bitterly.

Aidan didn't know if he should laugh or not. It was funny, but Zeke was in a dark place. "I guess not."

Lucky licked Aidan's hand, trying to figure out why they'd stopped. Zeke was holding the leash, and Aidan went around both of them to go knock on the front door. No one knew him, and he needed to be sure. He knocked, thinking about what he'd say if someone answered. He began to panic, not being able to think of a cover story, but it didn't matter. As Zeke said, no one was home. He motioned to Zeke, who hadn't moved from the spot. Zeke's face twitched as he headed across the street.

They went around the back of the house. Zeke wiggled the gate latch just so, making it swing open. He shut it behind them and approached the back door. He turned the handle and pushed it open, having to shove past stacks of garbage that hadn't been taken out. Aidan held his breath as they went in, less from anxiety and more from the stale smell of garbage, and the home which hadn't been aired out for years. If ever. They passed through a small kitchen with dishes piled in the sink. Zeke paused, glancing around and shook his head. Aidan was aghast at the filth of the place. Zeke was such a neat freak, Aidan couldn't imagine him living in this home. Maybe that was why he was that way now, or maybe Zeke had been the only one to clean then.

They stepped over items left where they'd been dropped, into a living room which was dark and reeked of thousands of smoked cigarettes. There was a decades-old, small, green couch and two brown armchairs. On the wall were pictures of children, none of whom looked exactly like Zeke. Zeke paused and stared at them, dropping his shoulders.

"They took that away, too. I have a brother and four sisters I'll never speak to again."

Aidan peered at the photos. This one had Zeke's smile and that one had his eyes. His brother appeared like a chubbier version of Zeke, with light brown hair and thin lips. His sisters all had different shades of brown hair and blank stares. At the end was a photo of the parents from their wedding. Zeke looked like his mother. She was young and pretty, with pale blond hair and light eyes. His father had brown hair and the thin lips of his brother. Even in the wedding photo, he appeared to be an unhappy person.

Zeke kneeled and was digging through photo albums on the bottom shelf of the bookcase. He'd been removed from all of them. He brushed away tears and sat on the ground, gazing around. He'd been erased from existence. Aidan thought about his own parents and how his mother was when he came out to them. How could a mother just remove their child? A thought occurred to him.

"Maybe someone hid them? Or moved them?"

Zeke glanced up at him defeated, then shrugged. "I doubt it, but we can look."

They checked the living room without any luck and went to the bedrooms. There were three bedrooms; the parents', one for the boys, and one for the girls. They checked the boys' room first, though Zeke struggled mentally being in there. He kept stopping and staring off. Even though all the kids were grown, his parents hadn't bothered to change anything or clean it. He stopped at a small dresser and slid the top drawer out. He reached behind and pulled out a stack of papers, handing them to Aidan. They were teenage writings by Zeke. How he wanted to kill himself and was so ashamed he existed. The one that broke Aidan's heart was a letter Zeke wrote, asking for his family to just love him as he was. Aidan slipped them into his backpack.

Zeke didn't want to be in the room anymore and pushed past Aidan to get out. Aidan took one last glance around the cramped, dirty room, then followed him out. Zeke was against the wall bent over and grabbed Aidan tightly as he came out. Aidan rubbed his back, repeating over and over how much Zeke meant to him. Zeke nodded and they headed into the parents' room, which also reeked of cigarette smoke. There were pictures of Jesus all over the room, making Aidan feel like he was being judged. They dug through the dresser and under the bed, finding nothing. The closet yielded the same.

Lastly, they went to the girls' room, bigger than the boys but only slightly. It had two sets of bunk beds, a dresser, and a desk. A large cross hung on the wall, like in the boys' room, but this one had faded, dingy lace around it. Zeke searched in the dresser and closet, but they held nothing, except clothes the girls had left behind. Zeke leaned against the bunk bed, rubbing his head. He was the youngest child. His sister Abigail had been the next oldest. They'd been as close as they'd been allowed to be, but he knew her best. She'd been married off at eighteen and was already pregnant with her second by the time Zeke left. She'd confessed she didn't love her husband but wanted to make their mother and father happy. To do right by the church. Abigail had been a stasher like Zeke, hiding her secrets from the world.

Zeke went over to the desk and yanked out the drawers. Below the bottom drawer was a space between the wooden base of the drawer and the floor. Zeke reached in and drew out a dusty box.

He brushed it off, removing the lid. Inside were all of his pictures. A letter was folded on top and he opened it. It was in Abigail's handwriting.

I told Daddy I destroyed these. I hid them here in case Ezekial comes back. I want him to come home. I miss him. The church says he is filthy and not worthy of forgiveness. I can't believe that. Ezekial is so loving and kind. I wish he would just marry Rebecca and come home. For things to go back to how they were. For us to be a family again.

The letter wasn't to anyone but herself. Zeke took the letter and put it back in the box. He stood up, meeting Aidan's eyes.

"I guess that's it. My sister Abigail hid them. She was the only one I could ever talk to."

"Do you think you could again?"

Zeke shook his head. "That was a long time ago. She's ingrained in the church. All is lost."

Aidan thought about what Chris had written in his journal. "All is not lost in the company of friends," he whispered.

Zeke eyed him, his pale eyes tired and sad. He cocked his head slightly. "There is that."

They went back to the living room where Zeke paused at the mantle. He picked up a pipe, turning it over his hand. "This was my grandfather's, my mother's father. He was nice at the end of his life. He'd sit smoking this pipe and tell me stories. He didn't like my father, but it was the church's wish for my parents to marry. When my grandfather died, my mother gave this to my father. I hated seeing him smoke it. He did it with such an air of condescension. Like he'd won over my grandfather."

Zeke slipped the pipe in his pocket, then grinned darkly at the act.

"Because it was your grandfather's?" Aidan asked.

Zeke nodded. "Well, yeah. That and because it will make my father insane to not be able to find it. Fuck him."

They headed back out, Zeke taking one last look around, sighing. "I was right to leave. This is a fucking prison."

They cut back through the backyard, letting Lucky pee on a folding chair with a can of cigarette butts next to it. They crossed the street and glanced back. Zeke had the box of pictures clutched close to him, turning away. His family wouldn't even know the son they'd shunned had been there, and he was fine with it. They weren't his family anymore.

Aidan took the next round of driving, while Zeke crashed out in the passenger seat with Lucky tucked under his arm. It was the sleep of mental exhaustion. Aidan knew it well. He peered over at Zeke in the seat with his head back, resting against the glass. He was breathing softly, his blond eyelashes catching the light. He seemed so innocent and untouched. Aidan held his breath. It was like the paintings of angels he'd seen in museums growing up. Powerful, yet gentle and pure. That was Zeke. They couldn't take that away from him.

After a few hours, Zeke woke up and offered to drive so Aidan could sleep. Aidan let him drive but had too much on his mind to sleep right off the bat. He went to the trailer and pulled out *Brave New World* from Chris's box, along with Chris's dog tags, bringing them to the Jeep. He reached over and put the dog tags over Zeke's neck. He'd been to war, too. Zeke smiled and touched them, tucking them under his shirt.

Once they were driving, Aidan opened the book to read and Zeke glanced over.

"That's Chris's book?"

"Yeah. Have you heard of it?"

Zeke laughed. "What do you think? Probably not church approved if Chris had it. Do you mind reading aloud?"

Aidan shrugged. "Sure, I can be your own personal book on tape. You want me to do the voices, too?"

Zeke shoved him, grinning. "Smartass."

Aidan opened the book and began to read. When he got to the passage where the Director is explaining the happiness of the utopian society they have created, by eliminating personal choice, Aidan paused and read it again.

"...that is the secret of happiness and virtue - liking what you've got to do. All conditioning aims at that: making people like their unescapable social destiny."

"Jesus," Zeke whispered from the driver's seat. "That sucks."

Aidan thought about their modern world. Aldous Huxley had written those words in 1932. He'd no idea what the world would become then. He wrote it before World War II. He wrote it before consumerism was on the books. How it was so pertinent to the current state of the country, boggled Aidan's mind. He continued reading until he could barely keep his eyes open and set the book down. He glanced at Zeke, who stared back, shaking his head.

"That is some crazy shit. Get some sleep, we can switch off when you wake up. I'll even read to you."

Aidan yawned, leaning back into the seat. The radio was playing old Johnny Cash and Zeke started singing softly along with it. He usually only did that when he thought he was alone, or Aidan was asleep. Aidan smiled to himself and nudged Zeke with his foot.

"You know, I like to hear you sing."

Zeke blushed and smiled bashfully. He went back to singing low, but with a little more confidence. He put his hand on Aidan's leg, rubbing it for a moment before putting his hand back on the wheel.

Aidan closed his eyes, allowing his thoughts to form into plans and ideas. Concrete concepts. Things he could put parameters around and timelines to. It made what they had to do seem within their grasp. Lucky curled up next to him, and as he dozed off he heard Zeke whisper to himself, deep in thought.

"Happiness is breaking free from the bonds which seek to control you, finding others like you out there. Happiness is truth."

Chapter Thirty-Two

Lucky went back and forth between Aidan and Zeke, sniffing their faces to convince at least one of them to wake up and put him out. Zeke climbed out of bed, opening the door in nothing but his boxer shorts. He stared out at the New Mexico landscape. They'd detoured after reading the book, and its mention of the New Mexico area where *The Savage* was discovered. Aidan stared at Zeke standing in the doorway, struck by his utter beauty. Zeke put his arms up on the door frame, leaning forward. Aidan slipped out of bed and came beside him, sliding his arm around Zeke's waist. Zeke grasped his arm and turned, bringing them face to face.

"This place is amazing. The desert is unreal," he murmured, putting his arms around Aidan.

It was. Neither of them had seen anything like it. New Mexico looked like a life-size painting of a beautiful planet. Lucky came running back in, jumping on their legs. Zeke let go of Aidan and filled Lucky's bowls. Aidan stared out at the mesas. They'd pulled off in the night and parked in a national park, not getting a chance to see the land around them. The sun rising over the formations was truly breathtaking. It was worth the detour. Aidan felt a tug on his arm and glanced over. Zeke was watching him and motioned to their bed.

"Come back to bed. I want you."

Aidan closed the door and climbed back into bed with Zeke. He slipped his hands down Zeke's chest and under the covers. Zeke put his hands on either side of Aidan's face, kissing him deeply without restraint. They took each other openly, as the sunlight poured over their naked bodies. As Aidan felt himself release, he thought about how he could just stay in New Mexico, making love to Zeke for the rest of his life.

Later, as they sipped coffee at their fold-out table and enjoyed the views, Aidan chuckled to himself. It wasn't New Mexico he wanted to stay in. It was Zeke. He'd live in a junkyard if Zeke was there. Zeke saw him laughing and cocked his head.

"What?"

"Oh, when we were making love, I thought about how I wanted to stay here with you forever. But what I truly want, is to be with *you* forever. It doesn't matter where. I want to see everything with you. The desert, the mountains, the oceans, the friggin' parking lots. I know you've been with other people, so maybe that sounds silly since you're my first."

Zeke shook his head. "I've never been with anyone like I've been with you. This isn't a sexual act, Aidan. It's love. It's family. It's knowing that the person I'm with, would go to the ends of the earth for me. And I for him. No one gets to trivialize what we have. Not even us. This is truth."

Aidan stared at Zeke, trying to put into words what he was feeling. "Zeke, I think this is it for me. I know I'm a couple of years younger than you, but you're the only one I'll ever want."

"So, not just your first. Your only?"

Aidan nodded. "I've found what is perfect for me. You give me everything I want; mentally, physically, emotionally. I've tested this relationship for sure, and you helped me when I was broken. You brought me back. How could I ever ask for more?"

Zeke was quiet for some time which made Aidan nervous. What if Zeke didn't feel the permanence Aidan did? Zeke got up to go inside and came back out with his box of pictures.

"Okay, I've seen your pictures and met your family, so now you need to meet mine." He poured his pictures on the table and sorted through them. He handed Aidan a picture of a bald baby, staring up at something out of view and pointing.

"This was me as a baby. I was curious and loved my sister Abigail more than my mother. After five other kids, I was an afterthought. A product of the church's stance on not using birth control. I wasn't wanted, nor could they afford me. Abigail was my primary caregiver, and she's only a couple of years older than me. I cried a lot but was left to cry because no one had the time for me."

He dug through and handed Aidan a picture of a filthy three or four-year-old, standing next to two equally dirty older children. "This was me at four, I guess, with Abigail and Sarah. My sisters. We're dirty because we were only allowed to bathe every other Sunday. I spent a lot of my childhood with lice."

A picture of what appeared to be his parents, his father scowling in the background. "Me at eight. The beatings were really bad then because I asked too many questions. My father told me regularly how I was a mistake, how he wished I was never born. My mother chain-smoked cigarettes and ignored us mostly. She talked to herself a lot. I remember being hungry all of the time."

Twelve or thirteen, a school photo of a thin, blond boy with a black eye, trying to smile for the camera. "My father punched me because I took a shower two minutes too long. I wasn't supposed to get my picture taken, but the teacher made me. I don't know why. My father kept the picture to threaten me with. To show me he wasn't scared of what people thought and would keep me in line."

Another school photo of a boy about sixteen. Somewhat defiantly meeting the camera dead-on, smiling almost wickedly. "I received a beating so bad after they saw this picture, I missed weeks of school."

"Why did they keep it then? If they hated it so much?" Aidan asked.

"They didn't. Abigail must have taken it out of the trash."

The last photo was of Zeke at about eighteen, with a plain girl about the same age. They were standing next to each other, at the front of the church.

"Two days before I left. That's Rebecca. We had to stand in front of the church to announce our intentions. We didn't get to say anything. They just made us go up there, and our parents announced our engagement. I was terrified."

Aidan peered at the picture. Zeke was smiling, but his eyes told a different story. Rebecca's eyes were dead, resigned. The next day or so, Zeke came out to his parents and his father beat him with the intent to kill. What if he *had* killed Zeke? Would he have even been sent to jail? Zeke read his face and his mind.

"Kids disappear, Aidan. We were truly never in the system. Born at home, educated by the church, not allowed out. When I left and tried to get a job, there was no info on me. In the eyes of the country, I didn't exist. Was never taken to a hospital. Broken bones healed at home. I was invisible."

Aidan had never heard of anything like that. How was it possible in a country that made it a point to track their every movement? "So, what did you do?"

"Eventually, I had to petition the court. Through that, I guess they went to the church and my parents, securing enough documentation to prove I existed. I don't really know. I worked with a social service group who helped."

"If they'd killed you, no one would've ever known?"

"Nope. Even if my body had been found, I would've gone unidentified and likely disposed of as a John Doe. I was nobody's child."

Nobody's child. Aidan stared at the photos. "I don't get it. Why did they even take these photos of you?"

"They didn't for the most part. My grandfather did, the school and church did."

"What the actual fuck?" Aidan yelled, his brain flashing with confusion and rage.

Zeke shrugged. "Now, you understand."

"No, I don't. I mean, I hear you, but I'll never understand. I want to drive back there and kill them!"

Zeke nodded. "Yeah, I know the feeling. I lived that way for years. But then I met you and knew what love was. Now, I want to expose them, but put it personally behind me. I want you, Aidan. I want to wake up next to you for the rest of my life. Nothing else matters."

Aidan stared at the pictures of Zeke at all ages. "Why didn't your grandfather stop it?"

"He loved me, but he also loved the church. I guess he loved the church more."

"Zeke, I'm so sorry. I don't even know what to say anymore. I want to hurt the people who hurt you, and I refuse to call them your family anymore. They don't deserve the honor of being that. I want to be your family. Officially," Aidan insisted.

"What does that mean?"

"It means, well...fuck." Aidan was getting tangled in his words. "I want to call you my husband. I want us to spend the rest of our lives together. I know we've only been together for some odd months, but that's how I feel."

"So, we missed going to the movies and eating at shitty restaurants," Zeke laughed, his voice soft and gentle. "Whatever. I think we've already done the sickness and health, I met your parents. We've fought off attackers, taken on the police, traveled cross country twice, and shared all of our miserable secrets. Hell, we even got a dog together."

Aidan chuckled. As if on queue, Lucky came over and wagged his tail. "What are you saying, Zeke?"

"If you're game, so am I."

"You will marry me?"

"I think you have the words turned around," Zeke teased.

Aidan squinted his eyes at Zeke and shook his head. He took Zeke's hand. "Zeke, will you marry me?"

Zeke leaned in to kiss him. "I already did a long time ago, but let's make it official."

Aidan texted TJ and Mia to let them know. Mia sent back hearts and TJ replied, "I saw it coming. Congrats, man."

Aidan texted Sam and Smitty, really wanting their approval. More so than his parents, who he'd wait to tell.

Their reply was, "You better have the ceremony here."

He showed the message to Zeke. Zeke took the phone and texted back, "Wouldn't have it any other way."

It was out there. Aidan couldn't contain the excitement he felt and wanted to shout it from the tops of the mesas. Instead, they packed up and got back on the road. The sooner they made it to North Carolina, the sooner they could start planning their future. Aidan drove the next leg and Zeke read from *Brave New World*. They switched off, pushing through, either sleeping as the other one drove or read out loud. By the time they hit the North Carolina border at the mountains, they came to the last page. As Aidan read the last words and shut the book, a silence fell between them. After a few minutes, Zeke spoke.

"I was hoping it would end differently. That he'd somehow change things."

Aidan knew what Zeke meant. The world would consume them if they let it. If they didn't fight back. The problem was the majority seemed to be happy with the lies. It allowed them to float through and not think about others, the earth, or how the choices they made were destroying everything.

"Chris was *The Savage*," Aidan murmured, thinking about how the book ended.

"Maybe. But *The Savage* was alone and that's where he had no power. We have each other, Chris had us," Zeke replied.

That was true. They had those around them who supported them, who wanted the same things for the world. Truth, fairness, justice. Aidan stared out the window, watching the world fly by. It was easier to stay quiet and go with the flow, ignoring suffering. He couldn't do it. He was destined to seek out the truth, to make the world see it. Even if it hurt him and cost him his own chance at mindless serenity. Denial was apathy, and apathy was a tool against the greater good. If *The Savage* had friends who believed with him, it would've ended differently. *All is not lost in the company of friends.*

As they crossed through North Carolina the long way, Aidan pieced it all together. Being a child, chasing Casey as Smitty and Casey rode away. Watching Casey's body being lowered into the ground, which led his family to move out west. Going to film school and meeting Mia, who'd sought Aidan out, creating a deep, lifelong friendship. TJ following him, then falling in love with Mia. Meeting Zeke and finding out who he truly was, who they both were. Enrique Garza being murdered as Aidan filmed helplessly. Sam and Smitty coming back into his life to protect him. The protests, and working with John to show the world what was going on. Coming out to his parents. To this moment, it was all about telling the truth. It was a chain that connected each of them indefinitely. From his first breath, it had begun and would grow until he took his last. It was up to him to honor each link.

"I was thinking, Zeke."

"Yeah?"

"I don't have a name for the film company yet, but like you said if *The Savage* hadn't been alone, he would've had power. I want to take that into the film company and change the ending. All is not lost in the company of friends, right? I want to call the company *The Savage Film Company*, using Chris's words as a motto. What do you think?"

"What do I think? I think that's fucking brilliant. Chris would be so proud of you."

Aidan smiled from the heart. Zeke reached out and took his hand. "You know, Aidan, you never allow yourself to see the courage you live with. From the beginning, you knew in your mind what you had to do and did it. You're so driven, but not out of ego or self-serving. Out of wanting it better for everyone else. That is an endless and exhausting task. Remember to take care of yourself, too."

Aidan grinned and winked at Zeke. "That's what I have you for."

"Indeed you do," Zeke replied, laughing.

When they hit the Outer Banks, Aidan was nearly bursting at the seams, ready to get everything rolling. Ideas that had been scattered were now formed, waiting to be implemented. This was the place which called to him. The beginning.

Home.

Chapter Thirty-Three

Zeke and Sam were bent over, sanding a long surfboard, when Aidan came in. He watched from the door, the two blond heads moving not in unison, but in a dance around each other. It'd been a couple of months since they'd come back to the Outer Banks, and Zeke had jumped right back in, helping Sam out in the shop. They now had two of his prototype skateboards for sale along with the surfboards, and they could hardly keep up with the demand. Aidan had been purchasing equipment and completed the filings for the film studio. Now, he just needed a home base to start the daunting task of editing his first official film. The RV was getting cramped for big jobs. Sam glanced up and saw him in the door. She pulled off her goggles.

"Hey, I'm glad you're here! I have something to show you!"

Zeke stopped what he was doing and looked up. He followed Sam around the board as she grabbed keys out of her bag. She motioned to Aidan to follow her, cutting down a narrow hall off the backroom. She fumbled through the keys, separating one to open a door in the hallway.

"These old buildings. They're like mazes once you start exploring. Jim and Marie own this building and when I mentioned you were searching for a space, they told me about this." She pushed open the door to a large room, probably four times the size of the shop. "It was an old manufacturing shop. The whole thing, the surf shop included. They just used this for storage, so they could keep utilities down."

Aidan walked in and peered around. It was spacious with a row of high windows, not visible in from the outside. There was a small room off to the side, which appeared like maybe it'd been a supervisor's office. The space was big enough to store all of his equipment, and the only access being through the surf shop would give added protection. No one would know he was back there unless he let them.

"What are they wanting for it?"

"They said if you cover the utilities they can give you a long term lease at three hundred a month?"

That was less than half the price of any other place he'd viewed and twice the size.

"Shared kitchen and bathroom with the surf shop. Back door down the hallway leads to the alleyway, where you can pull in to load and unload equipment," Sam explained.

"And you get to work near me," Zeke teased.

"That's the best part. Yeah, I'd love to take the space. When?"

Sam walked over and handed him the key. "I figured you'd say yes, so here's the key. It's all yours. I have the lease out front."

Sam left to get the lease, while Aidan walked around the space. It required a good cleaning, and there were a few things still stored there, but in his mind he could picture it. It allowed for growth and meeting space if it ever got to that. It would free up Sam and Smitty's garage, which was now acting as storage for his equipment. He could use some of the space for private screenings as well. It was perfect.

Sam came back with the lease and Aidan read over it. The lease was standard. Jim and Marie had owned the surf shop building for forty years. Sam ran the shop for them as the main surfboard artisan, and Zeke showed great promise as her protégé. They had plans to expand in the skateboarding department, due to his skill and ease of shipping the skateboards. Jim and Marie didn't need the money and wanted to support Aidan's endeavor.

Aidan signed the lease and paid for a year upfront. He was being careful with the money from the settlement but required money to start rolling in from film projects before he could stop living off of it. His phone rang and he peered at it. It was John, they hadn't spoken in almost a month.

"Hey, John."

"Aidan! Glad I caught you. A couple of things. First, Enrique Garza's family dropped the lawsuit."

"Wait, why?"

"Decided to move back to Mexico. They were getting harassed daily and couldn't take it anymore. Anna had her baby and decided it was safer in Mexico. They wanted to disappear and couldn't do that here with the lawsuit."

Aidan shook his head, ashamed of his country. "Shit. Okay. What else?"

"So, they won't defund the police. They *are* working on reforming the department though, for what that's worth. They said mental health calls will go to a different social service line, but since those calls aren't necessarily clear as mental health when they come in, not sure what good it will do. There is a push for mental health training for officers and psychological screening upon applying. Again, not sure what good it will do. Now, for the criminal charges against the officer, Blake Castor. I talked to the lawyers. You will be subpoenaed to testify about your presence there that night and what you filmed. This won't go to trial until next summer it looks like, but I thought you'd want to know."

"Thanks, John. I just signed a lease on studio space here, so I'm planning to start working as soon as possible. What do you know about my rights to use the footage I took both that night and at the protest? Is there any issue with me using it as I see fit?"

"No. I mean, you were on a public street in both cases and filming what was out in the public eye. As long as you don't alter the footage to look like something it wasn't, you're fine. People may try to claim defamation but there is no ground. I'll email you some cases to look over on the subject."

"I did film Chris's death from some guy's apartment."

"Did he ask you to leave his property?"

"No, he pretty much dragged me into his apartment when I was being chased, and showed me the view from the front window."

"Then you're fine."

"John, is anything going to change? Was this all for nothing?"

"Not at all, Aidan. It's two steps forward, one step back. We're still rewriting the script. It's slow, but it matters. The world saw what happened and demanded transparency. It's why we do this. I know you want to see change happen today, but unfortunately, there is too much bureaucracy and red tape for quick solutions. It's the consistent pounding on the door day after day, which will eventually sway things in the right direction. Just keep at it. If we can ensure that the officer pays for what he did to Enrique, it may make others think twice before drawing their guns. If we continue to let them know they're being watched and filmed, they may try other ways to do their job other than brute force. But don't give up. I promise you, what you're doing is making a difference."

Aidan sighed. "Thanks, John. I know you've been at this way longer than I have and have seen a lot."

"It ebbs and flows. Your generation is so much more in tune and outspoken. You're like the kids during the Vietnam war, who put their lives on the line to stand up against an unjust war on foreign soil. Except now, it's on your own soil."

"I appreciate the sentiment. Now, we have to be smarter. Use the technology and tools at our disposal."

"You're ridiculously bright, Aidan. I look forward to seeing what you do next. I'll send you that email and keep you updated on what happens next. Congrats on the new studio space. Now get to work." John chuckled as he hung up.

Aidan peered around the space. He needed to get to work. Zeke had headed back to work with Sam, leaving Aidan alone. He swept and mopped the space, moving any items left behind to the room by the back door. He made a makeshift desk out of saw horses and an old door. There were a couple of stools left behind he claimed and put by the table. Now he had a work table at least. He headed home and started loading equipment in the Jeep, making multiple trips until the garage was empty. On the last run, he picked up take out food to have with Zeke and Sam in the new space.

They joined him and sat on the floor of the studio to eat, as Aidan explained where everything was going to be.

"Over there will be the editing station and over here will be a screening place. Like a mini movie theatre. I'll set up a meeting area in that corner and equipment storage there."

Zeke nodded, picturing what Aidan was saying. "What about the office over there?"

"Honestly? I was thinking about putting a couch that folds out to a bed in there. I'm thinking I'll have some late nights here. You know how my brain is when I'm working through things."

"I do. You're a mad man." Zeke shook his head, laughing.

Aidan couldn't deny it. When he focused, he was all in. "Oh! TJ sent photos of the Chris Huber Village. They've built ten homes so far and put up a plaque for Chris." Aidan pulled out his phone, showing Sam and Zeke the tiny houses. TJ was grinning, holding up a hammer in one of the photos.

Sam sighed and touched the screen. "Man, I love TJ. He knows exactly who he is and where he needs to be. I miss him."

"They're coming in the spring for their honeymoon," Aidan replied.

Sam beamed, clapping her hands together. "We get to meet the infamous Mia?"

"You do. You'll love her. We all do," Zeke said.

They finished eating and cleaned up the space. Zeke was in such a good mood, Aidan didn't want to tell him the things John said and decided to save it for later. Once he was alone, he took out his laptop and started sorting through footage, pausing at the footage of Zeke outside the church in Utah. It was painful to watch, but he needed to get used to it to put together the documentary.

It had taken some digging, but he found an older woman, Betsy, who'd escaped the same church as Zeke after her husband found her in bed with another female parishioner. She'd been beaten and raped by the elders of the church. The other woman committed suicide a few days later, so Betsy took her child and ran. She was known as Martha by the church but changed their names and identities as soon as she was out. Now that her child was grown, she was ready to speak out. They'd only spoken on the phone, but she was willing to meet and be filmed.

Aidan switched to scan other footage. A segment from the protest caught his eye and he zoomed in. Tears sprang to his eyes as he watched in amazement. Zeke came to the door to see if he was ready to go. Aidan waved him over.

"Come see this, I never noticed it before."

Zeke grabbed a stool and sat down next to Aidan. Aidan went back on the footage to where Mia was climbing on the car at the protest. Aidan pointed to the lower right corner of the screen as she started to sing. Chris appeared from off-screen, walking towards her, his eyes locked in on her face. His own face in awe, his eyes big and shining, a smile touching the corners of his mouth. Chris paused and put his hand to his heart, mesmerized by her voice. For a moment, it was pure beauty before the police came in and knocked her down. The crowd consumed Chris into its depths after that. Zeke and Aidan watched it a few times, feeling close to their friend who gave everything that night. They knew very few people got to know the Chris they did.

Mia had given him the last gift of his life, without ever knowing it. Instead of only being surrounded by loud noises, tear gas, and hatred, Chris had an experience that profoundly touched his heart.

Less than fifteen minutes later, he was dead.

Chapter Thirty-Four

The wave crested over Aidan's head as he rode through the barrel. The taste of salt was embedded on his lips, and he pushed the wet hair out of his eyes. The water was cold but invigorating. Winter in North Carolina was chilly but rarely too cold. He eased himself down and rode into shore. As soon as his feet hit the sand, he shook his hair out and carried his board to the spread out blanket. He toweled off and reclined in the sun to dry, meditating with the shapes behind his eyelids. He felt wet lips press against his and peered up.

Zeke was grinning down at him, his wet hair making tiny drips onto Aidan's face. "Hey."

"Hey," Aidan replied, pulling Zeke down on top of him as they kissed.

"Ugh, gross," they heard a voice say. A woman walking by appeared truly disgusted at seeing them kiss. "Abomination."

Zeke rolled over onto one elbow and stared at her. "You know what, lady? Fuck you."

Aidan started to laugh uncontrollably, and the woman turned red as she hurried away. He drew Zeke back down to his mouth. An awareness that it might turn into more made him stop, as he bit his lip, glaring at Zeke.

"See what you do to me?" he sat up and covered his lap with a towel.

Zeke raised an eyebrow, reaching under the towel. "Yup."

Aidan pushed his hand away but held it in his own. "Damn, you get me going."

Zeke winked and kissed Aidan's fingers. "Well, you were the one lying there in all of your dark beauty."

"Dark beauty? Like because of my hair and skin? Or because of my personality?" Aidan teased.

"Both."

Sitting next to each other, Aidan could see the difference in their skin. His was a deep golden tan, Zeke's a light golden with white-blond hairs. Aidan's hair on his arms and legs were black like his head and eyebrows. When their eyes met, he was staring into Zeke's pale blue-grey eyes.

Zeke cocked his head, his eyes focused on Aidan's. "Your eyes are like pools of night. I could jump in and swim around, but I'd lose my mind."

Aidan blushed. It never got old, hearing Zeke tell him how beautiful he was. It also never got old, admiring Zeke's attributes. He shifted his eyes to the water, watching its unending beat against the earth.

"I heard from TJ. He and Mia are getting married at the end of April in California. Then about mid-May, they're coming out here for their honeymoon."

"Nice. Are we trying to go to their wedding?" Zeke asked.

"Not sure. We're invited, of course, and I'd like to. It's going to be huge with all of her family."

"Could be fun."

Aidan glanced over at Zeke. "You want to go?"

Zeke nodded. "Yeah. Also, I was thinking, since they'll be out here in May, anyway...you want to do the deed then?"

"Get married?"

"Yeah."

Aidan thought about it. It would make sense. They hadn't planned anything big, but they did want TJ and Mia to be there. He eyed Zeke and smiled. "Sure."

Zeke's eyes lit up and he grinned, staring out at the water. He took Aidan's hand in his, squeezing it. They picked May seventeenth, since it fell on a Saturday and TJ and Mia were in town that week. Zeke turned to Aidan.

"What about last names? Keep our own, or one of us takes the other's?"

It hadn't crossed Aidan's mind. He didn't want Zeke's last name, but only because it connected to the people who'd abused him. He didn't know how to say that without hurting Zeke in any way. Zeke cleared his throat.

"I don't want mine. I only use Zeke O. for board designs and stuff. Your last name starts with an O, so it wouldn't change anything if I took yours. If you're okay with it?"

"Of course, I am, Zeke," Aidan whispered. Zeke Osher. It caused butterflies in his stomach to even think about it. "I'd be fucking honored."

"Aidan and Zeke Osher," Zeke said out loud. "Sounds like a couple of badasses."

Aidan laughed. The lady from before was coming back down the beach, side-eying them and shaking her head as she tried to hustle past. Aidan called out to her.

"Hey, guess what? We're getting married. Legally. Zeke here is going to be my husband and take my name. Lovely isn't it?"

She turned a deep shade of purple and stomped off. Zeke was cracking up beside Aidan, rolling back on the sand. Aidan leaned over and kissed him full on the mouth. The world was changing, some people would just have to deal with it. He wasn't going to hide for their comfort. He slid his arms around his sandy, soon-to-be husband and lay with him, staring up at the sky.

They told Smitty and Sam at dinner that they'd set a date for when TJ and Mia were going to be there. Smitty smiled broadly, leaning back in his chair.

"That is fantastic. We'll have to throw down. Where?"

Aidan shrugged, they hadn't gotten that far. The beach seemed cheesy, even though they loved it. It had become the site for destination weddings, and they wanted more meaning than that. It was going to be a small event. Aidan would invite his parents, but he doubted they'd come. They'd accepted Zeke but still viewed him more as Aidan's live-in friend than anything. They were trying but still weren't comfortable with displays of affection. TJ and Mia would be there, Sam and Smitty, probably Jim and Marie, who had treated them like family. That was about it. No need for anything major.

"We can have it here in the back if you want?" Sam offered.

The backyard was long and beautiful with old-growth trees. Aidan looked at Zeke, who nodded. Simple, pretty, and private.

"Thanks. That actually would be very nice," Aidan answered.

Sam smiled slyly. Aidan could see the wheels were already turning in her mind. She leaned forward and whispered to Zeke, "I have some ideas. We can talk at work tomorrow."

"Hey, my wedding, too," Aidan said.

Sam grinned. "Okay, *we* will talk at work tomorrow. I'm always just face to face with Zeke over the boards. You know he won't do anything without you, anyway."

"True story, " Zeke replied.

Smitty asked Aidan to go for a walk with him after dinner. They headed down the road in silence and Smitty turned to Aidan, taking him by the shoulders.

"I'm acting as Casey and myself, right now. I've known you since you were just a small kid, playing in the front yard of my friend's house. Your little, dark eyes under those black eyebrows, watching the world. You were so serious and intimidating. I could see it then, but didn't know what it was. You were determined to know everything and expected the same from everyone. Casey once told me you were the smartest person he knew, and it scared him. He said you could read into people's souls, and he didn't want you to see what was in his. He didn't want to let you down."

Smitty stopped and pinched the top of his nose, doing his best to hold back tears. He cleared his throat and stared down at Aidan, meeting his eyes. "I loved Casey. I was too stupid to see we were going down a bad road. We were just kids and by the time we weren't, we were in too deep. I'm sorry we both let you down, Aidan. Casey because he was scared of what he saw inside himself, his vulnerability, and me because of my fucking ego, thinking I had everything under control. I was so far from shore and didn't even know it. Casey knew it but didn't know how to get back. This left you standing there, not being able to reach us, and for that, I'm truly, deeply ashamed for everything you lost. I know what Casey meant about you being able to read into souls. Every time you look at me, I feel exposed. But I gladly bear my soul to you, if it gives you back anything I took from you. Which was a lot."

Aidan stared up at Smitty, unblinking. Smitty *had* been a reason Aidan lost so much, but Aidan didn't blame him. Anymore. Casey and Smitty had been in the same place, and he couldn't expect Smitty to have been any more able to deal with the loneliness of his life than Casey was. They'd been in the same place because they'd been so alike. Aidan looked away before he spoke.

"You know when I was little and would run after Casey? It wasn't because I didn't want to be left behind. It was because each time, I was convinced he'd never come back. Like inside me, I knew. Each time, though, he came back. Until he didn't. I was mad at you, Smith, because it was easier than being mad at him for going away. For leaving me. For me not being enough to stick around for." Aidan didn't try to fight the tears which rolled down his cheeks. It was a hard truth of not feeling valued. Of not mattering.

"Fuck," Smitty whispered, gathering Aidan in his arms. "Is that how you have been feeling all these years? That's what you've been carrying? Casey loved you more than anything. He told me that. He was afraid of screwing you up, of being such a failure you would follow him down that road. He did what he did because in his fucked up brain, he was saving you from himself. It wasn't right, but it was what he thought. Aidan, believe this, Casey lived for you. When he died, it was because he felt worthless and lost. He didn't want you feeling that way. In his own messed up way, he thought he was taking his life to save yours."

Aidan leaned in against Smitty and sobbed. How could Casey have thought that? Why didn't he let Aidan help him? Why didn't he let Aidan in? *Because he was tormented by his own fears.* The boy Aidan had been, and the man he'd become, came together to let Casey go and forgive himself. He sighed, wiping the tears from his face.

"You know I'm around the same age Casey was when he died?" he asked, more to himself than anything.

Smitty nodded. "Yeah. I was just thinking about that. Casey at your age was spiraling out of control. Trying to hold on and let go at the same time. It's like watching a speeding car coming at someone, and not being able to push them out of the way."

Aidan remembered the car running Chris down; for a moment he pictured Casey, instead. They both were dealing with a world they didn't feel they belonged in, trying to push others out of the way. Casey believed he'd pushed Aidan out of the way, and maybe he had. Aidan's life wasn't the same as it would've been had Casey lived and his parents never moved. TJ, Smitty, Sam, were all changed by the choice Casey made subsequently. Then Zeke and Mia because they were all interlinked. Even Chris, who died a hero instead of nameless. Maybe Casey had sacrificed himself to save others, like Chris. For a moment he pictured Chris and Casey together, and it made him smile. They would've been about the same age, now.

Aidan glanced at Smitty, who was watching him. "Thank you for believing in me."

Smitty laughed, low and gentle. "That's like saying thank you for believing in the sun. You shine brighter than most, Aidan."

They walked back to the house and joined Zeke and Sam on the front porch. Zeke slid his arm around Aidan's waist as he sat down next to him. Zeke smelled like salt and home.

"You alright?" he whispered.

Aidan nodded, resting his head on Zeke's shoulder. "I am, now."

Zeke started to hum a tune Aidan didn't recognize but liked. The vibration passed from Zeke into Aidan, creating a soothing sync. Aidan peered up at the stars and remembered running down the road after Casey. One time, when Aidan was about five, Casey had stopped and scooped him up, holding him in his arms. Aidan had clung tightly to Casey's neck, hiccuping with tears. Casey had rubbed his back, whispering so his friends couldn't hear.

"My Aidan. I'm coming back to you. I need to go to far off lands and fight off the monsters, but when I come back we'll drink hot cocoa and lie in my bed. Then I'll tell you the tales of my victories. Wait for me, okay? I'll never leave you."

Aidan glanced around at Smitty sitting close with Sam, and Zeke holding him, humming. Casey had gone off to fight the monsters, but he was in the hum of Zeke's chest, the steadiness of Smitty's arms, Sam's gentle laugh, Mia's lyrical voice, TJ's undying loyalty, Chris's fearless bravery. He was in Aidan's beating heart. He was present and he was free.

Now, it was Aidan's turn to pick up the sword and fight off the monsters.

Epilogue

Change moves at a snail's pace. But it moves. Two years after Enrique was gunned down in the street, the officer who pulled the trigger was charged with manslaughter and sentenced to twenty years in prison. He'd still have more of a life than he allowed Enrique, but he didn't walk. Aidan had flown out for a day to testify, the footage spoke for itself. The other officers on the scene were not charged and were reinstated, even though they stood by and let it happen. The fact that Blake Castor was charged and sentenced shocked most people, and they quickly took sides. Families were divided. Neighbors quit speaking to one another. Talk around the water cooler became fistfights.

The Savage Film Company gained notoriety...and death threats. Especially after it released a cult church tell-all, "In the Eyes of God" exposing the abuse, mind control, and political ties of some of the country's most influential religions. People started to come forward to tell their stories of torment and escape. Aidan had been smart to have his mail and contacts routed through an outside service. If people tried to find him, they'd end up at a small closet-sized room in L.A., containing nothing more than a server. His second film, "Created Equal" used footage from Enrique's shooting and the protests, connecting the dots between corporations and politics, with a direct connection to supremacy and hate groups. He won awards for both films.

His parents had to move.

Zeke and Aidan tied the knot in Sam and Smitty's backyard with just a handful of close friends. His parents had at least sent good excuses as to why they couldn't make it. His father was out of town on business, his mother didn't want to fly alone. Fair enough. They sent an engraved wooden plaque with *The Oshers,* their wedding date, and Zeke and Aidan's names on it, showing they accepted their union. Lucky was the ring bearer and TJ the best man. Mia sang *Oh Mio Bab Bino Caro* by Puccini, which brought everyone to tears. After they exchanged rings and were announced married, they danced the night away under the strings of lights and the trees. Aidan liked the weight of the ring on his finger. They made love as husbands, holding each other in the magic of what had become.

The next day, all of them had gone surfing together, even Jim and Marie, who put the rest of them to shame with their moves. They were old but were surfers first. As Aidan paused to film from the beach, he found blessings in the reality that his circle had continued to grow, and he was never truly alone. One by one, as they came in from the ocean, his heart grew. By nightfall, Jim was playing his guitar around a fire on the beach while Zeke, Marie, and Mia sang along. Smitty was dancing with Sam off in the dark.

TJ was lying back, staring at the stars, smiling. Aidan filmed them, so he wouldn't forget that exact moment.

After the celebration of both nuptials, TJ and Mia had gone back to Seattle. Months passed, and life moved on. Zeke and Aidan worked hard, sometimes almost missing each other for days. Aidan liked it when he needed to go get footage somewhere in the country because Zeke would come along, and it would be like those first trips together. Just the two of them and Lucky. A year passed from their wedding date, and Mia announced she was expecting a baby. She was working as a teacher and performing with orchestras around the country when she could. TJ had moved up to Director and oversaw multiple assistance groups in Seattle. Another half a year passed. They saw each other maybe once a year. Life was continuing at a steady pace forward.

Aidan began to feel an old familiar sadness creep in, as he spent a night alone editing in the studio. He stared at the mural painted on the wall with the company logo; an old school film camera with the legs made of swords and the motto, *All is Not Lost in the Company of Friends.*

He missed TJ and Mia. He missed Chris. He missed Casey. Zeke was as busy as he was, as were Sam and Smitty. They were all making a name for themselves, but at what cost? They were changing the world, however, losing each other in the process. He texted Mia.

"I fucking miss you."

"I miss you, too," she texted back.

"What do we do?"

"We try harder."

"Fair. Next month we'll come to Seattle. After the baby, you come to the Outer Banks. Every three months one of us has to come to the other."

"Deal, but soon I'll have a baby in tow."

"I can't wait to meet the baby."

"Her."

"Her, aw. That's awesome. See you next month."

"I love you, Aidan."

"I love you, Mia. Tell TJ drinks are on him when we get there."

"You know it."

He saved his work and closed his computer. TJ and Mia were having a baby girl. She'd be one of the lucky ones. Loving parents who'd teach her to care about the world around her. Accept her for who she was. All children should have the right to grow up knowing they were safe and loved. He locked up the studio and headed home. The house and trailer were dark when he got there. Smitty was still at the restaurant because their car wasn't in the driveway. He'd opened a second restaurant and was working a lot of late nights to get it off the ground.

Aidan was supposed to work all night, too, but he decided he had something better to do. Zeke was already in bed asleep when Aidan slipped into the trailer. He could hear the soft sigh of Zeke breathing as he slept and smiled to himself. He took off his clothes, hanging them on the back of the chair and slid in next to his reason. Zeke rolled sleepily over to him, touching Aidan's face.

"Hey, I thought you were working all night," he murmured.

"Saving the world can wait. Right now, all I want is you."

Acknowledgements

First and foremost, I need to extend my ultimate gratitude to Austin Granger for letting me use his original protest photo for the cover. I knew what I had in my mind and when I saw this photo it said it all. To see his original photo and his other amazing photography visit **austingranger.com**

Thank you to Lizzy Johnston for her support and feedback! She is the best motivator and cheerleader! Thank you to Alex Baker for being a sounding board and friend.

For all those who feel they can't be themselves around their family, I thank you for your bravery and commitment to yourself. Family doesn't have to be blood.

For all the families who love and embrace their LGBTQIA+ children, knowing they are special no matter what, I thank you for your kind hearts and recognizing the only way to change the world is through love and acceptance.

For my own children fighting for their identity in this world, I have loved you forever, and you have taught me so much. I know the world is tough, but you are tougher.

For Justin, thank you for supporting my drive and focus on this which is so important.